THE WINDS OF CHANGE AND OTHER STORIES

DOUBLEDAY COLLECTIONS
OF SCIENCE FICTION SHORT STORIES
BY
ISAAC ASIMOV

I, Robot
The Martian Way and Other Stories
Earth Is Room Enough
Nine Tomorrows
The Rest of the Robots
Asimov's Mysteries
Nightfall and Other Stories
The Early Asimov
Buy Jupiter and Other Stories
The Bicentennial Man and Other Stories
The Complete Robot
The Winds of Change and Other Stories

ISAAC ASIMOV

THE WINDS
OF
CHANGE
and Other Stories

801010

DOUBLEDAY & COMPANY, INC.
GARDEN CITY, NEW YORK
1983

ACKNOWLEDGMENTS

About Nothing—Copyright © 1977 by Davis Publications, Inc.
A Perfect Fit—Copyright © 1981 by EDN
Belief—Copyright 1953 by Street & Smith Publications, Inc.; Copyright renewed by Isaac Asimov, 1980
Death of a Foy—Copyright © 1980 by Mercury Press, Inc.
Fair Exchange?—Copyright © 1978 by Davis Publications, Inc.
For the Birds—Copyright © 1980 by Davis Publications, Inc.
Found!—Copyright © 1978 by OMNI Publications International Ltd.
Good Taste—Copyright © 1976 by Isaac Asimov
How It Happened—Copyright © 1978 by Davis Publications, Inc.
Ideas Die Hard—Copyright © 1957 by Galaxy Publishing Corporation
Ignition Point!—Copyright © 1981, American Society of Association Executives
It Is Coming—Copyright © 1979, Field Enterprises, Inc.
Last Answer, The—Copyright © 1979 by the Condé Nast Publications, Inc.
Last Shuttle, The—Copyright © 1981 by Cape Publications, Inc.
Lest We Remember—Copyright © 1982 by Davis Publications, Inc.
Nothing for Nothing—Copyright © 1979 by Davis Publications, Inc.
One Night of Song—Copyright © 1982 by Mercury Press, Inc.
Smile That Loses, The—Copyright © 1982 by Mercury Press, Inc.
Sure Thing—Copyright © 1977 by Davis Publications, Inc.
To Tell at a Glance—(hitherto unpublished in this form)
Winds of Change, The—Copyright © 1982 by Laura W. Haywood and Isaac Asimov

Library of Congress Cataloging in Publication Data

Asimov, Isaac, 1920–
The winds of change and other stories.

1. Science fiction, American.   I. Title.
PS3551.S5W5   813'.54
ISBN 0-385-18099-3   AACR2
Library of Congress Catalog Card Number 81–43912

DEDICATED TO:

Dagmar Guarino and her G & S parodies.

CONTENTS

INTRODUCTION

Well, here we are again!

This is the dozenth collection of science fiction short stories of mine that Doubleday has published and there isn't much, by this time, that I can say. —Well, just a few things, and I will number them to keep myself from going on at too great length.

One. I suppose I feel defensive about the perpetual accusation that I "no longer write science fiction." It's true that I no longer write science fiction only, or even chiefly. However, I *do* write it. Please notice that of the twenty-one stories included in this volume only two were published before 1976.

Two. In several previous collections, I have included the stories in chronological order, either in the order in which they were written, or in the order in which they were published. This time, for the sake of variety, if nothing else, I am including them in alphabetical order.

Three. I will introduce each of the stories with a few words which I trust Doubleday will take the trouble to put into a different typeface, so that they will not be confused with the stories themselves.

There, that's it! Who says I'm long-winded!

THE WINDS OF CHANGE AND OTHER STORIES

Introduction to

ABOUT NOTHING

The vagaries of the alphabet place the shortest story in the book at the very start. Just as well. You can read it in a minute and if you don't like it, you can throw the book away. (Pay for it first, if you don't mind.)

What happened was that back in 1975 I was asked to write a two-hundred-and-fifty-word story that could fit on a postcard. The idea was to have "story-postcards" just the way you have "picture-postcards." I obliged (since I am a most obliging fellow) and "About Nothing" was the result.

I don't know what happened to the project. It probably failed. In any case, I finally offered "About Nothing" to *Isaac Asimov's Science Fiction Magazine* (which I will henceforth refer to as *Asimov's*) and George Scithers, the editor, graciously condescended to smile upon it and to include it in the Summer 1977 issue of the magazine.

And here it is in another incarnation. If you haven't seen it before, may you groan loudly.

1.

ABOUT NOTHING

All of Earth waited for the small black hole to bring it to its end. It had been discovered by Professor Jerome Hieronymus at the Lunar telescope in 2125 and it was clearly going to make an approach close enough for total tidal destruction.

All of Earth made its wills and wept on each other's shoulders, saying, "Good-bye, good-bye, good-bye." Husbands said good-bye to their wives, brothers said good-bye to their sisters, parents said good-bye to their children, owners said good-bye to their pets, and lovers whispered good-bye to each other.

But as the black hole approached, Hieronymus noted there was no gravitational effect. He studied it more closely and announced, with a chuckle, that it was not a black hole after all.

"It's nothing," he said. "Just an ordinary asteroid someone has painted black."

He was killed by an infuriated mob, but not for that. He was killed only after he publicly announced that he would write a great and moving play about the whole episode.

He said, "I shall call it *Much Adieu About Nothing*."

All humanity applauded his death.

END

Introduction to

A PERFECT FIT

These days, more often than not, I am asked to write a science fiction story to fit a particular theme, and then it becomes a matter of pride with me to come through, if the financial side of it is adequately nourishing.

In this particular case, a publication devoted to computer technology said they wanted twenty-five hundred words (for at the word-rate I suggested, that was the number of words they could budget) about a future society in which the inability to make use of computer technology was the equivalent to illiteracy in an earlier society. And that is what they got. The story was written in April 1981.

2.

A PERFECT FIT

Ian Bradstone, wandering his way sadly through one more town, was stopped by a cluster of people at the open door of an emporium. His first impulse was to turn and flee but he couldn't make himself do so. The fascination of horror drew him reluctantly toward the cluster.

His curiosity must have turned his face into one big question mark, for someone at the outskirts explained the matter pleasantly. "Three-D chess. It's a hot game."

Bradstone knew how it worked. There would be half a dozen people conferring at each move, all trying to beat the computer. The chances were that they would lose. Six wood-pushers add up to one wood-pusher. He caught the unbearable glitter of the graphic and closed his eyes against it. He turned away bitterly and noted a makeshift setup of eight chessboards balanced on pegs, one above the other.

Ordinary chessboards. Plastic chessmen.

"Hey," he said, in explosive surprise.

The young man at the mutiboard said, defensively, "We can't get close enough. I set this up myself so we can follow. Careful! Don't knock it down."

Bradstone said, "Is that the position as of now?"

"Yes. The guys have been arguing for ten minutes."

Bradstone looked eagerly at the position. He said, raptly, "If you move the rook from beta-B-6 to delta-B-6, you get the upper hand."

The young man studied the boards. "Are you sure?"

"Certainly I'm sure. No matter what the computer does, it's going to end up losing a move to protect its queen."

More studying. The young man shouted, "Hey, in there. Guy here says you should bump the rook up two levels."

There was a collective sigh from the inner group. One voice said, "I was thinking that."

Another said, "I get it. It leaves the queen with the potentiality of vulnerability. I didn't see that." The owner of this second voice turned. "You! The fellow who made the suggestion. Would you do the honor? Would you punch in the move?"

Bradstone backed away, his face contorted in sheer horror. "No— No— I don't play." He turned and hastened away.

He was hungry. Periodically he was hungry.

Occasionally, he came across fruit stands of the type set up by small entrepreneurs who found a disregarded space in the interstices of a thoroughly computerized economy. If Bradstone were careful, he could walk off with an apple or an orange.

It was a frightening thing. There was always the chance he might be caught and, if he were, he would be asked to pay. He had the money, of course—they were very kind to him—but how could he pay?

Yet every day on a dozen occasions, he would have to undergo a transfer of credits, to use his cash card. It meant endless humiliation.

He found himself outside a restaurant. It might have been the smell of the food that had reminded him he was hungry.

He peered cautiously through the window. There were a number of people eating. Too many. It was bad enough with one or two. He couldn't make himself the center of hordes of staring, pitying eyes.

He turned away, his stomach growling, and saw that he was not the only one staring into the window. A boy was doing the same. He was about ten years old and he didn't look particularly hungry.

Bradstone attempted a tone of hearty good-nature. "Hello there, young fellow. Hungry?"

The youngster looked at him suspiciously and edged away. "No!"

Bradstone made no move to come closer. If he did, the boy

would undoubtedly run. He said, "I'll bet you're big enough to do your own ordering. You can order a hamburger or anything else, I'm sure."

Pride overcame suspicion. The boy said, "Sure! Anytime!"

"But you don't have a card of your own, right? So you can't complete the order. Right?"

The boy stared at him warily out of brown eyes. He was neatly dressed and had an alert and intelligent air about him.

Bradstone said, "Tell you what. I have a card and you can use it to order. Get yourself a hamburger or anything else you want. Tell you what else. You can get me something, too. Nice T-bone steak, and a baked potato and some squash and some coffee. And two pieces of apple pie. You have one."

"I got to go home and eat," said the boy.

"Come on! You'll save your father some assets. They know you here, I'm sure."

"We eat here lots of times."

"There you are. Eat here again. Only this time, *you* handle the card. You do the selection—like a grown-up. Go ahead. You go in first."

There was a tense feeling in the pit of Bradstone's stomach. What he was doing made perfect sense to him and would not harm the child at all. Anyone who might be watching, however, might come to a horrible and quite wrong conclusion.

Bradstone could explain if given a chance, but how humiliating to have everyone see that he had to maneuver a little boy into doing something for him he could not do for himself.

The youngster hesitated, but he entered the restaurant and Bradstone followed, maintaining a careful distance. The youngster sat down at a table and Bradstone sat down opposite.

Bradstone smiled and handed him his card. It tingled his hands unpleasantly—as always, these days—and he was relieved to be able to let go of it. It had a hard, metallic glitter that made the muscles round his eyes twitch. He couldn't bear to look at it.

"Go ahead, boy. Make the selection," he said in a low voice. "Anything you want."

The boy hadn't lied. He could handle the small computer-outlet perfectly, his fingers flying over the controls.

"Steak for you, mister. Baked potato. Squash. Apple pie. Coffee.

—You want salad, mister?" His voice had taken on a fussy I'm-grown-up sound. "My mom always orders salad, but I don't like it."

"I guess I'll try it, though. Mixed green salad. They got that? Vinaigrette dressing. They got that? You can handle that?"

"Don't see about the vin-something. —Maybe this is it."

Bradstone ended up with French dressing as it later turned out, but it did well enough.

The boy inserted the card with ease and a skill that roused Bradstone's bitter envy, even as his picturing the act made his stomach lurch.

The boy handed back the card. "I guess you had enough money," he said, importantly.

Bradstone said, "Did you notice the figure?"

"Oh no. You're not supposed to look; that's what my dad says. I mean it didn't get rejected so there's enough for the food."

Bradstone crushed down the feeling of disappointment. He couldn't read the figures and he couldn't make himself ask others. Eventually, he might have to go to a bank and try to invent some way of maneuvering them into telling him.

He tried to make conversation. "What's your name, sonny?"

"Reginald."

"What are you studying at home these days, Reggie?"

"Arithmetic mostly because Dad says I have to, and dinosaurs because I want to. Dad says if I stick to my arithmetic I can get the dinosaurs, too. I can program my computer to get the graphics of dinosaur motion. You know how a brontosaurus walks on land? It has to balance its neck so the center of gravity is in the hips. It holds its head way up like a giraffe unless it's in water. Then—Here's my hamburger. And your stuff, too."

It had all come along the moving belt and had stopped at the appropriate place.

The thought of one full meal without humiliation overcame Bradstone's wistfulness at the thought of manipulating a computer in the free search for information.

Reginald said, quite politely, "I'll eat the hamburger at the counter, mister."

Bradstone waved. "I hope it's a good hamburger, Reggie." Bradstone needed him no more and was relieved to have him go. Someone from the kitchen, undoubtedly a Computer-Maintenance technician, had emerged and engaged Reginald in friendly conversation—which was also a relief.

There was no question about the profession. You could always tell a Comp-Maint by his lazy air of importance, his exuded sense of knowledge that the world rested on his shoulder.

But Bradstone was concentrating on his dinner—the first full meal he had enjoyed normally in a month.

It was only after he finished—quite finished in the most leisurely possible fashion—that he studied his surroundings again. The boy was long gone. Bradstone thought sadly that the boy, at least, had not pitied, had not condescended, had not patronized. He had not been old enough to find the event an odd one; had only concentrated on his own adulthood in being able to handle the computer outlet.

Adulthood!

The place was not very crowded now. The Comp-Maint was still behind the counter, presumably studying the wiring of the computerization.

It was, thought Bradstone with a pang, the major occupation of technologists virtually the world over; always programming, reprogramming, adjusting, checking the tiny electric currents that controlled the work of the world for everyone—for almost everyone.

The comfortably warm internal feeling produced by an excellent steak stirred the feeling of rebellion within Bradstone. Why not act? Why not do something about it?

He caught the Comp-Maint's eye and said in an attempt at lightness that didn't ring true even in his own ears, "Pal, I guess there are lawyers in this town?"

"You guess right."

"You couldn't suggest a good one not too far away, could you?"

The Comp-Maint said politely, "You'll find a town directory at the post office. Just punch in the request for lawyers."

"I mean a good one. Clever guy. Lost causes. Like that." He laughed, hoping to get at least a smile out of the other.

He didn't. The Comp-Maint said, "They're all described. List your needs, and you'll get evaluations, ages, addresses, case loads, fee levels. Anything you want you can get, if you play the keys properly. And it's working. I vetted it last week."

"That's not what I mean, buddy." The suggestion that he play the keys properly sent the usual frisson skidding up his spine. "I want your personal recommendation. You know?"

The Com-Maint shook his head. "I'm not a directory."

Bradstone said, "Damn it. What's wrong with you? Name a lawyer. Any lawyer. Is there a law against knowing something without a computer to play with?"

"Use of the directory is a dime. If you've got more than a dime registered on your card, what's the problem? Don't you know how to use your card? Or are you—" His eyes widened in sudden thought. "Oh— Son of a— *That's* why you got Reggie to order your meal for you! Listen, I didn't know—"

Bradstone shrank away. He turned to hurry out of the place and nearly collided with a large man who had a ruddy complexion and a balding head.

The large man said softly, "One moment, please. Aren't you the person who bought my son a hamburger a while ago?"

Bradstone hesitated, then nodded dry-mouthed.

"I would like to pay you for it. It's all right. I know who you are and I'll handle your card for you."

The Comp-Maint interposed sharply, "If you want a lawyer, fella, Mr. Gold is a lawyer."

The sharpened interest in Bradstone's eyes made itself evident at once.

Gold said, "I *am* a lawyer if you're looking for one. It's how I knew you. I followed your case with painful attention, I assure you, and when Reggie came home with a tale of having eaten dinner already and of having used the computer, I guessed who you might be from his description. And I recognize you now, of course."

Bradstone said, "Can we talk privately?"

"My home is a five-minute walk from here."

It was not a luxurious living room, but it was a comfortable one. Bradstone said, "Do you want a retainer? I can afford one."

"I know you have ample funds," said Gold. "Tell me first, though, what the problem is."

Bradstone leaned forward in his chair and said, intensely, "If you've followed my case, you must know I have been subjected to cruel and unusual punishment. I'm the first person who has received this kind of sentence. The combination of hypnosis and direct neuroconditioning has only been perfected recently. The nature of the punishment to which I have been sentenced could not be understood. It must be lifted."

Gold said, "You underwent due process in great detail, and there was no reasonable doubt that you were guilty—"

"Even so! Look! We live in a computerized world. I can't do a thing anywhere—I can't get information—I can't be fed—I can't amuse myself—I can't pay for anything, or check on anything, or just plain *do* anything—without using a computer. And I have been adjusted, as you surely know, so that I am incapable of looking at a computer without hurting my eyes, or touching one without blistering my fingers. I can't even handle my cash card or even *think* of using it without nausea."

Gold said, "Yes, I know all that. I also know you have been given ample funds for the duration of your punishment, and that the general public has been asked to sympathize and be helpful. I believe they do this."

"I don't *want* that. I don't *want* their help and their pity. I don't want to be a helpless child in a world of adults. I don't want to be an illiterate in a world of people who can read. Help me end the punishment. It's been almost a month of hell. I can't go through eleven more."

Gold sat in thought for a while. "Well, I will charge you a retainer so that I can become your legal representative, and I will do what I can for you. I must warn you, though, that I don't think the chances for success are great."

"Why? All I did was divert five thousand dollars—"

"You planned to divert far more, it was decided, but were caught before you could. It was an ingenious computer fraud, quite worthy of your well-known skill at chess, but it was still a crime. And, as you say, everything is computerized and no step, however small, can be taken these days without a computer. To defraud by means of a computer, then, is to break down what is now the essential framework of civilization. It is a terrible crime and it must be discouraged."

"Don't preach."

"I'm not. I'm explaining. You tried to break down a system and in punishment the system has been broken down for you alone and you are not otherwise mistreated. If you find your life unbearable, that merely shows you how unbearable it is that you tried, after a fashion, to break it down for everyone."

"But a year is too much."

"Well, perhaps less will still serve as a strong enough example to deter others from making the same attempt. I will try—but I'm afraid I can guess what the law will say."

"What?"

"It will say that if punishments should be made to fit the crime, yours is a perfect fit."

Introduction to

BELIEF

"Belief" was published originally in the October 1953 issue of *Astounding Science Fiction* and here is how it came to avoid publication in one or another of my collections.

In 1966, Ted Carnell, a British literary agent, told me that New English Library would like to put out a collection of my stories and you can be sure that I found no good reason for objecting. In 1967, therefore, New English Library published *Through a Glass, Clearly*, which included four of my stories. In the decade and a half since, the book has remained in print (both hard cover and soft cover) through a number of reprintings.

It turned out, though, that the book could be circulated only in Great Britain and in a few other nations that did *not* include the United States. I therefore decided there was no reason I couldn't place the four stories into one or another of my American collections. Three of them, "Breeds There a Man?," "The C-Chute," and "It's Such a Beautiful Day," all appeared in my collection *Nightfall and Other Stories* in 1969. "Belief" escaped somehow, and I don't know why. Certainly, I liked the story, even though John Campbell, the editor of *Astounding*, forced some changes I did not entirely approve of. (No, I don't have the original manuscript, or I would use it.) In any case, here it is—a dozen years later.

Incidentally, I don't mean to imply "Belief" has been unavailable to American readers all this time. It has appeared in seven different anthologies—but that isn't the same as appearing in one of my own collections. At least, not to *me* it isn't.

3.

BELIEF

"Did you ever dream you were flying?" asked Dr. Roger Toomey of his wife.

Jane Toomey looked up. "Certainly!"

Her quick fingers didn't stop their nimble manipulations of the yarn out of which an intricate and quite useless doily was being created. The television set made a muted murmur in the room and the posturings on its screen were, out of long custom, disregarded.

Roger said, "Everyone dreams of flying at some time or other. It's universal. I've done it many times. That's what worries me."

Jane said, "I don't know what you're getting at, dear. I hate to say so." She counted stitches in an undertone.

"When you think about it, it makes you wonder. It's not really flying that you dream of. You have no wings; at least I never had any. There's no effort involved. You're just floating. That's it. Floating."

"When I fly," said Jane, "I don't remember any of the details. Except once I landed on top of City Hall and hadn't any clothes on. Somehow no one ever seems to pay any attention to you when you're dream-nude. Ever notice that? You're dying of embarrassment but people just pass by."

She pulled at the yarn and the ball tumbled out of the bag and half across the floor. She paid no attention.

Roger shook his head slowly. At the moment, his face was pale and absorbed in doubt. It seemed all angles with its high cheekbones, its long straight nose and the widow's-peak hairline that was growing more pronounced with the years. He was thirty-five.

He said, "Have you ever wondered what makes you dream you're floating?"

"No, I haven't."

Jane Toomey was blonde and small. Her prettiness was the fragile kind that does not impose itself upon you but rather creeps on you unaware. She had the bright blue eyes and pink cheeks of a porcelain doll. She was thirty.

Roger said, "Many dreams are only the mind's interpretation of a stimulus imperfectly understood. The stimuli are forced into a reasonable context in a split second."

Jane said, "What are you talking about, darling?"

Roger said, "Look, I once dreamed I was in a hotel, attending a physics convention. I was with old friends. Everything seemed quite normal. Suddenly, there was a confusion of shouting and for no reason at all I grew panicky. I ran to the door but it wouldn't open. One by one, my friends disappeared. They had no trouble leaving the room, but I couldn't see how they managed it. I shouted at them and they ignored me.

"It was borne in upon me that the hotel was on fire. I didn't smell smoke. I just knew there was a fire. I ran to the window and I could see a fire escape on the outside of the building. I ran to each window in turn but none led to the fire escape. I was quite alone in the room now. I leaned out the window, calling desperately. No one heard me.

"Then the fire engines were coming, little red smears darting along the streets. I remember that clearly. The alarm bells clanged sharply to clear traffic. I could hear them, louder and louder till the sound was splitting my skull. I awoke and, of course, the alarm clock was ringing.

"Now I can't have dreamed a long dream designed to arrive at the moment of the alarm-clock ring in a way that builds the alarm neatly into the fabric of the dream. It's much more reasonable to suppose that the dream began at the moment the alarm began and crammed all its sensation of duration into one split second. It was just a hurry-up device of my brain to explain this sudden noise that penetrated the silence."

Jane was frowning now. She put down her crocheting. "Roger! You've been behaving queerly since you got back from the college. You didn't eat much and now this ridiculous conversation. I've

never heard you so morbid. What you need is a dose of bicar-
bonate."

"I need a little more than that," said Roger in a low voice. "Now,
what starts a floating dream?"

"If you don't mind, let's change the subject."

She rose, and with firm fingers turned up the sound on the television set. A young gentleman with hollow cheeks and a soulful tenor
suddenly raised his voice and assured her, dulcetly, of his never-
ending love.

Roger turned it down again and stood with his back to the instrument.

"Levitation!" he said. "That's it. There is some way in which
human beings can make themsleves float. They have the capacity
for it. It's just that they don't know how to use that capacity—except when they sleep. Then, sometimes, they lift up just a little bit,
a tenth of an inch maybe. It wouldn't be enough for anyone to notice even if they were watching, but it would be enough to deliver
the proper sensation for the start of a floating dream."

"Roger, you're delirious. I wish you'd stop. Honestly."

He drove on. "Sometimes we sink down slowly and the sensation
is gone. Then again, sometimes the float control ends suddenly and
we drop. Jane, did you ever dream you were falling?"

"Yes, of c—"

"You're hanging on the side of a building or you're sitting at the
edge of a seat and suddenly you're tumbling. There's the awful
shock of falling and you snap awake, your breath gasping, your
heart palpitating. You *did* fall. There's no other explanation."

Jane's expression, having passed slowly from bewilderment to
concern, dissolved suddenly into sheepish amusement.

"Roger, you *devil*. And you fooled me! Oh, you rat!"

"What?"

"Oh no. You can't play it out any more. I know exactly what
you're doing. You're making up a plot to a story and you're trying
it out on me. I should know better than to listen to you."

Roger looked startled, even a little confused. He strode to her
chair and looked down at her, "No, Jane."

"I don't see why not. You've been talking about writing fiction as
long as I've known you. If you've got a plot, you might as well

write it down. No use just frightening me with it." Her fingers flew as her spirits rose.

"Jane, this is no story."

"But what else—"

"When I woke up this morning, *I dropped to the mattress!*"

He stared at her without blinking. "I dreamed I was flying," he said. "It was clear and distinct. I remember every minute of it. I was lying on my back when I woke up. I was feeling comfortable and quite happy. I just wondered a little why the ceiling looked so queer. I yawned and stretched and *touched* the ceiling. For a minute, I just stared at my arm reaching upward and ending hard against the ceiling.

"Then I turned over. I didn't move a muscle, Jane. I just turned all in one piece because I wanted to. There I was, five feet above the bed. There you were on the bed, sleeping. I was frightened. I didn't know how to get down, but the minute I thought of getting down, I dropped. I dropped slowly. The whole process was under perfect control.

"I stayed in bed fifteen minutes before I dared move. Then I got up, washed, dressed and went to work."

Jane forced a laugh, "Darling, you had *better* write it up. But that's all right. You've just been working too hard."

"Please! Don't be banal."

"People work too hard, even though to say so is banal. After all, you were just dreaming fifteen minutes longer than you thought you were."

"It wasn't a dream."

"Of course it was. I can't even count the times I've dreamed I awoke and dressed and made breakfast; then really woke up and found it was all to do over again. I've even dreamed I was dreaming, if you see what I mean. It can be awfully confusing."

"Look, Jane. I've come to you with a problem because you're the only one I feel I can come to. Please take me seriously."

Jane's blue eyes opened wide. "Darling! I'm taking you as seriously as I can. You're the physics professor, not I. Gravitation is what you know about, not I. Would *you* take it seriously if I told you *I* had found myself floating?"

"No. *No!* That's the hell of it. I don't want to believe it, only I've got to. It was no dream, Jane. I tried to tell myself it was. You have no idea how I talked myself into that. By the time I got to class, I was sure it was a dream. You didn't notice anything queer about me at breakfast, did you?"

"Yes, I did, now that I think about it."

"Well, it wasn't very queer or you would have mentioned it. Anyway, I gave my nine o'clock lecture perfectly. By eleven, I had forgotten the whole incident. Then, just after lunch, I needed a book. I needed Page and— Well, the book doesn't matter; I just needed it. It was on an upper shelf, but I could reach it. Jane—"

He stopped.

"Well, go on, Roger."

"Look, did you ever try to pick up something that's just a step away? You bend and automatically take a step toward it as you reach. It's completely involuntary. It's just your body's over-all coordination."

"All right. What of it?"

"I reached for the book and automatically took a step upward. On air, Jane! On empty air!"

"I'm going to call Jim Sarle, Roger."

"I'm not sick, damn it."

"I think he ought to talk to you. He's a friend. It won't be a doctor's visit. He'll just talk to you."

"And what good will that do?" Roger's face turned red with sudden anger.

"We'll see. Now sit down, Roger. Please." She walked to the phone.

He cut her off, seizing her wrist. "You don't believe me."

"Oh, Roger."

"You don't."

"I believe you. Of course, I believe you. I just want—"

"Yes. You just want Jim Sarle to talk to me. That's how much you believe me. I'm telling the truth but you want me to talk to a psychiatrist. Look, you don't have to take my word for anything. I can prove this. I can prove I can float."

"I *believe* you."

"Don't be a fool. I know when I'm being humored. Stand still! Now watch me."

He backed away to the middle of the room and without preliminary lifted off the floor. He *dangled;* with the toes of his shoes six empty inches from the carpet.

Jane's eyes and mouth were three round O's. She whispered, "Come down, Roger. Oh, dear heaven, come down."

He drifted down, his feet touching the floor without a sound. "You see?"

"Oh, my. Oh, my."

She stared at him, half-frightened, half-sick.

On the television set, a chesty female sang mutedly that flying high with some guy in the sky was her idea of nothing at all.

Roger Toomey stared into the bedroom's darkness. He whispered, "Jane."

"What?"

"You're not sleeping?"

"No."

"I can't sleep, either. I keep holding the headboard to make sure I'm . . . you know."

His hand moved restlessly and touched her face. She flinched, jerking away as though he carried an electric charge.

She said, "I'm sorry. I'm a little nervous."

"That's all right. I'm getting out of bed anyway."

"What are you going to do? You've got to sleep."

"Well, I can't, so there's no sense keeping you awake, too."

"Maybe nothing will happen. It doesn't have to happen every night. It didn't happen before last night."

"How do I know? Maybe I just never went up so high. Maybe I just never woke up and caught myself. Anyway, now it's different."

He was sitting up in bed, his legs bent, his arms clasping his knees, his forehead resting on them. He pushed the sheet to one side and rubbed his cheek against the soft flannel of his pajamas.

He said, "It's bound to be different now. My mind's full of it. Once I'm asleep, once I'm not holding myself down consciously, why, up I'll go."

"I don't see why. It must be such an effort."

"That's the point. It isn't."

"But you're fighting gravity, aren't you?"

"I know, but there's still no effort. Look, Jane, if I only *could* understand it, I wouldn't mind so much."

He dangled his feet out of bed and stood up. "I don't want to talk about it."

His wife muttered, "I don't want to, either." She started crying, fighting back the sobs and turning them into strangled moans, which sounded much worse.

Roger said, "I'm sorry, Jane. I'm getting you all wrought up."

"No, don't touch me. Just . . . just leave me alone."

He took a few uncertain steps away from the bed.

She said, "Where are you going?"

"To the studio couch. Will you help me?"

"How?"

"I want you to tie me down."

"Tie you down?"

"With a couple of ropes. Just loosely, so I can turn if I want to. Do you mind?"

Her bare feet were already seeking her mules on the floor at her side of the bed. "All right," she sighed.

Roger Toomey sat in the small cubbyhole that passed for his office and stared at the pile of examination papers before him. At the moment, he didn't see how he was going to mark them.

He had given five lectures on electricity and magnetism since the first night he had floated. He had gotten through them somehow, though not swimmingly. The students asked ridiculous questions so probably he wasn't making himself as clear as he once did.

Today he had saved himself a lecture by giving a surprise examination. He didn't bother making one up; just handed out copies of one given several years earlier.

Now he had the answer papers and would have to mark them. Why? Did it matter what they said? Or anyone? Was it so important to know the laws of physics? If it came to that, what were the laws? Were there any, really?

Or was it all just a mass of confusion out of which nothing orderly could ever be extracted? Was the universe, for all its appearance, merely the original chaos, still waiting for the Spirit to move upon the face of its deep?

Insomnia wasn't helping him, either. Even strapped in upon the couch, he slept only fitfully, and then always with dreams.

There was a knock at the door.

Roger cried angrily, "Who's there?"

A pause, and then the uncertain answer. "It's Miss Harroway, Dr. Toomey. I have the letters you dictated."

"Well, come in, come in. Don't just stand there."

The department secretary opened the door a minimum distance and squeezed her lean and unprepossessing body into his office. She had a sheaf of papers in her hand. To each was clipped a yellow carbon and a stamped, addressed envelope.

Roger was anxious to get rid of her. That was his mistake. He stretched forward to reach the letters as she approached and felt himself leave the chair.

He moved two feet forward, still in sitting position, before he could bring himself down hard, losing his balance and tumbling in the process. It was too late.

It was entirely too late. Miss Harroway dropped the letters in a fluttering handful. She screamed and turned, hitting the door with her shoulder, caroming out into the hall and dashing down the corridor in a clatter of high heels.

Roger rose, rubbing an aching hip. "Damn," he said forcefully.

But he couldn't help seeing her point. He pictured the sight as she must have seen it; a full-grown man, lifting smoothly out of his chair and gliding toward her in a maintained squat.

He picked up the letters and closed his office door. It was quite late in the day; the corridors would be empty; she would probably be quite incoherent. Still— He waited anxiously for the crowd to gather.

Nothing happened. Perhaps she was lying somewhere in a dead faint. Roger felt it a point of honor to seek her out and do what he could for her, but he told his conscience to go to the devil. Until he found out exactly what was wrong with him, exactly what this wild nightmare of his was all about, he must do nothing to reveal it.

Nothing, that is, more than he had done already.

He leafed through the letters; one to every major theoretical physicist in the country. Home talent was insufficient for this sort of thing.

He wondered if Miss Harroway grasped the contents of the letters. He hoped not. He had couched them deliberately in technical language; more so, perhaps, than was quite necessary. Partly, that was to be discreet; partly, to impress the addressees with the fact that he, Toomey, was a legitimate and capable scientist.

One by one, he put the letters in the appropriate envelopes. The best brains in the country, he thought. Could they help?

He didn't know.

The library was quiet. Roger Toomey closed the *Journal of Theoretical Physics*, placed it on end and stared at its backstrap somberly. The *Journal of Theoretical Physics!* What did any of the contributors to that learned bit of balderdash understand anyway? The thought tore at him. Until so recently they had been the greatest men in the world to him.

And still he was doing his best to live up to their code and philosophy. With Jane's increasingly reluctant help, he had made measurements. He had tried to weigh the phenomenon in the balance, extract its relationships, evaluate its quantities. He had tried, in short, to defeat it in the only way he knew how—by making of it just another expression of the eternal modes of behavior that all the Universe must follow.

(*Must* follow. The best minds said so.)

Only there was nothing to measure. There was absolutely no sensation of effort to his levitation. Indoors—he dared not test himself outdoors, of course—he could reach the ceiling as easily as he could rise an inch, except that it took more time. Given enough time, he felt, he could continue rising indefinitely; go to the Moon, if necessary.

He could carry weights while levitating. The process became slower, but there was no increase in effort.

The day before he had come on Jane without warning, a stop watch in one hand.

"How much do you weigh?" he asked.

"One hundred ten," she replied. She gazed at him uncertainly.

He seized her waist with one arm. She tried to push him away but he paid no attention. Together, they moved upward at a creeping pace. She clung to him, white and rigid with terror.

"Twenty-two minutes thirteen seconds," he said, when his head nudged the ceiling.

When they came down again, Jane tore away and hurried out of the room.

Some days before he had passed a drug-store scale, standing shabbily on a street corner. The street was empty, so he stepped on and put in his penny. Even though he suspected something of the sort, it was a shock to find himself weighing thirty pounds.

He began carrying handfuls of pennies and weighing himself under all conditions. He was heavier on days on which there was a brisk wind, as though he required weight to keep from blowing away.

Adjustment was automatic. Whatever it was that levitated him maintained a balance between comfort and safety. But he could enforce conscious control upon his levitation just as he could upon his respiration. He could stand on a scale and force the pointer up to almost his full weight and down, of course, to nothing.

He bought a scale two days before and tried to measure the rate at which he could change weight. That didn't help. The rate, whatever it was, was faster than the pointer could swing. All he did was collect data on moduli of compressibility and moments of inertia.

Well—what did it all amount to anyway?

He stood up and trudged out of the library, shoulders drooping. He touched tables and chairs as he walked to the side of the room and then kept his hand unobtrusively on the wall. He had to do that, he felt. Contact with matter kept him continually informed as to his status with respect to the ground. If his hand lost touch with a table or slid upward against the wall—that was it.

The corridor had the usual sprinkling of students. He ignored them. In these last days, they had gradually learned to stop greeting him. Roger imagined that some had come to think of him as queer and most were probably growing to dislike him.

He passed by the elevator. He never took it any more; going down, particularly. When the elevator made its initial drop, he found it impossible not to lift into the air for just a moment. No matter how he lay in wait for the moment, he hopped and people would turn to look at him.

He reached for the railing at the head of the stairs and just before his hand touched it, one of his feet kicked the other. It was the most ungainly stumble that could be imagined. Three weeks earlier, Roger would have sprawled down the stairs.

This time his autonomic system took over and, leaning forward, spread-eagled, fingers wide, legs half-buckled, he sailed down the flight gliderlike. He might have been on wires.

He was too dazed to right himself, too paralyzed with horror to do anything. Within two feet of the window at the bottom of the flight, he came to an automatic halt and hovered.

There were two students on the flight he had come down, both now pressed against the wall, three more at the head of the stairs, two on the flight below, and one on the landing with him, so close they could almost touch one another.

It was very silent. They all looked at him.

Roger straightened himself, dropped to the ground and ran down the stairs, pushing one student roughly out of his way.

Conversation swirled up into exclamation behind him.

"Dr. Morton wants to see me?" Roger turned in his chair, holding one of its arms firmly.

The new department secretary nodded. "Yes, Dr. Toomey."

She left quickly. In the short time since Miss Harroway had resigned, she had learned that Dr. Toomey had something "wrong" with him. The students avoided him. In his lecture room today, the back seats had been full of whispering students. The front seats had been empty.

Roger looked into the small wall mirror near the door. He adjusted his jacket and brushed some lint off but that operation did little to improve his appearance. His complexion had grown sallow. He had lost at least ten pounds since all this had started, though, of course, he had no way of really knowing his exact weight loss. He was generally unhealthy-looking, as though his digestion perpetually disagreed with him and won every argument.

He had no apprehensions about this interview with the chairman of the department. He had reached a pronounced cynicism concerning the levitation incidents. Apparently, witnesses didn't talk. Miss Harroway hadn't. There was no sign that the students on the staircase had.

With a last touch at his tie, he left his office.

Dr. Philip Morton's office was not too far down the hall, which was a gratifying fact to Roger. More and more, he was cultivating the habit of walking with systematic slowness. He picked up one foot and put it before him, watching. Then he picked up the other and put it before him, still watching. He moved along in a confirmed stoop, gazing at his feet.

Dr. Morton frowned as Roger walked in. He had little eyes, wore a poorly trimmed grizzled mustache and an untidy suit. He had a moderate reputation in the scientific world and a decided penchant for leaving teaching duties to the members of his staff.

He said, "Say, Toomey, I got the strangest letter from Linus Deering. Did you write to him on"—he consulted a paper on his desk—"the twenty-second of last month. Is this your signature?"

Roger looked and nodded. Anxiously, he tried to read Deering's letter upside down. This was unexpected. Of the letters he had sent out the day of the Miss Harroway incident, only four had so far been answered.

Three of them had consisted of cold one-paragraph replies that read, more or less: "This is to acknowledge receipt of your letter of the twenty-second. I do not believe I can help you in the matter you discuss." A fourth, from Ballantine of Northwestern Tech, had bumblingly suggested an institute for psychic research. Roger couldn't tell whether he was trying to be helpful or insulting.

Deering of Princeton made five. He had had high hopes of Deering.

Dr. Morton cleared his throat loudly and adjusted a pair of glasses. "I want to read you what he says. Sit down, Toomey, sit down. He says: 'Dear Phil—'"

Dr. Morton looked up briefly with a slightly fatuous smile. "Linus and I met at Federation meetings last year. We had a few drinks together. Very nice fellow."

He adjusted his glasses again and returned to the letter: "'Dear Phil: Is there a Dr. Roger Toomey in your department? I received a very queer letter from him the other day. I didn't quite know what to make of it. At first, I thought I'd just let it go as another crank letter. Then I thought that since the letter carried your department heading, you ought to know of it. It's just possible someone may be using your staff as part of a confidence game. I'm enclosing Dr. Toomey's letter for your inspection. I hope to be visiting your part of the country—'

"Well, the rest of it is personal." Dr. Morton folded the letter, took off his glasses, put them in a leather container and put that in his breast pocket. He twined his fingers together and leaned forward.

"Now," he said, "I don't have to read you your own letter. Was it a joke? A hoax?"

"Dr. Morton," said Roger, heavily, "I was serious. I don't see anything wrong with my letter. I sent it to quite a few physicists. It speaks for itself. I've made observations on a case of . . . of levitation and I wanted information about possible theoretical explanations for such a phenomenon."

"Levitation! Really!"

"It's a legitimate case, Dr. Morton."

"You've observed it yourself?"

"Of course."

"No hidden wires? No mirrors? Look here, Toomey, you're no expert on these frauds."

"This was a thoroughly scientific series of observations. There is no possibility of fraud."

"You might have consulted me, Toomey, before sending out these letters."

"Perhaps I should have, Dr. Morton, but, frankly, I thought you might be—unsympathetic."

"Well, thank you. I should hope so. And on department stationery. I'm really surprised, Toomey. Look here, Toomey, your life is your own. If you wish to believe in levitation, go ahead, but strictly on your own time. For the sake of the department and the college, it should be obvious that this sort of thing should not be injected into your scholastic affairs.

"In point of fact, you've lost some weight recently, haven't you, Toomey? Yes, you don't look well at all. I'd see a doctor, if I were you. A nerve specialist, perhaps."

Roger said, bitterly, "A psychiatrist might be better, you think?"

"Well, that's entirely your business. In any case, a little rest—"

The telephone had rung and the secretary had taken the call. She caught Dr. Morton's eye and he picked up his extension.

He said, "Hello. . . . Oh, Dr. Smithers, yes. . . . Um-m-m. . . . Yes. . . . Concerning whom? . . . Well, in point of fact, he's with me right now. . . . Yes. . . . Yes, immediately."

He cradled the phone and looked at Roger thoughtfully. "The Dean wants to see both of us."

"What about, sir?"

"He didn't say." He got up and stepped to the door. "Are you coming, Toomey?"

"Yes, sir." Roger rose slowly to his feet, cramming the toe of one foot carefully under Dr. Morton's desk as he did so.

Dean Smithers was a lean man with a long, ascetic face. He had a mouthful of false teeth that fitted just badly enough to give his sibilants a peculiar half-whistle.

"Close the door, Miss Bryce," he said, "and I'll take no phone calls for a while. Sit down, gentlemen."

He stared at them portentously and added, "I think I had better get right to the point. I don't know exactly what Dr. Toomey is doing, but he must stop."

Dr. Morton turned upon Roger in amazement. "What have you been doing?"

Roger shrugged dispiritedly. "Nothing that I can help." He had underestimated student tongue-wagging after all.

"Oh, come, come." The Dean registered impatience. "I'm sure I don't know how much of the story to discount, but it seems you must have been engaging in parlor tricks; silly parlor tricks quite unsuited to the spirit and dignity of this institution."

Dr. Morton said, "This is all beyond me."

The Dean frowned. "It seems you haven't heard, then. It is amazing to me how the faculty can remain in complete ignorance of matters that fairly saturate the student body. I had never realized it before. I myself heard of it by accident; by a very fortunate accident, in fact, since I was able to intercept a newspaper reporter who arrived this morning looking for someone he called 'Dr. Toomey, the flying professor.'"

"What?" cried Dr. Morton.

Roger listened haggardly.

"That's what the reporter said. I quote him. It seems one of our students had called the paper. I ordered the newspaper man out and had the student sent to my office. According to him, Dr. Toomey flew—I use the word, 'flew,' because that's what the student insisted on calling it—down a flight of stairs and then back up again. He claimed there were a dozen witnesses."

"I went down the stairs only," muttered Roger.

Dean Smithers was tramping up and down along his carpet now. He had worked himself up into a feverish eloquence. "Now mind you, Toomey, I have nothing against amateur theatricals. In my stay in office I have consistently fought against stuffiness and false dignity. I have encouraged friendliness between ranks in the faculty and have not even objected to reasonable fraternization with students. So I have no objection to your putting on a show for the students *in your own home*.

"Surely you see what could happen to the college once an irresponsible press is done with us. Shall we have a flying-professor craze succeed the flying-saucer craze? If the reporters get in touch with you, Dr. Toomey, I will expect you to deny all such reports categorically."

"I understand, Dean Smithers."

"I trust that we shall escape this incident without lasting damage. I must ask you, with all the firmness at my command, never to repeat your . . . uh . . . performance. If you ever do, your resignation will be requested. Do you understand, Dr. Toomey?"

"Yes," said Roger.

"In that case, good day, gentlemen."

Dr. Morton steered Roger back into his office. This time, he shooed his secretary and closed the door behind her carefully.

"Good heavens, Toomey," he whispered, "has this madness any connection with your letter on levitation?"

Roger's nerves were beginning to twang. "Isn't it obvious? I was referring to myself in those letters."

"You can fly? I mean, levitate?"

"Either word you choose."

"I never heard of such— Damn it, Toomey, did Miss Harroway ever see you levitate?"

"Once. It was an accid—"

"Of course. It's obvious now. She was so hysterical it was hard to make out. She said you had jumped at her. It sounded as though she were accusing you of . . . of—" Dr. Morton looked embarrassed. "Well, I didn't believe that. She was a good secretary, you understand, but obviously not one designed to attract the attention of a young man. I was actually relieved when she left. I thought she would be carrying a small revolver next, or accusing *me*— You . . . you levitated, eh?"

"Yes."

"How do you do it?"

Roger shook his head. "That's my problem. I don't know."

Dr. Morton allowed himself a smile. "Surely, you don't repeal the law of gravity?"

"You know, I think I do. There must be antigravity involved somehow."

Dr. Morton's indignation at having a joke taken seriously was marked. He said, "Look here, Toomey, this is nothing to laugh at."

"*Laugh* at. Great Scott, Dr. Morton, do I look as though I were laughing?"

"Well—you need a rest. No question about it. A little rest and this nonsense of yours will pass. I'm sure of it."

"It's not nonsense." Roger bowed his head a moment, then said, in a quieter tone, "I tell you what, Dr. Morton, would you like to go in to this with me? In some way this will open new horizons in physical science. I don't know how it works; I just can't conceive of any solution. The two of us together—"

Dr. Morton's look of horror penetrated by that time.

Roger said, "I know it all sounds queer. But I'll demonstrate for you. It's perfectly legitimate. I wish it weren't."

"Now, now," Dr. Morton sprang from his seat. "Don't exert yourself. You need a rest badly. I don't think you should wait till June. You go home right now. I'll see that your salary comes through and I'll look after your course. I used to give it myself once, you know."

"Dr. Morton. This is important."

"I know. I know." Dr. Morton clapped Roger on the shoulder. "Still, my boy, you look under the weather. Speaking frankly, you look like hell. You need a long rest."

"I *can* levitate." Roger's voice was climbing again. "You're just trying to get rid of me because you don't believe me. Do you think I'm lying? What would be my motive?"

"You're exciting yourself needlessly, my boy. You let me make a phone call. I'll have someone take you home."

"I tell you I *can* levitate," shouted Roger.

Dr. Morton turned red. "Look, Toomey, let's not discuss it. I don't care if you fly up in the air right this minute."

"You mean seeing isn't believing as far as you're concerned?"

"Levitation? Of course not." The department chairman was bellowing. "If I saw you fly, I'd see an optometrist or a psychiatrist. I'd sooner believe myself insane than that the laws of physics—"

He caught himself, harrumphed loudly. "Well, as I said, let's not discuss it. I'll just make this phone call."

"No need, sir. No need," said Roger. "I'll go. I'll take my rest. Good-bye."

He walked out rapidly, moving more quickly than at any time in days. Dr. Morton, on his feet, hands flat on his desk, looked at his departing back with relief.

James Sarle, M.D., was in the living room when Roger arrived home. He was lighting his pipe as Roger stepped through the door, one large-knuckled hand enclosing the bowl. He shook out the match and his ruddy face crinkled into a smile.

"Hello, Roger. Resigning from the human race? Haven't heard from you in over a month."

His black eyebrows met above the bridge of his nose, giving him a rather forbidding appearance that somehow helped him establish the proper atmosphere with his patients.

Roger turned to Jane, who sat buried in an armchair. As usual lately, she had a look of wan exhaustion on her face.

Roger said to her, "Why did you bring him here?"

"Hold it! Hold it, man," said Sarle. "Nobody brought me. I met Jane downtown this morning and invited myself here. I'm bigger than she is. She couldn't keep me out."

"Met her by coincidence, I suppose? Do you make appointments for all your coincidences?"

Sarle laughed, "Let's put it this way. She told me a little about what's been going on."

Jane said, wearily, "I'm sorry if you disapprove, Roger, but it was the first chance I had to talk to someone who would understand."

"What makes you think he understands? Tell me, Jim, do you believe her story?"

Sarle said, "It's not an easy thing to believe. You'll admit that. But I'm trying."

"All right, suppose I flew. Suppose I levitated right now. What would you do?"

"Faint, maybe. Maybe I'd say, 'Holy Pete.' Maybe I'd bust out laughing. Why don't you try, and then we'll see?"

Roger stared at him. "You really want to see it?"

"Why shouldn't I?"

"The ones that have seen it screamed or ran or froze with horror. Can you take it, Jim?"

"I think so."

"O.K." Roger slipped two feet upward and executed a slow ten-fold *entrechat*. He remained in the air, toes pointed downward, legs together, arms gracefully outstretched in bitter parody.

"Better than Nijinski, eh, Jim?"

Sarle did none of the things he suggested he might do. Except for catching his pipe as it dropped, he did nothing at all.

Jane had closed her eyes. Tears squeezed quietly through the lids.

Sarle said, "Come down, Roger."

Roger did so. He took a seat and said, "I wrote to physicists, men of reputation. I explained the situation in an impersonal way. I said I thought it ought to be investigated. Most of them ignored me. One of them wrote to old man Morton to ask if I were crooked or crazy."

"Oh, Roger," whispered Jane.

"You think that's bad? The Dean called me into his office today. I'm to stop my parlor tricks, he says. It seems I had stumbled down the stairs and automatically levitated myself to safety. Morton says he wouldn't believe I could fly if he saw me in action. Seeing isn't believing in this case, he says, and orders me to take a rest. I'm not going back."

"Roger," said Jane, her eyes opening wide. "Are you serious?"

"I can't go back. I'm sick of them. Scientists!"

"But what will you do?"

"I don't know." Roger buried his head in his hands. He said in a muffled voice, "You tell me, Jim. You're the psychiatrist. Why won't they believe me?"

"Perhaps it's a matter of self-protection, Roger," said Sarle, slowly. "People aren't happy with anything they can't understand. Even some centuries ago when many people *did* believe in the existence of extranatural abilities, like flying on broomsticks, for instance, it was almost always assumed that these powers originated with the forces of evil.

"People still think so. They may not believe literally in the devil, but they do think that what is strange is evil. They'll fight against believing in levitation—or be scared to death if the fact is forced down their throats. That's true, so let's face it."

Roger shook his head. "You're talking about people, and I'm talking about scientists."

"Scientists are people."

"You know what I mean. I have here a phenomenon. It isn't witchcraft. I haven't dealt with the devil. Jim, there must be a natural explanation. We don't know all there is to know about gravitation. We know hardly anything, really. Don't you suppose it's just barely conceivable that there is some biological method of nullifying gravity? Perhaps I am a mutation of some sort. I have a . . . well, call it a muscle . . . which can abolish gravity. At least it can abolish the effect of gravity on myself. Well, let's investigate it. Why sit on our hands? If we have antigravity, imagine what it will mean to the human race."

"Hold it, Rog," said Sarle. "Think about the matter awhile. Why are *you* so unhappy about it? According to Jane, you were almost mad with fear the first day it happened, *before* you had any way of knowing that science was going to ignore you and that your superiors would be unsympathetic."

"That's right," murmured Jane.

Sarle said, "Now why should that be? Here you had a great, new, wonderful power; a sudden freedom from the deadly pull of gravity."

Roger said, "Oh, don't be a fool. It was—horrible. I couldn't understand it. I still can't."

"Exactly, my boy. It was something you couldn't understand and *therefore* something horrible. You're a physical scientist. You *know* what makes the universe run. Or if you don't know, you know someone else knows. Even if no one understands a certain point, you know that some day someone will know. The key word is *know*. It's part of your life. Now you come face to face with a phenomenon which you consider to violate one of the basic laws of the universe. Scientists say: Two masses will attract one another according to a fixed mathematical rule. It is an inalienable property of matter and space. There are no exceptions. And now you're an exception."

Roger said, glumly, "And how."

"You see, Roger," Sarle went on, "for the first time in history, mankind really has what he considers unbreakable rules. I mean, unbreakable. In primitive cultures, a medicine man might use a spell to produce rain. If it didn't work, it didn't upset the validity of magic. It just meant that the shaman had neglected some part of his spell, or had broken a taboo, or offended a god. In modern theocratic cultures, the commandments of the Deity are unbreakable. Still if a man were to break the commandments and yet prosper, it would be no sign that that particular religion was invalid. The ways of Providence are admittedly mysterious and some invisible punishment awaits.

"Today, however, we have rules that *really* can't be broken, and one of them is the existence of gravity. It works even though the man who invokes it has forgotten to mutter em-em-over-ahr-square."

Roger managed a twisted smile. "You're all wrong, Jim. The unbreakable rules have been broken over and over again. Radioactivity was impossible when it was discovered. Energy came out of nowhere; incredible quantities of it. It was as ridiculous as levitation."

"Radioactivity was an objective phenomenon that could be communicated and duplicated. Uranium would fog photographic film for anyone. A Crookes tube could be built by anyone and would deliver an electron-stream in identical fashion for all. You—"

"I've tried communicating—"

"I know. But can you tell me, for instance, how *I* might levitate."

"Of course not."

"That limits others to observation only, without experimental duplication. It puts your levitation on the same plane with stellar evolution, something to theorize about but never experiment with."

"Yet scientists are willing to devote their lives to astrophysics."

"Scientists are people. They can't reach the stars, so they make the best of it. But they can reach you and to be unable to touch your levitation would be infuriating."

"Jim, they haven't even tried. You talk as though I've been studied. Jim, they won't even consider the problem."

"They don't have to. Your levitation is part of a whole class of phenomena that won't be considered. Telepathy, clairvoyance, prescience and a thousand other extranatural powers are practically never seriously investigated, even though reported with every appearance of reliability. Rhine's experiments on E.S.P. have annoyed far more scientists than they have intrigued. So you see, they don't have to study you to know they don't want to study you. They know that in advance."

"Is this funny to you, Jim? Scientists refuse to investigate facts; they turn their back on the truth. And you just sit there and grin and make droll statements."

"No, Roger, I know it's serious. And I have no glib explanations for mankind, really. I'm giving you my thoughts. It's what I think. But don't you see? What I'm doing, really, is to try to look at things as they are. It's what you must do. Forget your ideals, your theories, your notions as to what people *ought* to do. Consider what they *are* doing. Once a person is oriented to face facts rather than delusions, problems tend to disappear. At the very least, they fall into their true perspective and become soluble."

Roger stirred restlessly. "Psychiatric gobbledygook! It's like putting your fingers on a man's temple and saying, 'Have faith and you will be cured!' If the poor sap isn't cured, it's because he didn't drum up enough faith. The witch doctor can't lose."

"Maybe you're right, but let's see. What *is* your problem?"

"No catechism, please. You know my problem so let's not horse around."

"You levitate. Is that it?"

"Let's say it is. It'll do as a first approximation."

"You're not being serious, Roger, but actually you're probably right. It's only a first approximation. After all you're tackling that problem. Jane tells me you've been experimenting."

"Experimenting! Ye Gods, Jim, I'm not experimenting. I'm drifting. I need high-powered brains and equipment. I need a research team and I don't have it."

"Then what's your problem? Second approximation."

Roger said, "I see what you mean. My problem is to get a research team. But I've tried! Man, I've tried till I'm tired of trying."

"How have you tried?"

"I've sent out letters. I've asked— Oh, stop it, Jim. I haven't the heart to go through the patient-on-the-couch routine. You know what I've been doing."

"I know that you've said to people, 'I have a problem. Help me.' Have you tried anything else?"

"Look, Jim. I'm dealing with mature scientists."

"I know. So you reason that the straightforward request is sufficient. Again it's theory against fact. I've told you the difficulties involved in your request. When you thumb a ride on a highway you're making a straightforward request, but most cars pass you by just the same. The point is that the straightforward request has failed. Now what's your problem? Third approximation!"

"To find another approach which won't fail? Is that what you want me to say?"

"It's what you have said, isn't it?"

"So I know it without your telling me."

"Do you? You're ready to quit school, quit your job, quit science. Where's your consistency, Rog? Do you abandon a problem when your first experiment fails? Do you give up when one theory is shown to be inadequate? The same philosophy of experimental science that holds for inanimate objects should hold for people as well."

"All right. What do you suggest I try? Bribery? Threats? Tears?"

James Sarle stood up. "Do you really want a suggestion?"

"Go ahead."

"Do as Dr. Morton said. Take a vacation and to hell with levitation. It's a problem for the future. Sleep in bed and float or don't float; what's the difference. Ignore levitation, laugh at it or even enjoy it. Do anything but worry about it, because it isn't your problem. That's the whole point. It's not your immediate problem. Spend your time considering how to make scientists study something they don't want to study. That is the immediate problem and that is exactly what you've spent no thinking time on as yet."

Sarle walked to the hall closet and got his coat. Roger went with him. Minutes passed in silence.

Then Roger said without looking up, "Maybe you're right, Jim."

"Maybe I am. Try it and then tell me. Good-bye, Roger."

Roger Toomey opened his eyes and blinked at the morning brightness of the bedroom. He called out, "Hey, Jane, where are you?"

Jane's voice answered, "In the kitchen. Where do you think?"

"Come in here, will you?"

She came in. "The bacon won't fry itself, you know."

"Listen, did I float last night?"

"I don't know. I slept."

"You're a help." He got out of bed and slipped his feet into his mules. "Still, I don't think I did."

"Do you think you've forgotten how?" There was sudden hope in her voice.

"I haven't forgotten. See!" He slid into the dining room on a cushion of air. "I just have a feeling I haven't floated. I think it's three nights now."

"Well, that's good," said Jane. She was back at the stove. "It's just that a month's rest has done you good. If I had called Jim in the beginning—"

"Oh, please, don't go through that. A month's rest, my eye. It's just that last Sunday I made up my mind what to do. Since then I've relaxed. That's all there is to it."

"What are you going to do?"

"Every spring Northwestern Tech gives a series of seminars on physical topics. I'll attend."

"You mean, go way out to Seattle."

"Of course."

"What will they be discussing?"

"What's the difference? I just want to see Linus Deering."

"But he's the one who called you crazy, isn't he?"

"He did." Roger scooped up a forkful of scrambled eggs. "But he's also the best man of the lot."

He reached for the salt and lifted a few inches out of his chair as he did so. He paid no attention.

He said, "I think maybe I can handle him."

The spring seminars at Northwestern Tech had become a nationally known institution since Linus Deering had joined the faculty. He was the chairman and lent the proceedings their distinctive tone. He introduced the speakers, led the questioning periods, summed up at the close of each morning and afternoon session and was the soul of conviviality at the concluding dinner at the end of the week's work.

All this Roger Toomey knew by report. He could now observe the actual workings of the man. Professor Deering was rather under middle height, was dark of complexion and had a luxuriant and quite distinctive mop of wavy brown hair. His wide, thin-lipped mouth when not engaged in active conversation looked perpetually on the point of a sly smile. He spoke quickly and fluently, without notes, and seemed always to deliver his comments from a level of superiority that his listeners automatically accepted.

At least, so he had been on the first morning of the seminar. It was only during the afternoon session that the listeners began to notice a certain hesitation in his remarks. Even more, there was an uneasiness about him as he sat on the stage during the delivery of the scheduled papers. Occasionally, he glanced furtively toward the rear of the auditorium.

Roger Toomey, seated in the very last row, observed all this tensely. His temporary glide toward normality that had begun when he first thought there might be a way out was beginning to recede.

On the Pullman to Seattle, he had not slept. He had had visions of himself lifting upward in time to the wheel-clacking, of moving out quietly past the curtains and into the corridor, of being awakened into endless embarrassment by the hoarse shouting of a porter. So he had fastened the curtains with safety pins and had achieved nothing by that; no feeling of security; no sleep outside of a few exhausting snatches.

He had napped in his seat during the day, while the mountains slipped past outside, and arrived in Seattle in the evening with a stiff neck, aching bones, and a general sensation of despair.

He had made his decision to attend the seminar far too late to have been able to obtain a room to himself at the Institute's dormitories. Sharing a room was, of course, quite out of the question. He registered at a downtown hotel, locked the door, closed and locked all the windows, shoved his bed hard against the wall and the bureau against the open side of the bed; then slept.

He remembered no dreams, and when he awoke in the morning he was still lying within the manufactured enclosure. He felt relieved.

When he arrived, in good time, at Physics Hall on the Institute's campus, he found, as he expected, a large room and a small gathering. The seminar sessions were held, traditionally, over the Easter vacation and students were not in attendance. Some fifty physicists sat in an auditorium designed to hold four hundred, clustering on either side of the central aisle up near the podium.

Roger took his seat in the last row, where he would not be seen by casual passersby looking through the high, small windows of the auditorium door, and where the others in the audience would have had to twist through nearly a hundred eighty degrees to see him.

Except, of course, for the speaker on the platform—and for Professor Deering.

Roger did not hear much of the actual proceedings. He concentrated entirely on waiting for those moments when Deering was alone on the platform; when only Deering could see him.

As Deering grew obviously more disturbed, Roger grew bolder. During the final summing up of the afternoon, he did his best.

Professor Deering stopped altogether in the middle of a poorly constructed and entirely meaningless sentence. His audience, which had been shifting in their seats for some time stopped also and looked wonderingly at him.

Deering raised his hand and said, gaspingly, "You! You there!"

Roger Toomey had been sitting with an air of complete relaxation—in the very center of the aisle. The only chair beneath him was composed of two and a half feet of empty air. His legs were stretched out before him on the armrest of an equally airy chair.

When Deering pointed, Roger slid rapidly sidewise. By the time fifty heads turned, he was sitting quietly in a very prosaic wooden seat.

Roger looked this way and that, then stared at Deering's pointing finger and rose.

"Are you speaking to me, Professor Deering?" he asked, with only the slightest tremble in his voice to indicate the savage battle he was fighting within himself to keep that voice cool and wondering.

"What are you doing?" demanded Deering, his morning's tension exploding.

Some of the audience were standing in order to see better. An unexpected commotion is as dearly loved by a gathering of research physicists as by a crowd at a baseball game.

"I'm not doing anything," said Roger. "I don't understand you."

"Get out! Leave this hall!"

Deering was beside himself with a mixture of emotions, or perhaps he would not have said that. At any rate, Roger sighed and took his opportunity prayerfully.

He said, loudly and distinctly, forcing himself to be heard over the gathering clamor, "I am Professor Roger Toomey of Carson College. I am a member of the American Physical Association. I have applied for permission to attend these sessions, have been accepted, and have paid my registration fee. I am sitting here as is my right and will continue to do so."

Deering could only say blindly, "Get out!"

"I will not," said Roger. He was actually trembling with a synthetic and self-imposed anger. "For what reason must I get out? What have I done?"

Deering put a shaking hand through his hair. He was quite unable to answer.

Roger followed up his advantage. "If you attempt to evict me from these sessions without just cause, I shall certainly sue the Institute."

Deering said, hurriedly, "I call the first day's session of the Spring Seminars of Recent Advances in the Physical Sciences to a close. Our next session will be in this hall tomorrow at nine in—"

Roger left as he was speaking and hurried away.

There was a knock at Roger's hotel-room door that night. It startled him, froze him in his chair.

"Who is it?" he cried.

The answering voice was soft and hurried. "May I see you?"

It was Deering's voice. Roger's hotel as well as his room number were, of course, recorded with the seminar secretary. Roger had hoped, but scarcely expected, that the day's events would have so speedy a consequence.

He opened the door, said stiffly, "Good evening, Professor Deering."

Deering stepped in and looked about. He wore a very light topcoat that he made no gesture to remove. He held his hat in his hand and did not offer to put it down.

He said, "Professor Roger Toomey of Carson College. Right?" He said it with a certain emphasis, as though the name had significance.

"Yes. Sit down, Professor."

Deering remained standing. "Now what is it? What are you after?"

"I don't understand."

"I'm sure you do. You aren't arranging this ridiculous foolery for nothing. Are you trying to make me seem foolish or is it that you expect to hoodwink me into some crooked scheme? I want you to know it won't work. And don't try to use force now. I have friends who know exactly where I am at this moment. I'll advise you to tell the truth and then get out of town."

"Professor Deering! This is my room. If you are here to bully me, I'll ask you to leave. If you don't go, I'll have you put out."

"Do you intend to continue this . . . this persecution?"

"I have not been persecuting you. I don't know you, sir."

"Aren't you the Roger Toomey who wrote me a letter concerning a case of levitation he wanted me to investigate?"

Roger stared at the man. "What letter is this?"

"Do you deny it?"

"Of course I do. What are you talking about? Have you got the letter?"

Professor Deering's lips compressed. "Never mind that. Do you deny you were suspending yourself on wires at this afternoon's sessions?"

"On wires? I don't follow you at all."

"You were levitating!"

"Would you please leave, Professor Deering? I don't think you're well."

The physicist raised his voice. "Do you deny you were levitating?"

"I think you're mad. Do you mean to say I made magician's arrangements in your auditorium? I was never in it before today and when I arrived you were already present. Did you find wires or anything of the sort after I left?"

"I don't know how you did it and I don't care. *Do* you deny you were levitating?"

"Why, of course I do."

"I saw you. Why are you lying?"

"You saw me levitate? Professor Deering, will you tell me how that's possible? I suppose your knowledge of gravitational forces is enough to tell you that true levitation is a meaningless concept except in outer space. Are you playing some sort of joke on me?"

"Good heavens," said Deering in a shrill voice, "why won't you tell me the truth?"

"I am. Do you suppose that by stretching out my hand and making a mystic pass . . . so . . . I can go sailing off into air?" And Roger did so, his head brushing the ceiling.

Deering's head jerked upward, "Ah! There . . . there—"

Roger returned to earth, smiling. "You *can't* be serious."

"You did it again. You just did it."

"Did what, sir?"

"You levitated. You just levitated. You can't deny it."

Roger's eyes grew serious. "I think you're sick, sir."

"I know what I saw."

"Perhaps you need a rest. Overwork—"

"It was *not* a hallucination."

"Would you care for a drink?" Roger walked to his suitcase while Deering followed his footsteps with bulging eyes. The toes of his shoes touched air two inches from the ground and went no lower.

Deering sank into the chair Roger had vacated.

"Yes, please," he said, weakly.

Roger gave him the whiskey bottle, watched the other drink, then gag a bit. "How do you feel now?"

"Look here," said Deering, "have you discovered a way of neutralizing gravity?"

Roger stared. "Get hold of yourself, Professor. If I had antigravity, I wouldn't use it to play games on you. I'd be in Wash-

ington. I'd be a military secret. I'd be— Well, I wouldn't be here!
Surely all this is obvious to you."

Deering jumped to his feet. "Do you intend sitting in on the
remaining sessions?"

"Of course."

Deering nodded, jerked his hat down upon his head and hurried
out.

For the next three days, Professor Deering did not preside over
the seminar sessions. No reason for his absence was given. Roger
Toomey, caught between hope and apprehension, sat in the body
of the audience and tried to remain inconspicuous. In this, he was
not entirely successful. Deering's public attack had made him noto-
rious while his own strong defense had given him a kind of David
versus Goliath popularity.

Roger returned to his hotel room Thursday night after an unsatisfactory dinner and remained standing in the doorway, one foot
over the threshold. Professor Deering was gazing at him from
within. And another man, a gray fedora shoved well back on his
forehead, was seated on Roger's bed.

It was the stranger who spoke. "Come inside, Toomey."

Roger did so. "What's going on?"

The stranger opened his wallet and presented a cellophane window to Roger. He said, "I'm Cannon of the FBI."

Roger said, "You have influence with the government, I take it,
Professor Deering."

"A little," said Deering.

Roger said, "Well, am I under arrest? What's my crime?"

"Take it easy," said Cannon. "We've been collecting some data
on you, Toomey. Is this your signature?"

He held a letter out far enough for Roger to see, but not to
snatch. It was the letter Roger had written to Deering which the
latter had sent on to Morton.

"Yes," said Roger.

"How about this one?" The federal agent had a sheaf of letters.

Roger realized that he must have collected every one he had sent
out, minus those that had been torn up. "They're all mine," he said,
wearily.

Deering snorted.

Cannon said, "Professor Deering tells us that you can float."

"Float? What the devil do you mean, float?"

"Float in the air," said Cannon, stolidly.

"Do you believe anything as crazy as that?"

"I'm not here to believe or not to believe, Dr. Toomey," said Cannon. "I'm an agent of the government of the United States and I've got an assignment to carry out. I'd cooperate if I were you."

"How can I cooperate in something like this? If I came to you and told you that Professor Deering could float in air, you'd have me flat on a psychiatrist's couch in no time."

Cannon said, "Professor Deering has been examined by a psychiatrist at his own request. However, the government has been in the habit of listening very seriously to Professor Deering for a number of years now. Besides, I might as well tell you that we have independent evidence."

"Such as?"

"A group of students at your college have seen you float. Also, a woman who was once secretary to the head of your department. We have statements from all of them."

Roger said, "What kind of statements? Sensible ones that you would be willing to put into the record and show to my congressman?"

Professor Deering interrupted anxiously, "Dr. Toomey, what do you gain by denying the fact that you can levitate? Your own dean admits that you've done something of the sort. He has told me that he will inform you officially that your appointment will be terminated at the end of the academic year. He wouldn't do that for nothing."

"That doesn't matter," said Roger.

"But why won't you admit I saw you levitate?"

"Why should I?"

Cannon said, "I'd like to point out, Dr. Toomey, that if you have any device for counteracting gravity, it would be of great importance to your government."

"Really? I suppose you have investigated my background for possible disloyalty."

"The investigation," said the agent, "is proceeding."

"All right," said Roger, "let's take a hypothetical case. Suppose I admitted I could levitate. Suppose I didn't know how I did it. Suppose I had nothing to give the government but my body and an insoluble problem."

"How can you know it's insoluble?" asked Deering, eagerly.

"I once asked you to study such a phenomenon," pointed out Roger, mildly. "You refused."

"Forget that. Look," Deering spoke rapidly, urgently. "You don't have a position at the moment. I can offer you one in my department as Associate Professor of Physics. Your teaching duties will be nominal. Full-time research on levitation. What about it?"

"It sounds attractive," said Roger.

"I think it's safe to say that unlimited government funds will be available."

"What do I have to do? Just admit I can levitate?"

"I know you can. I saw you. I want you to do it now for Mr. Cannon."

Roger's legs moved upward and his body stretched out horizontally at the level of Cannon's head. He turned to one side and seemed to rest on his right elbow.

Cannon's hat fell backward onto the bed.

He yelled, "He floats."

Deering was almost incoherent with excitement. "Do you see it, man?"

"I sure see something."

"Then report it. Put it right down in your report, do you hear me? Make a complete record of it. They won't say there's anything wrong with me. I didn't doubt for a minute that I had seen it."

But he couldn't have been so happy if that were entirely true.

"I don't even know what the climate is like in Seattle," wailed Jane, "and there are a million things I have to do."

"Need any help?" asked Jim Sarle from his comfortable position in the depths of the armchair.

"There's nothing you can do. Oh, dear." And she flew from the room, but unlike her husband, she did so figuratively only.

Roger Toomey came in. "Jane, do we have the crates for the books yet? Hello, Jim. When did you come in? And where's Jane?"

"I came in a minute ago and Jane's in the next room. I had to get past a policeman to get in. Man, they've got you surrounded."

"Um-m-m," said Roger, absently. "I told them about you."

"I know you did. I've been sworn to secrecy. I told them it was a matter of professional confidence in any case. Why don't you let the movers do the packing? The government is paying, isn't it?"

"Movers wouldn't do it right," said Jane, suddenly hurrying in again and flouncing down on the sofa. "I'm going to have a cigarette."

"Break down, Roger," said Sarle, "and tell me what happened."

Roger smiled sheepishly. "As you said, Jim, I took my mind off the wrong problem and applied it to the right one. It just seemed to me that I was forever being faced with two alternatives. I was either crooked or crazy. Deering said that flatly in his letter to Morton. The dean assumed I was crooked and Morton suspected that I was crazy.

"But supposing I could show them that I could really levitate. Well, Morton told me what would happen in that case. Either I would be crooked or the *witness* would be insane. Morton said that —he said that if he saw me fly, he'd prefer to believe himself insane than accept the evidence. Of course, he was only being rhetorical. No man would believe in his own insanity while even the faintest alternative existed. I counted on that.

"So I changed my tactics. I went to Deering's seminar. I didn't *tell* him I could float; I showed him, *and then denied I had done it.* The alternative was clear. I was either lying or he—not I, mind you, but *he*—was mad. It was obvious that he would sooner believe in levitation than doubt his own sanity, once he was really put to the test. All his actions thereafter, his bullying, his trip to Washington, his offer of a job, were all intended only to vindicate his own sanity, not to help me."

Sarle said, "In other words you had made your levitation his problem and not your own."

Roger said, "Did you have anything like this in mind when we had our talk, Jim?"

Sarle shook his head. "I had vague notions but a man must solve his own problems if they're to be solved effectively. Do you think they'll work out the principle of levitation now?"

"I don't know, Jim. I still can't communicate the subjective aspects of the phenomenon. But that doesn't matter. We'll be investigating them and that's what counts." He struck his balled right fist into the palm of his left hand. "As far as I'm concerned the important point is that I made them help me."

"Is it?" asked Sarle, softly. "I should say that the important point is that you let them make *you* help *them*, which is a different thing altogether."

Introduction to

DEATH OF A FOY

Every once in a while, George Scithers of *Asimov's* likes to publish short and outrageous stories, and, every once in a while, I like to write one. So I wrote "Death of a Foy" and sent it off to George, hardly able to stop laughing long enough to seal the envelope.

You can imagine my indignation when George rejected it. (Actually, it was good that he did. I don't want anyone to think that the appearance in my own magazine of any story I write is a foregone conclusion. George has strict orders to reject anything of mine he doesn't like. He accepts that situation, and so do I.)

Making a few cursory remarks under my breath, I sent the story on to Ed Ferman at *The Magazine of Fantasy and Science Fiction*, hereafter to be referred to as *F & SF*. Fortunately, he managed to stop laughing long enough to write out a check, and it appeared in the October 1980 *F & SF*.

4.

DEATH OF A FOY

It was extremely unusual for a Foy to be dying on Earth. They were the highest social class on their planet (with a name which was pronounced—as nearly as Earthly throats could make the sounds—Sortibackenstrete) and were virtually immortal.

Every Foy, of course, came to voluntary death eventually, and this one had given up because of an ill-starred love affair, if you can call it a love affair where five individuals, in order to reproduce, must indulge in a year-long mental contact. Apparently, he himself had not fit into the contact after several months of trying and it had broken his heart—or hearts, for he had five.

All Foys had five large hearts and there was speculation that it was this that made them virtually immortal.

Maude Briscoe, Earth's most renowned surgeon, wanted those hearts. "It can't be just their number and size, Dwayne," she said to her chief assistant. "It has to be something physiological or biochemical. I must have them."

"I don't know if we can manage that," said Dwayne Johnson. "I've been speaking to him earnestly, trying to overcome the Foy taboo against dismemberment after death. I've had to play on the feeling of tragedy any Foy would have over death away from home. And I've had to lie to him, Maude."

"Lie?"

"I told him that after death, there would be a dirge sung for him by the world-famous choir led by Harold J. Gassenbaum. I told him that by Earthly belief this would mean that his astral essence would be instantaneously wafted back, through hyperspace, to his home planet of Sortib-what's its name. —Provided he would sign a release allowing you, Maude, to have his hearts for scientific investigation."

"Don't tell me he believed that horse excrement!" said Maude.

"Well, you know this modern attitude about accepting the myths and beliefs of intelligent aliens. It wouldn't have been polite for him not to believe me. Besides, the Foys have a profound admiration for terrestrial science and I think this one is a little flattered that we should want his hearts. He promised to consider the suggestion, and I hope he decides soon because he can't live more than another day or so, and we must have his permission by interstellar law, and the hearts must be fresh, and— Ah, his signal."

Dwayne Johnson moved in with smooth and noiseless speed.

"Yes?" he whispered, unobtrusively turning on the holographic recording device in case the Foy wished to grant permission.

The Foy's large, gnarled, rather tree-like body lay motionless on the bed. The bulging eyes palpitated (all five of them) as they rose, each on its stalk, and turned toward Dwayne. The Foy's voice had a strange tone and the lipless edges of his open, round mouth did not move, but the words formed perfectly. His eyes were making the Foyan gesture of assent as he said:

"Give my big hearts to Maude, Dwayne. Dismember me for Harold's choir. Tell all the Foys on Sortibackenstrete that I will soon be there—"

Introduction to

FAIR EXCHANGE?

I am a member of the Gilbert & Sullivan Society of New York, a most enthusiastic one, and never miss a meeting if I can help it.

Once, when I was in the apartment of one of the members, rehearsing something we were going to do at one of the meetings, the play *Thespis* was mentioned. It was the first of the Gilbert and Sullivan collaborations and almost all the music to it is lost. At once I got the thought of weaving the matter into a science fiction story. I got to work on it in January 1978 to the delight of the society generally.

There was only one catch. I intended to write a funny story, but as every writer knows, stories have a bad habit of writing themselves, and you will have to accept the result the story seemed to want. It appeared in the Fall 1979 issue of *Asimov's Science Fiction Adventure Magazine* (or *Asfam*), a short-lived (alas!) sister magazine of *Asimov's*.

"Fair Exchange?" also appeared, in 1981, in a small three-story collection of mine called *Three by Asimov*. This was published by William Targ in a very limited edition of two hundred and fifty, at sixty dollars a copy. Presumably, they are now all gone, so I see nothing wrong with including it in a collection that will be considerably larger, cheaper, and more available.

One of the other two stories in *Three by Asimov* also appears in this collection, by the way, and I will point it out when I get to it.

5.

FAIR EXCHANGE?

I kept drifting in and out and every once in a while I'd hear a brief snatch of tune in my head.

The words came. "While noodles are baroned and earled, there's nothing for clever obscurity."

I was aware of light, then John Sylva's face bending over me. "Hello, Herb," its mouth said.

I didn't hear the words, but I saw the mouth forming them. I nodded and drifted out again.

It was dark when I drifted in once more. A nurse was fussing over me but I lay quietly and she drifted away.

I was in a hospital, of course.

I wasn't surprised. John had warned me and I had taken the risk. I moved my legs, then my arms—very gently. They didn't hurt. They had sensation. My head throbbed but that was to be expected, too.

—*While noodles are baroned and earled, there's nothing*—

Thespis, I thought jubilantly. I had heard *Thespis.* I drifted off again.

It was dawn. There was the taste of orange juice on my lips. I sipped at the straw and was grateful.

Time machine!

John Sylva didn't like to have me call it that. Temporal transference, he called it.

I could hear him saying it and I luxuriated in it. My brain seemed perfectly normal. I tried to solve problems in my head and worked away, mentally, at the square root of five hundred and forty-three. Name the Presidents in order! I *seemed* to be in good mental shape. Could I tell? I assured myself I could.

Brain damage had been the great worry, of course, and I don't think I'd have risked it except for *Thespis*. You'd have to be a Gilbert and Sullivan fanatic to understand that. I was, and so was Mary. We had met at a G & S Society meeting, wooed each other through further meetings and while attending performances by the Village Light Opera Group. When we married at last, a chorus of our G & S friends sang "When a Merry Maiden Marries" from *The Gondoliers*.

My brain was normal. I was sure of it and I stared out at the cold gray dawn that coated the window and listened to my steadily strengthening memory of what had happened.

"Not a time machine," I heard John's voice saying in my mind. "That's an automobile you drive up and down the corridors of time and it's theoretically impossible. What we have here is temporal transference. Minds can exert their influence across time. Or, rather, subatomic particles can, and if organized as complexly as in an advanced brain, their influence is multiplied to the point where it can be detected and, I think, used. If two minds are similar enough, they can resonate to the point where consciousness can shift back and forth across the time gap. Temporal transference."

"Can you actually control that?"

"I think so. I dare say each mind resonates with many others and God knows what this would account for in terms of dreams, of feelings of *déjà vu*, of sudden inspiration and so on. —But to make an actual transfer means an overriding resonance between two particular minds, and requires the proper amplification."

I was one of hundreds he tested. There was no use trying animals. Only the human brain set up a field strong enough to detect. —Dolphins, perhaps, but how would one go about working with them?

"Just about everyone shows detectable resonance," said John. "You show a strong one, for instance, in one particular direction."

"With whom?" I asked, interested.

"Impossible to tell that, Herb," he said, "and we can't be sure how accurate our estimates of time and place are, but you seem to resonate with someone in London in 1871."

"In London in 1871?"

"Yes. We can't check our measurements through until we can subject someone to amplification great enough to effect a transfer and frankly I don't expect to find many volunteers."

"I'll volunteer," I said.

It took me some time to convince him I was serious. We were old friends and he knew of my attachment to the G & S mystique but I imagine he could not conceive its depth.

Mary could! She was as excited as I was.

I said to her, "Imagine the luck of the draw! *Thespis* was produced in London in 1871. If I suddenly found myself in that place at that time, I could *hear* it. I could—"

It was an overwhelming thought. *Thespis* was the first of the fourteen Gilbert & Sullivan operettas, a slight piece, and certainly unsuccessful, but it *was* Gilbert & Sullivan just the same and the music was irretrievably lost. —All except one introductory chorus which was used in *Pirates of Penzance* very successfully, and one ballad.

If I could hear it!

I said, enthusiastically, "And not just hear it. If I could lay my hands on the score and study it. If I could put a copy in a safe-deposit box and somehow get to open it now. If I could—"

Mary's eyes were gleaming but she did not lose her sense of the practical. "But could it be done? Granted that anything from *Thespis* would be the G & S find of the century, there's still no use having false hopes. If you got into the mind of whoever it is in 1871, could you make him do what you want?"

"I could try," I said. "He would have to be much like me if our minds resonated so strongly over a time-gap of more than a century. He would have my tastes."

"But what if something happened to you?"

"Some goals are worth the risk," I said firmly, and she agreed. She wouldn't have been my Mary if she hadn't in this case.

Just the same I didn't tell her that John had warned me that brain damage was the great risk. "There's no way of predicting how great the risk of damage is," he said, "or if there's any at all, till we try it. I'd rather not try it with my best friend."

"Your best friend insists," I said, and signed all the releases that the lawyers of John's Temporal Transfer Foundation had set up.

But I took one precaution. I didn't tell Mary exactly when it would happen. If something went wrong, I didn't want her there at the time. She would soon be making her annual trek to Canada to visit her parents and why not then?

"John won't be ready till the fall at the earliest," I said, and did my best to look disappointed.

Three days after Mary left, it was all ready.

I wasn't conscious of any nervousness at all, even when John said, "The sensations may be unpleasant."

I shrugged it off. "John," I said, "when I'm in England will I be able to do anything? Voluntarily, I mean?"

John said, "That's another question I can't answer categorically until you return—which will be automatic by the way. Even if I drop dead or the power fails, the resonance will eventually snap and you'll be back here. It's fail-safe because your physical body never leaves. You understand?"

"I understand." John was convinced that to relax me on this point would relieve tension and lower the chance of brain damage. He had reassured me over and over. I said, "Will I be able to do anything?"

"I don't think so. You'll only be able to observe."

"Can I affect history?"

"That would introduce paradoxes, which is what makes the ordinary notion of time-travel impossible. You can observe, bring those observations back and change history from this point on—and that introduces no paradoxes."

"Better than nothing," I muttered.

"Of course," he said. "You'll be able to hear that operetta of yours possibly and that would be something."

Something, but not enough. I wasn't a trained musician; I couldn't reproduce every note.

I consoled myself with the hope that John was wrong or, perhaps, was lying. If there *were* the possibility of changing history the Office of Technological Assessment would not allow the experiments to continue. Surely, John had to maintain there was no such possibility or his research funds would be cut off.

They wheeled in my breakfast and the nurse said, with synthetic cheer, "Well, you seem quite yourself now."

She had broken into my memories and it wasn't much of a breakfast but I was hungry enough for even the hot oatmeal to taste
good.

It was a good sign and in my mind a voice sang, "Well, well,
that's the way of the world, and will be through all its futurity;
while noodles are baroned and earled, there's nothing for clever obscurity."

I recognized it. It was the chorus to Mercury's solo from the first
act of *Thespis*. Or at least I recognized the words. The music was
new to me—but it was Sullivan. No question about it.

John Sylva arrived at 10 A.M. He said, "They called to tell me
you're off the intravenous and you're still asking for me. How do
you feel? You look pretty normal." His relief seemed limited. There
was a worried look in his eye.

"I was asking for you?" I tried to remember.

"Constantly, while you were semiconscious. I was here yesterday,
but you weren't quite awake."

"I think I remember," I said, then brushed it aside. "Listen,
John," I said. My voice was rather weak but I started from the beginning of Mercury's solo. "Oh, I'm the celestial drudge, From
morning to night I must stop at it; On errands all day—" and
carried it through to the end.

John nodded, having kept time as I sang. "Pretty," he said.

"*Pretty!* It's *Thespis*. I attended three performances in London. I
didn't even have to work to do it. My alter ego—a stockbroker by
the way, named Jeremy Bentford—did it on his own. I even tried
to get a copy of the score. I managed to get Bentford to break into
Sullivan's dressing room during the third performance. It didn't
take much. It was his own urge, too; we were very much alike,
which is why we resonated, of course.

"Trouble is, he was caught and ejected. He actually had the
score in his hand but couldn't hang on to it. So you're right. We
can't change past history. —But we can change future history because I've got all the important tunes of *Thespis* right in my
head. . . .

John said, "What are you talking about, Herb?"

"England! 1871! —For God's sake, John. Temporal transference!"

John nearly jumped. "Is *that* why you wanted to see me?"

"Yes, of course. How can you question that? Weren't you here all the time? My God, you sent me back in time. My mind, anyway."

John looked absolutely at sea. Wasn't I making sense? Had my brain been damaged after all? Is what I'm saying not what I think I am saying?

He said, "We talked about temporal transference a good deal. Yes, Herb. But—"

"But what?"

"It never worked. You remember that, don't you? It was a failure."

It was my turn to feel stupefied. "How can it be a failure? You sent me back."

John thought awhile, then got up. "Let me get the doctor, Herb."

I tried to grasp his sleeve. "No, you did! How else do I know the tunes to *Thespis*? You don't think I'm making them up, do you? Do you think I'm capable of inventing the tune I just sang?"

But he had rung for the nurse, and he left. Eventually the doctor arrived and went through the ridiculous ritual of examination.

Why was John lying? Had he had trouble with the government over sending my mind back into time? Was he going to save his project by forcing me to lie too? Or representing me to be insane?

It was an upsetting and depressing thought. I had the music to *Thespis,* but could I prove that that was what it was? Would it not be much easier to suppose it a forgery? Would the Gilbert and Sullivan Society be able to help out? There would have to be people there who could judge Sullivan's musical fingerprints, so to speak. Or would *anything* carry conviction if John remained firm in his denial?

By the next morning, I felt pugnacious about it. In fact, I thought of nothing else. I called John (or had the nurse call him, at any rate) and told him I had to see him again. And I forgot completely to ask him to bring my mail, which would have to include letters from Mary, among other things.

When John arrived, I said, as soon as the door opened and his face appeared in the opening, "John, I have the music to *Thespis*. I sang it to you. Do you deny I'm telling the truth about that?"

"No, of course not, Herb," he said, placatingly. "I know the tunes, too."

That almost stopped me. I swallowed and said, "How can you—"

"Look, Herb, I understand. I can imagine that you would want the music to *Thespis* to be missing. But it isn't. You've got to face that. Look at this."

He held out a book with its soft covers in blue. The title was *Thespis,* lyrics by William Schwenck Gilbert, music by Arthur Sullivan.

I opened it and leafed through it in utter astonishment.

"Where did you get this?"

"In a music store near Lincoln Center. You can get it anywhere that sells the Gilbert and Sullivan scores."

I was silent for a while. Then I said, petulantly, "I want you to make a call for me."

"To whom?"

"To the president of the Gilbert and Sullivan Society."

"Certainly, if you'll give me his name and number."

"Ask him to come see me. Just as soon as he can. It's very important."

Again I forgot to ask about my mail. —No. *Thespis* first.

Saul Reeve was in my room immediately after lunch, his gentle face and comfortable paunch an element of solidity I clung to with relief. He was virtually the personification of the Society and I was mildly astonished that he wasn't wearing his Gilbert and Sullivan T-shirt.

He said, "I'm awfully glad you pulled through, Herb. The Society has been worried sick."

(Pulled through what? Worried over what? How did they know about the temporal transference experiment? If they did know, why was John lying and saying there hadn't been one?)

I said, sharply, "What's this about *Thespis?*"

"What's what about *Thespis?*"

"Does the music exist?"

Poor Saul is no actor. He knows everything there is to know about Gilbert and Sullivan, but if he knows anything else, he's fooled everyone. The look of astonishment on his face had to be the mark of a genuine, unfaked emotion.

He said, "Of course it exists—but it nearly didn't, if that's what you mean."

"What do you mean, nearly."

"You know the story."

"Tell me, anyway. —*Tell* me!"

"Well, Sullivan was disgusted at the reception of the play and he wasn't going to publish the score. Then there was an attempted burglary. Some stockbroker tried to steal the score, actually had it in his hand when he was caught. Sullivan said that if the score was good enough to steal, it was good enough to publish. If it hadn't been for the stockbroker, we might not have the music today. —Not that it's popular. It's hardly ever performed. *You* know that."

I didn't listen after that.

—If it hadn't been for the stockbroker!

I *had* changed history, then.

Did that explain matters? Did even so small a thing as the publication of *Thespis* set up its ripples and create an alternate time-path, and was I in that alternate time-path?

Where did the ripples come from? Did the music matter so much? Did it inspire someone to do something or say something that would otherwise have been undone or unsaid? Or did the stockbroker's career take a turn as a result of apprehension for attempted burglary, and did that set up the ripples?

And did that somehow so alter events that John Sylva had never worked out the technology of temporal transference so that I was trapped forever in the new world?

I was alone by now. I hadn't even been conscious of Saul's leaving.

I shook my head. How was it possible? How could the yes of temporal transference become a no? John Sylva hadn't changed. Saul Reeve hadn't changed. How could there be so large a change without there being many small changes?

I rang for the nurse. "Can you get me a copy of the *Times*, please. Today's, yesterday's, last week's. It doesn't matter."

Would she find an excuse not to bring one? Was there a conspiracy to keep me confused for some reason I couldn't fathom?

She brought one at once.

I looked at the date. It was four days after the temporal transference experiment.

The headlines seemed normal—President Carter—the Mideast crisis—satellite launchings.

I went from page to page, looking for discrepancies I could recognize. Senator Abzug had introduced a bill that would bring federal aid to a financially troubled New York City.

Senator Abzug?

Hadn't she lost the Democratic senatorial primary to Patrick Moynihan in 1976?

I had changed history. I had saved *Thespis*, and in doing that I had somehow wiped out John's working out of temporal transference, and won the primary and election for Bella Abzug.

What other changes? Millions of trifling changes to trifling people that I wouldn't recognize? If I had a New York *Times* for this day from my world and could compare it with the *Times* I was holding, would even a single inch of the paper in any column on any page be exactly duplicated?

If that were so, what about my own life? I *felt* exactly the same. Of course, I could only remember my life from the other time-path. My own. In this one— I could have kids. —My father could still be alive. —I might be unemployed.

Now I remembered my mail, and I needed it. I rang for my nurse and had her call John Sylva again. He was to bring me my mail. He had a key to my apartment. (Did he in this time-path?) Particularly, he was to bring me the letters from Mary.

John never came, but long after dinner, the doctor came in. It was not entirely for the usual routine of prod and poke. He sat down and looked at me thoughtfully.

He said, "Mr. Sylva tells me you were under the impression that the music to the play *Thespis* was lost."

I was on my guard at once. They were not going to have me in a mental institution. I said, "Are you a Gilbert and Sullivan enthusiast, Doctor?"

"Not an enthusiast, but I've seen several of the operettas; including, in fact, *Thespis,* about a year ago. Have you ever seen *Thespis?*"

I nodded my head, "I have," and I hummed Mercury's solo. I didn't think I had to tell him that the only times I had seen *Thespis* were in 1871.

He said, "Then you don't think the music to *Thespis* was lost?"

"Obviously not, since I know the music."

That stopped him. He cleared his throat and tried a new tack.

"Mr. Sylva seems to think you were under the impression you had gone back in time—"

I felt like a matador withstanding the rush of the bull. I almost enjoyed it. "Private joke," I said.

"Joke?"

"Mr. Sylva and I used to discuss time travel."

"Still," said the doctor with a kind of heavy patience, "it was this particular matter you decided to joke about? That the music to *Thespis* was lost?"

"Why not?"

"Do you have any reason for wishing the music did not exist?"

"No, of course not."

He stared at me thoughtfully. "You said you saw a production of *Thespis*. When?"

I shrugged. "I can't pinpoint it offhand. Must I?"

"Could it have been a year ago December?"

"Is that when you saw it, Doctor?"

"Yes."

"It's very possible I saw it then."

The doctor said, "It was a very bad day when I saw it. Freezing rain. Does that help you remember?"

Was he trying to trap me? Would I be agreeing to nonsense if I pretended to remember that?

I said, "Doctor, I'm obviously not well and I won't pretend I have every detail of my memories clear. What do *you* remember?" That put the ball clearly in his court.

He said, "I understand that there was a full house that day despite the weather. Many went only because it was *Thespis*, a play very rarely performed, and therefore one that most had not heard. It was the only reason I had gone. If the music to *Thespis* were lost, and if it had been any other play, I probably would not have gone. —Is that why you told Mr. Sylva when you regained consciousness that the music did not exist?"

"What do you mean?"

"That then *you* wouldn't have gone? Or been in the taxi coming back?"

"I don't understand you."

"But you were in an accident, sir."

"Are you telling me that that's why I'm here?" I stared at him, hostilely.

"No, sir. That was a year ago. It was your wife."

I felt the stab as though the word had been an ice pick. I tried to struggle to one elbow but there was a nurse at my side, holding me. I hadn't seen her come in.

The doctor said, "Do you remember?"

What was I *supposed* to remember? What was the worst? I said, "My wife was killed?"

Deny it. Please deny it.

But the doctor's vague tension diminished. He sighed a little. "Then you do remember."

I stopped struggling. There was one flaw in the story. "Then why am *I* in the hospital? Now!"

"Then you *don't* remember?"

"Tell me."

He was going to make me face reality. *His* reality. *This* time-path's reality. I waited for his words.

He said, "You've been depressed ever since. You attempted suicide. We saved you. —We will help you."

I didn't move. I didn't speak. Where could there be help?

I had changed history. I could never go back.

I had gained *Thespis*.

I had lost Mary.

Introduction to

FOR THE BIRDS

Back in 1978 a French fashion magazine wanted to put out an American edition. The American editor asked me to do a science fiction story which featured a clothes designer.

Well, you can take all I know about clothes designing, or about clothes, for that matter, and stuff it between the keys of a typewriter without affecting their working in any way, but I was being offered a generous sum, and it was a challenge. In November 1978, therefore, I wrote "For the Birds," received my payment, and sat back complacently to experience the novelty of having a story of mine appear in a fashion magazine.

I was dreadfully disappointed, therefore, when it turned out that, for some reason never revealed to me, the French publishers changed their minds. (And if any of you wise guys out there have just invented a theory, let me tell you that the editor assured me my story had nothing at all to do with the decision.)

In any case, I sent the story on to George Scithers, and it appeared in the May 1980 *Asimov's*.

6.

FOR THE BIRDS

Charles Modine, despite the fact that he was in his late thirties, and in perfect health, had never been in space. He had seen space settlements on television and had occasionally read about them in the public prints but it went no further than that.

To tell the truth, he was not interested in space. He had been born on Earth, and Earth was enough for him. When he wanted a change of environment, he turned to the sea. He was an avid and skilled sailor.

He was therefore repelled when the representative of Space Structures, Limited, finally told him that in order for him to do the job they were asking him to do, he would have to leave Earth.

Modine said, "Listen. I'm not a space person. I design clothes. What do I know about rockets and acceleration and trajectories and all the rest of it?"

"*We* know about that. You don't have to," said the other, urgently. Her name was Naomi Baranova and she had the queer, tentative walk of someone who had been in space so long she wasn't sure what the gravitational situation was at the moment.

Her clothes, Modine noted with some irritation, functioned as coverings and as little else. A tarpaulin would have done as well.

"But why need I come out to a space station?" he said.

"For what *you* know. We want you to design something for us."

"Clothes?"

"Wings."

Modine thought about it. He had a high, pale forehead and the process of thought always seemed to flush it somewhat. He had been told that at any rate. This time, if it flushed, it was partly in annoyance. "I can do that here, can't I?"

Baranova shook her head firmly. She had hair with a dark reddish tinge that was slowly being invaded by gray. She didn't seem to mind. She said, "We want you to understand the situation, Mr. Modine. We've consulted the technicians and the computer experts and they've built the most efficient possible wings, they tell us. They've taken into account stresses and surfaces and flexibilities and maneuverabilities and everything else you can imagine—but it doesn't help. We think perhaps a few frills—"

"Frills, Ms. Baranova?"

"Something other than scientific perfection. Something to rouse interest. Otherwise, the space settlements won't survive. That's why I want you there; to appreciate the situation for yourself. We're prepared to pay you very well."

It was the promised pay, including a healthy retainer, win or lose, that brought Modine into space. He was no more money-mad than the average human being, but he was not money-insensitive either, and he liked to see his reputation appreciated.

Nor was it actually as bad as he had expected. In the early days of space travel, there had been short periods of high acceleration and long cramped periods in small modules. Somehow that was what Earth-bound people still thought of in connection with space travel. But a century had passed and the shuttles were commodious, while the hydraulic seats seemed to sop up the acceleration as though it were nothing more than a coffee spill.

Modine spent the time studying photographs of the wings in action and in watching holographic videotapes of the flyers.

He said, "There's a certain grace to the performance."

Naomi Baranova smiled rather sadly. "You're watching experts—athletes. If you could see me trying to handle those wings and manage to tumble and sideslip, I'm afraid you would laugh. And yet I'm better than most."

They were approaching Space Settlement Five. Its name was Chrysalis, officially, but everyone called it Five.

"You might suppose," said Baranova, "that it would be the other way around, but there's no feeling of poetry about the place. That's the trouble. It's not a home; it's just a job, and it is hard to make people establish families and settle down. Until it's a home—"

Five showed up as a small sphere, far away, looking much as Modine had seen it on television on Earth. He knew it was larger than it looked, but that was only an intellectual knowledge. His eyes and his emotions were not prepared for the steady increase in size as they approached. The spaceship and he dwarfed steadily and, eventually, they were circling an enormous object of glass and aluminum.

He watched for a long time before he became aware that they were still circling. He said, "Aren't we going to land on it?"

"Not that easy," said Baranova. "Five rotates on an axis about once in two minutes. It has to in order to set up a centrifugal effect that will keep everything inside pressed against the inner wall and create an artificial gravity. We have to match that speed before we can land. It takes time."

"Must it spin that quickly?"

"To have the centrifugal effect mimic Earth-strength gravity, yes. That's the basic problem. It would be much better if we could use a slow spin to produce a tenth-normal gravity or even less, but that interferes with human physiology. People can't take low gravity for too long."

The ship's speed had nearly matched the rotation period of Five. Modine could clearly see the curve of the outer mirror that caught the sunlight and with it illuminated Five's interior. He could make out the solar power station that supplied the energy for the station, with enough left over for export to Earth.

And they finally entered at one of the poles of the sphere and were inside Five.

Modine had spent a full day on Five and he was tired—but he had, rather unexpectedly, enjoyed it. They were sitting now on lawn furniture—on a wide stretch of grass—against a vista of suburbia.

There were clouds overhead—sunshine, without a clear view of the Sun itself—a wind—and, in the distance, a small stream.

It was hard to believe he was on a sphere floating in space in the

Moon's orbit, circling Earth once a month. He said, "It's like a world."

Baranova said, "So it seems when you're new here. When you've been here a time, you discover you know every corner of it. Everything repeats."

Modine said, "If you live in a particular town on Earth, everything repeats too."

"I know. But on Earth you can travel widely if you wish. Even if you don't travel, you know you can. Here you can't. That's—not so good; but it's not the worst."

"You don't have the Earth's worst," said Modine. "I'm sure you don't have weather extremes."

"The weather, Mr. Modine, is indeed Garden of Edenish, but you get used to that. —Let me show you something. I have a ball here. Could you throw it high up; straight up, and catch it?"

Modine smiled. "Are you serious?"

"Quite. Please do."

Modine said, "I'm not a ball player, but I think I can throw a ball. I might even catch it when it comes down."

He threw the ball upward. It curved parabolically, and Modine found himself drifting forward in order to catch it, then running. It fell out of reach.

Baranova said, "You didn't throw it straight up, Mr. Modine."

"Yes I did," gasped Modine.

"Only by Earth standards," said Baranova. "The difficulty is that what we call the Coriolis force is involved. Here at the inner surface of Five, we're moving quite rapidly in a great circle about the axis. If you throw the ball upward it moves nearer the axis where things make a smaller circle and move more slowly. However, the ball retains the speed it had down here, so it moves ahead and you couldn't catch it. If you had wanted to catch it, you would have had to throw it up and back so that it would loop and return to you like a boomerang. The details of motion are different here on Five than on Earth."

Modine said, thoughtfully, "You get used to it, I suppose."

"Not entirely. We live in the equatorial regions of our small sphere. That's where the motion is fastest and where we get the effect of normal gravity. If we move upward toward the axis, or along the surface toward the poles, the gravitational effect decreases rapidly. We frequently have to go up or poleward and, whenever we do, the Coriolis effect must be taken into account. We have small monorails that must move spirally toward either pole; one track poleward, another returning. In the trip we feel ourselves perpetually canted to one side. It takes a long time to get used to it and some people never learn the trick of it. No one likes to live here for that reason."

"Can you do something about that twisting effect?"

"If we could make our rotation slower, we would lessen the Coriolis, but we would also lessen the feel of gravitation and we can't do that."

"Damned if you do, damned if you don't."

"Not entirely. We could get along with less gravitation, if we exercise, but it would mean exercise every day for considerable periods. That would have to be fun. People won't indulge in daily calisthenics that are troublesome or a bore. We used to think that flying would be the answer. When we go to the low-gravity regions near the poles, people are almost weightless. They can almost rise into the air by flapping their arms. If we attach light plastic wings to each arm, stiffened by flexible rods, and if those wings are folded and extended in just the right rhythm, people can fly like birds."

"Will that work as exercise?"

"Oh, yes. Flying is hard work, I assure you. The arm and shoulder muscles may not have to do much to keep you aloft but they must be in continuous use to maneuver you properly. It keeps up the muscle tone and bone calcium, *if* it's done on a regular basis. —But people won't do it."

"I should think they'd love to fly."

Baranova sniffed. "They would, if it were easy enough. The trouble is that it requires skillful coordination of muscles to keep steady. The slightest errors result in tumbling and spinning and almost inevitable nausea. Some can learn how to fly gracefully as you saw on the holo-cassettes, but very few."

"Birds don't get seasick."

"Birds fly in normal gravity fields. People on Five don't."

Modine frowned and grew thoughtful.

Baranova said, "I can't promise that you'll sleep. People don't usually their first few nights on a space settlement. Still, please try to do so and tomorrow we'll go to the flying areas."

Modine could see what Baranova had meant by saying the Coriolis force was unpleasant. The small monorail coach that took them poleward seemed constantly to be sliding leftward and his entrails seemed to be doing the same. He held on to the hand-grips, white-knuckled.

"I'm sorry," said Baranova, sympathetically. "If we went more slowly, it wouldn't be so bad, but we're holding up traffic as it is."

"Do you get used to this?" groaned Modine.

"Somewhat. Not enough."

He was glad to stop finally, but only limitedly so. It took a while to get used to the fact that he seemed to be floating. Each time he tried to move, he tumbled, and each time he tumbled he didn't fall but drifted slowly forward or upward and returned only gradually. His automatic kicking made things worse.

Baranova left him to himself for a while, then caught at him and drew him slowly back. "Some people enjoy this," she said.

"I don't," gasped Modine, miserably.

"Many don't. Please put your feet into these stirrups on the ground and don't make any sudden movements."

There were five of them flying in the sky. Baranova said, "Those five birds are here just about every day. There are a few hundred who are there now and then. We could accommodate at this pole and at the other, as well as along the axis, something like five thousand at a time. We could use all the space to keep Five's thirty thousand people in condition. What do we do?"

Modine gestured and his body swayed backward in response. "They must have learned how, those birds up there. They weren't born birds. Can't the others learn it, too?"

"Those up there have natural coordination."

"What can I do then? I'm a fashion designer. I don't create natural coordination."

"Not having natural coordination doesn't stop you altogether. It just means working hard, practicing longer. Is there any way you could make the process more—fashionable? Could you design a flying costume; suggest a psychological campaign to get the people out? If we could arrange proper programs of exercise and physical fitness, we could slow Five's rotation, weaken the Coriolis effect, make this place a home."

"You may be asking for a miracle. —Could you have them come closer?"

Baranova waved and one of the birds saw her, and swooped toward them in a long graceful curve. It was a young woman. She hovered ten feet away, smiling, her wings flicking slightly at the tips.

"Hi," she called out. "What's up?"

"Nothing," said Baranova. "My friend wants to watch you handle the wings. Show him how they work."

The young woman smiled and, twisting first one wing, then the other, performed a slow somersault. She straightened to a halt with both wings given a backhanded twist, then rose slowly, her feet dangling and her wings moving slowly. The wing motion grew more rapid and she was off in wild acceleration.

Modine said, after a while, "Rather like ballet dancing, but the wings are ugly."

"Are they? Are they?"

"Certainly," said Modine. "They look like bat wings. The associations are all wrong."

"Tell us what to do then? Should we put a feather design on them? Would that bring out the fliers and make them try harder to learn?"

"No." Modine thought for a while. "Maybe we can make the whole process easier."

He took his feet out of the stirrups, gave himself a little push and floated into the air. He moved his arms and legs experimentally and rocked erratically. He tried to scramble back for the stirrups and Baranova reached up to pull him down.

Modine said, "I'll tell you. I'll design something and if someone here can help me construct it according to the design, I'll try to fly. I've never done any such thing; you've just seen me try to wriggle in the air and I can't even do that. Well, if I use my design and *I* can fly, then anyone can."

"I should think so, Mr. Modine," said Baranova, in a tone that seemed suspended between skepticism and hope.

By the end of the week, Modine was beginning to feel that Space Settlement Five was home. As long as he stayed at ground level in the equatorial regions, where the gravitational effect was normal, there was no Coriolis effect to bother him and he felt his surroundings to be very Earth-like.

"The first time out," he said, "I don't want to be watched by the population generally because it may be harder than I think and I don't want to get this thing off to a bad start. —But I would like to be watched by some of the officials of the Settlement, just in case I make it."

Baranova said, "I should think we would try in private first. A failure the first time, whatever the excuse—"

"But a success would be *so* impressive."

"What are the chances of success? Be reasonable."

"The chances are good, Ms. Baranova. Believe me. What you have been doing here is all wrong. You're flying in air—like birds—and it's so hard. You said it yourself. Birds on Earth operate under gravity. The birds up here operate without gravity—so everything has to be designed differently."

The temperature, as always, was perfectly adjusted. So was the humidity. So was the wind speed. The atmosphere was so perfect it was as though it weren't there. —And yet Modine was perspiring with a bad case of stage fright. He was also gasping. The air was thinner in these gravity-free regions than at the equator—not by much, but enough thinner for him to have trouble gathering enough with his heart pounding so.

The air was empty of the human birds; the audience was a handful—the Coordinator, the Secretary of Health, the Commissioner of Safety and so on. There were a dozen men and women present. Only Baranova was familiar.

He had been outfitted with a small mike and he tried to keep his voice from shaking.

He said, "We are flying without gravity and neither birds nor bats are a good model for us. They fly *with* gravity. —It's different in the sea. There's little effective gravity in water, since buoyancy lifts you. When we fly through no-gravity water, we call it swimming. In Space Station Five, where there's no gravity in this region, the air is for swimming, not for flying. We must imitate the dolphin and not the eagle."

He sprang into the air as he spoke, wearing a graceful one-piece suit that neither clung skintight nor bellied. He began to tumble at once, but stretching one arm was sufficient to activate a small gas cartridge. A smoothly curved fin emerged along his spinal column, while a shallow keel marked the line of his abdomen.

The tumbling ceased. "Without gravity," he said, "this is enough to stabilize your flight. You can still tip and turn, but always under control. I may not do it well at first, but it won't take much practice."

He stretched his other arm and each foot was suddenly outlined by a flipper—each elbow by another.

"These," he said, "offer the propulsive force. You needn't flap the arms. Gentle motions will suffice for everything, but you have to bend your body and arch your neck in order to make turns and veers. You have to twist and alter the angle of your arms and legs. The whole body is engaged, but smoothly and nonviolently. —Which is all the better, for every muscle in your body is involved and you can keep it up for hours without tiring."

He could feel himself moving more surely and gracefully—and faster. Up, up, he was suddenly going, with the air rushing past him until he was almost in a panic for fear he would not be able to slow up. But he turned his heels and elbows almost instinctively and felt himself curve and slow.

Dimly, through the pounding of his heart, he could hear the applause.

Baranova said, admiringly, "How did you see this when our technicians couldn't?"

"The technicians started with the inevitable assumption of wings, thanks to birds and airplanes, and designed the most efficient ones possible. That's a technician's job. The job of a fashion designer is to see things as an artistic whole. I could see that the wings didn't fit the conditions of the space settlement. Just my job."

Baranova said, "We'll make these dolphin suits and get the population out into the air. I'm sure we can now. And then we can lay our plans to begin to slow Five's rotation."

"Or stop it altogether," said Modine. "I suspect that everyone will want to swim all the time instead of walking." He laughed. "They may not ever want to walk again. *I* may not."

They made out the large check they had promised and Modine, smiling at the figure, said, "Wings are for the birds."

Introduction to
FOUND!

In 1978, the *Penthouse* people were planning to put out a magazine that would feature futurism and science fiction. The magazine was to be called *Omni*. They asked me for a story for the first issue and offered me generous payment.

I was in a quandary. By the terms of my agreement with Joel Davis, the genial publisher of *Asimov's*, I had to give that magazine the refusal on any of my science fiction, which is, after all, only right. So I put it up to Joel, asking if I might have permission to do a science fiction story for *Omni* this one time, and explaining that if he said "No," it was "No," and there would be no argument.

As it happens, however, Joel never tries to get in the way of my earning a living. He suggested that *Omni* give him favorable terms for a one-shot advertisement of *Asimov's* in the magazine and *Omni* was perfectly willing.

Therefore, with cooperation and good-humor all around, I wrote "Found!" and it appeared in the very first issue (November 1978) of *Omni*, which has since gone on to score a considerable success. (No, I don't think *that* was because of my story, either.)

7.

FOUND!

Computer-Two, like the other three that chased each other's tails in orbit round the Earth, was much larger than it had to be.

It might have been one tenth its diameter and yet contained all the volume it needed to store the accumulated and accumulating data needed to control space flight.

They needed the extra space, however, so that Joe and I could get inside, if we had to.

And we had to.

Computer-Two was perfectly capable of taking care of itself. Ordinarily, that is. It was redundant. It worked everything out three times in parallel and all three programs had to mesh perfectly; all three answers had to match. If they did not, the answer was delayed for nano-seconds while Computer-Two checked itself, found the malfunctioning part and replaced it.

There was no sure way in which ordinary people would know how many times it caught itself. Perhaps never. Perhaps twice a day. Only Computer-Central could measure the time delay induced by error and only Computer-Central knew how many of the component spares had been used as replacements. And Computer-Central never talked about it. The only good public image is perfection.

And for all practical purposes, it's *been* perfection, for there was never any call for Joe and me.

We're the trouble-shooters. We go up there when something really goes wrong and Computer-Two or one of the others can't correct itself. It's never happened in the five years we've been on the job. It did happen now and again in the early days of their existence, but that was before our time.

We keep in practice. Don't get me wrong. There isn't a computer made that Joe and I can't diagnose. Show us the error and we'll show you the malfunction. Or Joe will, anyway. I'm not the kind who sings one's own praises.

Anyway, this time, neither of us could make the diagnosis.

The first thing that happened was that Computer-Two lost internal pressure. That's not unprecedented and it's certainly not fatal. Computer-Two can work in a vacuum after all. An internal atmosphere was established in the old days when it was expected there would be a steady flow of repairmen fiddling with it. And it's been kept up out of tradition. Who told you scientists aren't chained by tradition? In their spare time from being scientists, they're human, too.

From the rate of pressure loss, it was deduced that a gravel-sized meteoroid had hit Computer-Two. Its exact radius, mass and energy was reported by Computer-Two itself, using that rate of pressure loss, and a few other things, as data.

The second thing that happened was that the break was not sealed and the atmosphere was not regenerated. After that came the errors and they called us in.

It made no sense. Joe let a look of pain cross his homely face and said, "There must be a dozen things out of whack."

Someone at Computer-Central said, "The hunk of gravel ricocheted, very likely."

Joe said, "With that energy of entry, it would have passed right through the other side. No ricochets. Besides, even with ricochets, I figure it would have had to take some very unlikely strikes."

"Well, then, what do we do?"

Joe looked uncomfortable. I think that it was at this point that he realized what was coming. He had made it sound peculiar enough to require the trouble-shooters on the spot—and Joe had never been up in space. If he had told me once that his chief reason for taking the job was that he knew it meant he would never have to go up in space, he had told it to me 2^x times, with x a pretty high number.

So I said it for him. I said, "We'll have to go up there."

Joe's only way out would have been to say he didn't think he could handle the job, and I watched his pride slowly come out ahead of his cowardice. Not by much, you understand—by a nose, let's say.

To those of you who haven't been on a spaceship in the last fifteen years—and I suppose Joe can't be the only one—let me emphasize that the initial acceleration is the only troublesome thing. You can't get away from that, of course.

After that it's nothing, unless you want to count possible boredom. You're just a spectator. The whole thing is automated and computerized. The old romantic days of space pilots are gone totally. I imagine they'll return briefly when our space settlements make the shift to the asteroid belt as they constantly threaten to do—but then only until additional Computers are placed in orbit to set up the necessary additional capacity.

Joe held his breath throughout the acceleration, or at least he seemed to. (I must admit that I wasn't very comfortable myself. It was only my third trip. I've taken a couple of vacations on Settlement-Rho with my husband, but I'm not exactly a seasoned hand.)

After that, he was relieved for a while, but only for a while. He got despondent.

"I hope this thing knows where it's going," he said, pettishly.

I extended my arms forward, palms up, and felt the rest of me sway backward a bit in the zero-gravity field. "You," I said, "are a computer specialist. Don't you *know* it knows?"

"Sure, but Computer-Two is off."

"We're not hooked into Computer-Two," I said. "There are three others. And even if only one were left functional, it could handle all the space flights undertaken on an average day."

"All four might go off. If Computer-Two is wrong, what's to stop the rest?"

"Then we'll run this thing manually."

"You'll do it, I suppose? You know how—I think not?"

"So they'll talk me in."

"For the love of Eniac," he groaned.

There was no problem, actually. We moved out to Computer-Two as smooth as vacuum and less than two days after takeoff, we were placed into a parking orbit not ten meters behind it.

What was not so smooth was that, about twenty hours out, we got the news from Earth that Computer-Three was losing internal pressure. Whatever had hit Computer-Two was going to get the rest, and when all four were out, space flight would grind to a halt. It could be reorganized on a manual basis, surely, but that would take months as a minimum, possibly years, and there would be serious economic dislocation on Earth. Worse yet, several thousand people now out in space would surely die.

It wouldn't bear thinking of and neither Joe nor I talked about it, but it didn't make Joe's disposition sweeter and, let's face it, it didn't make me any happier.

Earth hung over 200,000 kilometers below us, but Joe didn't seem to be bothered by that. He was concentrating on his tether and was checking the cartridge in his reaction-gun. He wanted to make sure he could get to Computer-Two and back again.

You'd be surprised—if you've never tried it—how you can get your space legs if you absolutely have to. I wouldn't say there was nothing to it and we did waste half the fuel we used, but we finally reached Computer-Two. We hardly made any bump at all when we struck Computer-Two. (You hear it, of course, even in vacuum, because the vibration travels through the metalloid fabric of your space suits—but there was hardly any bump, just a whisper.)

Of course, our contact and the addition of our momentum altered the orbit of Computer-Two slightly, but tiny expenditures of fuel compensated for that and we didn't have to worry about it. Computer-Two took care of it, for nothing had gone wrong with it, as far as we could tell, that affected any of its external workings.

We went over the outside first, naturally. The chances were pretty overwhelming that a small piece of gravel had whizzed through Computer-Two and that would leave an unmistakable ragged hole. Two of them in all probability; one going in and one coming out.

Chances of that happening are one in two million on any given day—even money that it will happen at least once in six thousand years. It's not likely, but it can, you know. The chances are one in not more than ten billion that, on any one day, it will be struck by a meteoroid large enough to demolish it.

I didn't mention that because Joe might realize that we were exposed to similar odds ourselves. In fact, any given strike on us would do far more damage to our soft and tender bodies than to the stoical and much-enduring machinery of the computer, and I didn't want Joe more nervous than he was.

The thing is, though, it wasn't a meteoroid.

"What's this?" said Joe, finally.

It was a small cylinder stuck to the outer wall of Computer-Two, the first abnormality we had found in its outward appearance. It was about half a centimeter in diameter and perhaps six centimeters long. Just about cigarette-sized for any of you who've been caught up in the antique fad of smoking.

We brought our small flashlights into play.

I said, "That's not one of the external components."

"It sure isn't," muttered Joe.

There was a faint spiral marking running round the cylinder from one end to the other. Nothing else. For the rest, it was clearly metal, but of an odd, grainy texture—at least to the eye.

Joe said, "It's not tight."

He touched it gently with a fat and gauntleted finger and it gave. Where it had made contact with the surface of Computer-Two, it lifted and our flashes shone down on a visible gap.

"There's the reason gas pressure inside declined to zero," I said.

Joe grunted. He pushed a little harder and the cylinder dropped away and began to drift. We managed to snare it after a little trouble. Left behind was a perfectly round hole in the skin of Computer-Two, half a centimeter across.

Joe said, "This thing, whatever it is, isn't much more than foil."

It gave easily under his fingers, thin but springy. A little extra pressure and it dented. He put it inside his pouch, which he snapped shut, and said, "Go over the outside and see if there are any other items like that anywhere on it. I'll go inside."

It didn't take me very long. Then I went in. "It's clean," I said. "That's the only thing there is. The only hole."

"One is enough," said Joe, gloomily. He looked at the smooth aluminum of the wall and, in the light of the flash, the perfect circle of black was beautifully evident.

It wasn't difficult to place a seal over the hole. It was a little more difficult to reconstitute the atmosphere. Computer-Two's reserve gas-forming supplies were low and the controls required manual adjustment. The solar generator was limping but we managed to get the lights on.

Eventually, we removed our gauntlets and helmet, but Joe carefully placed the gauntlets inside his helmet and secured them both to one of his suit-loops.

"I want these handy if the air pressure begins to drop," he said, sourly.

So I did the same. No use being devil-may-care.

There was a mark on the wall just next to the hole. I had noted it in the light of my flash when I was adjusting the seal. When the lights came on, it was obvious.

"You notice that, Joe?" I said.

"I notice."

There was a slight, narrow depression in the wall, not very noticeable at all, but it was there beyond doubt if you ran your finger over it and it continued for nearly a meter. It was as though someone had scooped out a very shallow sampling of the metal and the surface where that had taken place was distinctly less smooth than elsewhere.

I said, "We'd better call Computer-Central downstairs."

"If you mean back on Earth, say so," said Joe. "I hate that phony space-talk. In fact, I hate everything about space. That's why I took an Earth-side job—I mean a job on Earth—or what was supposed to be one."

I said patiently, "We'd better call Computer-Central back on Earth."

"What for?"

"To tell them we've found the trouble."

"Oh? What did we find?"

"The hole. Remember?"

"Oddly enough, I do. And what caused the hole? It wasn't a meteoroid. I never saw one that would leave a perfectly circular hole with no signs of buckling or melting. And I never saw one that left a cylinder behind." He took the cylinder out of his suit pocket and smoothed the dent out of its thin metal, thoughtfully. "Well, what caused the hole?"

I didn't hesitate. I said, "I don't know."

"If we report to Computer-Central, they'll ask the question and we'll say we don't know and what will we have gained? Except hassle?"

"They'll call us, Joe, if we don't call them."

"Sure. And we won't answer, will we?"

"They'll assume something killed us, Joe, and they'll send up a relief party."

"You know Computer-Central. It will take them at least two days to decide on that. We'll have something before then and once we have something, we'll call them."

The internal structure of Computer-Two was not *really* designed for human occupancy. What was foreseen and allowed for was the occasional and temporary presence of trouble-shooters. That meant there was room for maneuvering and there were tools and supplies.

There weren't any armchairs, though. For that matter, there was no gravitational field, either, or any centrifugal imitation of one.

We both floated in midair, drifting very slowly this way or that. Occasionally, one of us touched the wall and rebounded very slowly. Or else part of one of us overlapped part of the other.

"Keep your foot out of my mouth," said Joe, and pushed it away violently. It was a mistake because we both began to turn. Of course, that's not how it looked to us. To us, it was the interior of Computer-Two that was turning, which was most unpleasant, and it took us a while to get relatively motionless again.

We had the theory perfectly worked out in our Earth-side training, but we were short on practice. A lot short.

By the time we had steadied ourselves, I felt unpleasantly nauseated. You can call it nausea, or astronausea, or space sickness, but whatever you call it, it's the heaves and it's worse in space than anywhere else, because there's nothing to pull the stuff down. It floats around in a cloud of globules and you don't want to be floating around with it. —So I held it back, and so did Joe.

I said, "Joe, it's clearly the computer that's at fault. Let's get at its insides." Anything to get my mind off *my* insides and let them quiet down. Besides, things weren't moving fast enough. I kept thinking of Computer-Three on its way down the tube; maybe Computers-One and -Four by now, too; and thousands of people in space with their lives hanging on what we could do.

Joe looked a little greenish, too, but he said, "First I've got to think. Something got in. It wasn't a meteroid, because whatever it was chewed a neat hole out of the hull. It wasn't cut out because I didn't find a circle of metal anywhere inside here. Did you?"

"No. But it hadn't occurred to me to look."

"*I* looked, and it's nowhere in here."

"It may have fallen outside."

"With the cyclinder covering the hole till I pulled it away? A likely thing. Did you see anything come flying out?"

"No."

Joe said, "We may still find it in here, of course, but I doubt it. It was somehow dissolved and something got in."

"What something? Whose is it?"

Joe's grin was remarkably ill-natured. "Why do you bother asking questions to which there is no answer. If this was last century, I'd say the Russians had somehow stuck that device onto the outside of Computer-Two. —No offense. If it were last century, you'd say it was the Americans."

I decided to be offended. I said, coldly, "We're trying to say something that makes sense *this* century, Iosif," giving it an exaggerated Russian pronunciation.

"We'll have to assume some dissident group."

"If so," I said, "we'll have to assume one with a capacity for space flight and with the ability to come up with an unusual device."

Joe said, "Space flight presents no difficulties, if you can tap into the orbiting Computers illegally—which has been done. As for the cylinder, that may make more sense when it is analyzed back on Earth—downstairs, as you space buffs would say."

"It doesn't make sense," I said. "Where's the point in trying to disable Computer-Two?"

"As part of a program to cripple space flight."

"Then everyone suffers. The dissidents, too."

"But it gets everyone's attention, doesn't it, and suddenly the cause of whatever-it-is makes news. Or the plan is to just knock out Computer-Two and then threaten to knock out the other three. No real damage, but lots of potential, and lots of publicity."

"I don't believe it," I said. "It's too dramatic."

"On the contrary," said Joe. "I'm trying to be nondramatic." He was studying all parts of the interior closely, edging over it square centimeter by square centimeter. "I *might* suppose the thing was of nonhuman origin."

"Don't be silly."

"You want me to make the case? The cylinder made contact, after which something inside ate away a circle of metal and entered Computer-Two. It crawled over the inside wall eating away a thin layer of metal for some reason. Does that sound like anything of human construction?"

"Not that I know of, but I don't know everything. Even you don't know everything."

Joe ignored that. "So the question is, how did it—whatever it is —get into the computer, which is, after all, reasonably well-sealed. It did so quickly, since it knocked out the resealing and air-regeneration capacities almost at once."

"Is *that* what you're looking for?" I said, pointing.

He tried to stop too quickly and somersaulted backward, crying, "That's it! That's it!"

In his excitement, he was thrashing his arms and legs which got him nowhere, of course. I grabbed him and, for a while, we were both trying to exert pushes in uncoordinated directions and that got us nowhere either. Joe called me a few names, but I called him some back and I had the advantage of him there. I understand English perfectly, better than he does, in fact; but his knowledge of Russian is—well, fragmentary would be a kind way of putting it. Bad language in an ununderstood language always sounds very dramatic.

"Here it is," he said, when we had finally sorted ourselves out.

Where the computer-shielding met the wall, there was a small circular hole left behind when Joe brushed aside a small cyclinder.

It was just like the one on the outer hull, but it seemed even thinner. In fact, it seemed to disintegrate when Joe touched it.

"We'd better get into the computer," said Joe.

The computer was a shambles.

Not obviously. I don't mean to say it was like a beam of wood that had been riddled by termites.

In fact, if you looked at the computer casually, you might swear it was intact.

Look closely, though, and some of the chips would be gone. The more closely you looked, the more you realized were gone. Worse yet, the stores which Computer-Two used in self-repair had dwindled to almost nothing. We kept looking and every once in a while, one of us would discover something else was missing.

Joe took the cylinder out of his pouch again and turned it end for end. He said, "I suspect it's after high-grade silicon in particular. I can't say for sure, of course, but my guess is that the sides are mostly aluminum but that the flat end is mostly silicon."

I said, "Do you mean the thing is a solar battery?"

"Part of it is. That's how it gets its energy in space; energy to get to Computer-Two, energy to eat a hole into it, energy to—to—I don't know how else to put it. Energy to stay alive."

"You call it alive?"

"Why not? Look, Computer-Two can repair itself. It can reject faulty bits of equipment and replace it with working ones, but it needs a supply of spares to work with. Given enough spares of all kinds, it could build a Computer just like itself, when properly programmed—but it needs the supply, so we don't think of it as alive. This object that entered Computer-Two is apparently collecting its own supplies. That's suspiciously life-like."

"What you're saying," I said, "is that we have here a microcomputer advanced enough to be considered alive."

"I don't honestly know what I'm saying," said Joe.

"Who on Earth could make such a thing?"

"Who *on Earth?*"

I made the next discovery. It looked like a stubby pen drifting through the air. I just caught it out of the corner of my eye and it registered as a pen.

In zero gravity, things will drift out of pockets and float off. There's no way of keeping anything in place unless it is physically confined. You expect pens and coins and anything else that can find an opening to drift their way through the opening eventually and go wherever air currents and inertia lead them.

So my mind registered "Pen" and I groped for it absently and, of course, my fingers didn't close on it. Just reaching for something sets up an air current that pushes it away. You have to reach over it and sneak behind it with one hand, and then reach for it with the other. Picking up any small object in midair is a two-hand operation.

I know some people can do it one-handed, but they're space hounds and I'm not.

I turned to look at the object and pay a little more attention to retrieval, then realized that my pen was safely in its pouch. I felt for it and it was there.

"Did you lose a pen, Joe?" I called out.

"No."

"Anything like that? Key? Cigarette?"

"I don't smoke. You know that."

A stupid answer. "Anything?" I said in exasperation. "I'm seeing things here."

"No one ever said you were stable."

"Look, Joe. Over there. Over there."

He lunged for it. I could have told him it would do no good.

By now, though, our poking around in the computer seemed to have stirred things up. We were seeing them wherever we looked. They were floating in the air currents.

I stopped one at last. Or, rather, it stopped itself, for it was on the elbow of Joe's suit. I snatched it off and shouted. Joe jumped in terror and nearly knocked it out of my hand.

I said, "Look!"

There was a shiny circle on Joe's suit where I had taken the thing off. It had begun to eat its way through.

"Give it to me," said Joe. He took it gingerly and put it against the wall to hold it steady. Then he shelled it, gently lifting the paper-thin metal.

There was something inside that looked like a line of cigarette ash. It caught the light and glinted, though, like lightly woven metal.

There was a moistness about it, too. It wriggled slowly, one end seeming to seek something blindly.

The end made contact with the wall and stuck. Joe's finger pushed it away. It seemed to require a small effort to do so. Joe rubbed his finger and thumb and said, "Feels oily."

The metal worm—I don't know what else I can call it—seemed limp now after Joe had touched it. It didn't move again.

I was twisting and turning, trying to look at myself.

"Joe," I said, "for heaven's sake, have I got one of them on me anywhere?"

"I don't see one," he said.

"Well, *look* at me. You've got to watch me, Joe, and I'll watch you. If our suits are wrecked we might not be able to get back to the ship."

Joe said, "Keep moving, then."

It was a grisly feeling, being surrounded by things hungry to dissolve your suit wherever they could touch it. When any showed up, we tried to catch them and stay out of their way at the same time, which made things almost impossible. A rather long one drifted close to my leg and I kicked at it, which was stupid, for if I had hit it, it might have stuck. As it was, the air current I set up brought it against the wall, where it stayed.

Joe reached hastily for it—too hastily. The rest of his body rebounded and as he somersaulted, one booted foot struck the wall near the cylinder lightly. When he finally managed to right himself, it was still there.

"I didn't smash it, did I?"

"No, you didn't," I said. "You missed it by a decimeter. It won't get away."

I had a hand on either side of it. It was twice as long as the other cylinder had been. In fact, it was like two cylinders stuck together lengthwise, with a constriction at the point of joining.

"Act of reproducing," said Joe as he peeled away the metal. This time what was inside was a line of dust. Two lines. One on either side of the constriction.

"It doesn't take much to kill them," said Joe. He relaxed visibly. "I think we're safe."

"They do seem alive," I said, reluctantly.

"I think they seem more than that. They're viruses. —Or the equivalent."

"What are you talking about?"

Joe said, "Granted I'm a computer technologist and not a virologist—but it's my understanding that viruses on Earth, or, downstairs, as you would say, consist of a nucleic acid molecule coated in a protein shell.

"When a virus invades a cell, it manages to dissolve a hole in the cell wall or membrane by the use of some appropriate enzyme and the nucleic acid slips inside, leaving the protein coat outside. Inside the cell it finds the material to make a new protein coat for itself. In fact, it manages to form replicas of itself and to form a new protein coat for each replica. Once it has stripped the cell of all it has, the cell dissolves and in place of the one invading virus there are several hundred daughter viruses. Sound familiar?"

"Yes. Very familiar. It's what's happening here. But where did it come from, Joe?"

"Not from Earth, obviously, or any Earth settlement. From somewhere else, I suppose. They drift through space till they find something appropriate in which they can multiply. They look for sizable objects ready-made of metal. I don't imagine they can smelt ores."

"But large metal objects with pure silicon components and a few other succulent matters like that are the products of intelligent life only," I said.

"Right," said Joe, "which means we have the best evidence yet that intelligent life is common in the Universe, since objects like the one we're on must be quite common or it couldn't support these viruses. And it means that intelligent life is old, too, perhaps ten billion years old—long enough for a kind of metal evolution, forming a metal/silicon/oil life as we have formed a nucleic/protein/water life. Time to evolve a parasite on space-age artifacts."

I said, "You make it sound as though every time some intelligent life form develops a space culture, it is subjected before long to parasitic infestation."

"Right. And it must be controlled. Fortunately, these things are easy to kill, especially now when they're forming. Later on, when they're ready to burrow out of Computer-Two, I suppose they will grow, thicken their shells, stabilize their interior and prepare, as the equivalent of spores, to drift a million years before they find another home. They might not be so easy to kill, then."

"How are you going to kill them?"

"I already have. I just touched that first one when it instinctively sought out metal to begin manufacturing a new shell after I had broken open the first one—and that touch finished it. I didn't touch the second, but I kicked the wall near it and the sound vibration in the metal shook its interior apart into metal dust. So they can't get us, now, or any more of the computer if we just shake them apart now!"

He didn't have to explain further—or as much. He put on his gauntlets slowly, and then banged at the wall with one. It pushed him away and he kicked at the wall where he next approached it.

"You do the same," he shouted.

I tried to, and for a while we both kept at it. You don't know how hard it is to hit a wall at zero gravity, at least on purpose, and do it hard enough to make it clang. We missed as often as not or just struck it a glancing blow that sent us whirling but made virtually no sound. We were panting with effort and aggravation in no time.

But we had acclimated ourselves (or at least I had) and the nausea didn't return. We kept it up and then when we gathered up some more of the viruses, there was nothing inside but dust in every case. They were clearly adapted to empty, automated space objects which, like modern computers, were vibration-free. That's what made it possible, I suppose, to build up the exceedingly rickety complex metallic structures that possessed sufficient instability to produce the properties of simple life.

I said, "Do you think we got them all, Joe?"

"How can I say? If there's one left, it will cannibalize the others for metal supplies and start all over. Let's bang around some more."

We did until we were sufficiently worn out not to care whether one was still left alive.

"Of course," I said, panting, "the Planetary Association for the Advancement of Science isn't going to be pleased with our killing them all."

Joe's suggestion as to what the P.A.A.S. could do with itself was forceful, but impractical. He said, "Look, our mission is to save

Computer-Two, a few thousand lives and, as it turned out, our own lives, too. Now they can decide whether to renovate this computer or rebuild it from scratch. It's their baby.

"The P.A.A.S. can get what they can out of these dead objects and that should be something. If they want live ones, I suspect they'll find them floating about in these regions. They can look for them if they want live specimens, but they'd better watch their suits at all times. I don't think they can vibrate them to death in open space."

I said, "All right. My suggestion is we tell Computer-Central we're going to jerry-rig this Computer and get it doing some work anyway, and we'll stay till a relief is up for main repairs or whatever in order to prevent any reinfestation. Meanwhile, they better get to each of the other Computers and set up a system that can set it to vibrating strongly as soon as the internal atmosphere shows a pressure drop."

"Simple enough," said Joe, sardonically.

"It's lucky we found them when we did."

"Wait awhile," said Joe, and the look in his eye was one of deep trouble. "We didn't find them. *They* found *us*. If metal life has developed, do you suppose it's likely that this is the only form it takes? Just this fragile kind?

"What if such life forms communicate somehow and, across the vastness of space, others are now converging on us for the picking? Other species, too; all of them after the lush new fodder of an as yet untouched space culture. *Other* species! Some that are sturdy enough to withstand vibration. Some that are large enough to be more versatile in their reactions to danger. Some that are equipped to invade our settlements in orbit. Some, for the sake of Univac, that may be able to invade the Earth for the metals of its cities.

"What I'm going to report, what I must report, is that we've been *found!*"

Introduction to

GOOD TASTE

In late 1975, Alan Bechtold, who ran a small semiprofessional publishing outfit he called Apocalypse Press, wanted to put out a series of limited printings of individual science fiction stories especially written for the purpose. After one year, all rights would revert to the author.

I was intrigued by the proposition and, in January 1976, wrote "Good Taste" which, frankly, pleased me a great deal. It seemed to me I had worked out a fascinating social background. Bechtold published the story, but others who had promised to deliver stories did not do so and the project failed, alas.

Nevertheless, once the year was up, I submitted the story to George Scithers, for my own magazine had just started, and it appeared in the Fall 1977 *Asimov's*.

8.

GOOD TASTE

1

I t was quite clear to everyone that it would not have happened
—the family would not have been disgraced and the world of
Gammer would not have been stunned and horrified—if
Chawker Minor had not made the Grand Tour.

It wasn't exactly illegal to make the Grand Tour but, on Gammer
at least, it was not really socially acceptable. Elder Chawker had
been against it from the start, to do him justice, but then Lady
Chawker took the side of her minor and mothers are, at times, not
to be withstood. Chawker was her second child (both of them sons,
as it happened) and she would have no more, of course, so it was
not surprising that she doted on him.

Her younger son had wanted to see the Other Worlds of the
Orbit and had promised to stay away no longer than a year. She
had wept and worried and gone into a tragic decline and then,
finally, had dried her eyes and spoken stiffly to Elder Chawker—
and Chawker Minor had gone.

Now he was back, one year to the day (he was always a young
man to keep his word, besides which the Elder's support would
have ceased the day after, never fear), and the family made holiday.

Elder wore a new black glossy shirt but would not permit the
prim lines of his face to relax, nor would he stoop to ask for details.
He had no interest—no interest *whatever*—in the Other Worlds
with their strange ways and with their primitive browsing (no better than the ways on Earth of which Gammerpeople *never* spoke).

He said, "Your complexion is dirtied and spoiled, Chawker
Minor." (The use of the full name showed his displeasure.)

Chawker laughed and the clear skin of his rather thin face crinkled. "I stayed out of the sun as much as I could, Elder-mine, but the Other Worlders would not always have it so."

Lady Chawker would have none of that either. She said warmly, "It isn't dirtied at all, Elder. It breathes a warmth."

"Of the Sun," grumbled Elder, "and it would be next that he would be grubbing in the filth they have there."

"No farming for me, Elder. That's hard work. I visited the fungus vats at times, though."

Chawker Major, older than Minor by three years, wider of face, heavier of body, but otherwise of close resemblance, was torn between envy at his younger brother's having seen different worlds of the Orbit and revulsion at the thought of it. He said, "Did you eat their Prime, Minor?"

"I had to eat something," said Chawker Minor. "Of course, there were your packages, Lady-mine. Lifesavers, sometimes."

"I suppose," said Elder Chawker with distaste, "the Prime was inedible there. Who can tell the filth that found its way into it."

"Come now, Elder-mine." Chawker Minor paused, as though attempting to choose words, then shrugged. "Well, it held body and soul together. One got used to it. I won't say more than that. —But Elder-Lady-mine, I am so glad to be home. The lights are so warm and gentle."

"You've had enough of the sun, I take it," said Elder. "But you would go. Well, welcome back to the inner world, with light and warmth under our control locked away from the patch and blaze of sunshine. Welcome back to the womb of the people, as the saying goes."

"Yet I'm glad I went," said Chawker Minor. "Eight different worlds, you know. It gives you a view you don't have otherwise."

"And would be better off not having," said Elder.

"I'm not sure about that," said Chawker Minor, and his right upper eyelid trembled just slightly as he looked at Major. Chawker Major's lips compressed but he said nothing.

2

It was a feast. Anyone would have had to admit that, and in the end it was Chawker Minor himself who had been the greediest to begin, who was the first to push away. He had no choice; Lady would else have kept on supplying him with samples out of what seemed to be a bottomless larder.

"Lady-mine," he said, affectionately, "my tongue wearies. I can no longer taste anything."

"You not taste?" said Lady. "What kind of nithling-story is that? You have the skill of the Grand-Elder himself. At the age of six, you were already a Gustator; we had endless proofs of that. There was not an additive you could not detect even when you could not pronounce them right."

"Taste buds blunt when not used," said Elder Chawker, darkly, "and jogging the Other Worlds can utterly spoil a man."

"Yes? Well, let us see," said Lady. "Minor-mine, tell your doubting Elder what you have eaten."

"In order?" said Chawker Minor.

"Yes. Show him you remember."

Chawker Minor closed his eyes. "It's scarcely a fair test," he said, "I so relished the taste I did not pause to analyze it; and it's been so long."

"He has excuses. See, Lady?" said Elder.

"But I will try," Chawker Minor said hastily. "In the first place, the Prime base for all of them is from the fungus vats of the East Section and the thirteenth corridor within it, I believe, unless great changes have been made in my absence."

"No, you are right," said Lady, with satisfaction.

"And it was expensive," said Elder.

"The prodigal returns," said Chawker Major, just a bit acidly, "and we must have the fatted fungus, as the saying goes. —Get the additives, Minor, if you can."

"Well," said Chawker Minor, "the first dab was strongly Spring Morning with added Leaves A-Freshened, and a touch, not more than a touch of Spara-Sprig."

"Perfectly right," said Lady, smiling happily.

Chawker Minor went on with the list, his eyes still closed, his taste-memory rolling backward and forward luxuriously over the tang and consistency of the samplings. He skipped the eighth and came back to it.

"That one," he said, "puzzles me."

Chawker Major grinned. "Didn't you get any of it?"

"Of course I did. I got most of it. There was Frisking Lamb—not

Leaping-Lamb, either. Frisking, even though it leaned just a little toward Leaping."

"Come on, don't try to make it hard. That's easy," said Chawker Major. "What else?"

"Green-Mint, with just a touch of Sour-Mint—*both*—and a dusting of Sparkle-Blood. —But there was something else I couldn't identify."

"Was it good?" asked Chawker Major.

"Good? This isn't the day to ask me that. Everything is good. Everything is succulent. And what I can't identify seems very succulent. It's close to Hedge-Bloom, but better."

"Better?" said Chawker Major, delighted. "It's mine!"

"What do you mean yours?" said Chawker Minor.

Elder said, with stiff approval, "My stay-at-home son has done well while you were gone. He devised a computer program that has designed and produced three new life-compatible flavor molecules of considerable promise. Grand-Elder Tomasz himself has given one of Major's constructions tongue-room, the very one you just tasted Flyaway-Minor-mine, and has given it his approval."

Chawker Major said, "He didn't actually say anything, Elder-mine."

Lady said, "His expression needed no words."

"It *is* good," said Chawker Minor, rather dashed at having the play taken away from him. "Will you be entering for the Awards?"

"It has been in my mind," said Chawker Major, with an attempt at indifference. "Not with this one—I call it Purple-Light, by the way—but I believe I will have something else, more worthy of the competition."

Chawker Minor frowned. "I had thought that—"

"Yes?"

"—That I am ready to stretch out and think of nothing. Come, half a dab more of Major's construction, Lady-mine, and let's see what I can deduce concerning the chemical structure of his Purple-Light."

3

For a week, the holiday atmosphere in the Chawker household continued. Elder Chawker was well-known in Gammer and it seemed that half the inhabitants of the world must have passed through his Section before all had had their curiosity sated and could see with their own eyes that Chawker Minor had returned unscathed. Most remarked on his complexion, and more than one young woman asked if she might touch his cheek, as though the light tan were a layer that could be felt.

Chawker Minor allowed the touch with lordly complacence, though Lady disapproved of these forward requests and said so.

Grand-Elder Tomasz himself came down from his aerie, as plump as a Gammerman ever permits himself to be and with no sign that age or white hair had blunted his talents. He was a Master Gustator such as Gammer might never have seen before despite the tales of Grand-Elder Faron of half a century ago. There was nothing that Tomasz tongued that did not open itself in detail to him.

Chawker Minor, who had no great tendency to underrate his own talent, felt no shame in admitting that what he himself had innately could not yet come anywhere near the old man's weight of experience.

The Grand-Elder, who for nearly twenty years now had governed the annual Awards festival by the force of his skill, asked closely after the Other Worlds which, of course, he himself had never visited.

He was indulgent, though, and smiled at Lady Chawker. "No need to fret, Lady," he said. "Young people these days are curious. In my time we were content to attend to our own cylinder of worth, as the saying goes, but these are new times and many are making what they call the Grand Tour. Good, perhaps. To see the Other Worlds—frivolous, Sun-drenched, browsive, nongustational, without a taste bud to content themselves with—makes one appreciate the eldest brother, as the saying goes."

Grand-Elder Tomasz was the only Gammerman whom Chawker Minor had ever heard actually speak of Gammer as "the eldest brother" although you could find it often enough in the videocassettes. It had been the third colony to be founded in the Moon's orbit back in the pioneering years of the twenty-first century, but the first two, Alfer and Bayter, had never become ecologically viable. Gammer had.

Chawker Minor said, with tactful caution, "The Other World

people never tired of telling me how much the experience of Gammer meant to all the worlds that were founded afterward. All had learned, they said, from Gammer."

Tomasz beamed. "Certainly. Certainly. Well said."

Chawker Minor said, with even greater caution, "And yet such is self-love, you understand, Grand-Elder, that a few thought they had improved on Gammer."

Grand-Elder Tomasz puffed his breath out through his nose (never breathe through your mouth any more than you can help, he would say over and over again, for that blunts the Gustator's tongue) and fixed Chawker with his deep blue eyes that looked the bluer for the snow-white eyebrows that curved above them.

"Improved in what way? Did they suggest a specific improvement?"

Chawker Minor, skating over thin ice and aware of Elder Chawker's awful frown, said softly, "In matters that they value, I gather I am not a proper judge of such things, perhaps."

"In matters that *they* value. Did you find a world that knows more about food chemistry than we do?"

"No! Certainly not, Grand-Elder. None concern themselves with that, as far as I could see. They all rely on our findings. They admit it openly."

Grand-Elder Tomasz grunted. "They can rely on us to know the effects and side effects of a hundred thousand molecules, and each year to study, define and analyze the effects of a thousand more. They rely on us to work out the dietary needs of elements and vitamins to the last syllable. Most of all, they rely on us to work out the art of taste to the final, most subtly convoluted touch. They do so, do they not?"

"They admit all this, without hesitation."

"And where do you find computers more reliable and more complex than ours?"

"As far as our field is concerned, nowhere."

"And what Prime did they serve?" With heavy humor, he added, "Or did they expect a young Gammerman to browse?"

"No, Grand-Elder, they had Prime. On all the worlds I visited they had Prime; and on all those I did not visit, I was told, there was also Prime. Even on the world where Prime was considered fit chiefly for the lower classes—"

Tomasz reddened. "Idiots!" he muttered.

"Different worlds, different ways," said Chawker Minor rather hurriedly. "But even then, Grand-Elder, Prime was popular when something was needed that was convenient, inexpensive and nourishing. And they got their Prime from us. All of them had a fungal strain brought originally from Gammer."

"Which strain?"

"Strain A-5," said Chawker Minor, apologetically. "It's the sturdiest, they said, and the most energy-sparing."

"And the coarsest," said Tomasz, with satisfaction. "And what flavor additives?"

"Very few," said Chawker Minor. He thought a moment, then said, "There was, on Kapper, a place where they had an additive that was popular with the Kapperpeople and that had—possibilities. Those were not properly developed, however, and when I distributed tastes of what Lady-mine had sent me they were forced to admit that it was to theirs as Gammer is to a space-pebble."

"You had not told me that," said Lady Chawker who, till then, had not ventured to interpose comments in a conversation that had the Grand-Elder as one of its participants. "The Other Worlders liked my preparation, did they?"

"I didn't often hand it out," said Chawker Minor. "I was too selfish to do it, but when I did, they liked it a great deal, Lady-mine."

4

It was several days before the two brothers managed to find a way of being alone together.

Major said, "Weren't you on Kee at all?"

Chawker Minor lowered his voice. "I was. Just a couple of days. It was too expensive to stay long."

"I have no doubt Elder would not have liked even the two days."

"I don't intend telling him. Do you?"

"A witless remark. Tell me about it."

Chawker Minor did, in semiembarrassed detail, and said, finally, "The point is, Major, it doesn't seem wrong to them. They don't think anything of it. It made me think that perhaps there is no real right and wrong. What you're used to, that's right. What you're not used to, that's wrong."

"Try telling that to Elder."

"What he thinks is right, and what he is used to, are precisely the same. You'll have to admit that."

"What difference does it make what *I* admit? Elder thinks that all rights and wrongs were written down by the makers of Gammer and that it's all in a book of which there is only one copy and we have it, so that all the Other Worlds are wrong forever. —I'm speaking metaphorically, of course."

"I believed that, too, Major—metaphorically. But it shook me up to see how calmly those Other World people took it. I could— watch them browse."

A spasm of distaste crossed Major's face. "Animals, you mean?"

"It doesn't look like animals when they browse on it. That's the point."

"You watched them kill, and dissect that—that—"

"No," hastily. "I just saw it when it was all finished. What they ate looked like some kinds of Prime and it smelled like some kinds of Prime. I imagine it tasted—"

Chawker Major twisted his expression into one of extreme revulsion, and Chawker Minor said, defensively, "But browsing came first, you know. On Earth, I mean. And it could be that when Prime was first developed on Gammer it was designed to imitate the taste of browse-food."

"I prefer not to believe that," said Chawker Major.

"What you prefer doesn't matter."

"Listen," said Chawker Major. "I don't care what they browse. If they ever got the chance to eat real Prime—not Strain A-5, but the fatted fungus, as the saying goes—and if they had the sophisticated additives and not whatever primitive trash they use, they would eat forever and never dream of browsing. If they could eat what *I* have constructed, and will yet construct—"

Chawker Minor said, wistfully, "Are you really going to try for the Award, Major?"

Chawker Major thought for a moment, then said, "I think I will, Minor. I really will. Even if I don't win, I eventually will. This program I've got is different." He grew excited. "It's not like any computer program I've ever seen or heard of; and it works. It's all in the—" But he pulled himself up sharply and said uneasily, "I hope, Minor, you don't mind if I *don't* tell you about it? I haven't told anyone."

Chawker Minor shrugged. "It would be foolish to tell anyone. If you really have a good program, you can make your fortune; you know that. Look at Grand-Elder Tomasz. It must be thirty-five years since he developed Corridor-Song and he still hasn't published his path."

Chawker Major said, "Yes, but there's a pretty good guess as to how he got to it. And it's not really, in my opinion—" He shook his head doubtfully, in preference to saying anything that might smack of lèse-majesté.

Chawker Minor said, "The reason I asked if you were going to try for the Award—"

"Well?"

"Is that I was rather thinking of entering myself."

"You? You're scarcely old enough."

"I'm twenty-two. But would you mind?"

"You don't know enough, Minor. When have you ever handled a computer?"

"What's the difference? A computer isn't the answer."

"No? What is?"

"The taste buds."

"Hit-and-miss-and-taste-buds-all-the-way. We all know that song and I will jump through the zero axis in a bound, too, as the saying goes."

"But I'm serious, Major. A computer is only the starting point, isn't it? It all ends with the tongue no matter where you start."

"And, of course, a Master Gustator like Minor-lad-here can do it."

Chawker Minor was not too tanned to flush. "Maybe not a Master Gustator, but a Gustator anyway, and you know it. The point is that being away from home for a year, I've gotten to appreciating good Prime and what might be done with it. I've learned enough— Look, Major, my tongue is all I've got, and I'd like to make back the money that Elder and Lady spent on me. Do you object to my entering? Do you fear the competition?"

Chawker Major stiffened. He was taller and heavier than Chawker Minor and he didn't look friendly. "There is no competition to fear. If you want to enter, do so, Minor-child. But don't come whimpering to me when you're shamed. And I tell you, Elder won't like your making a no-taste-batch of yourself, as the saying goes."

"Nobody has to win right away. Even if I don't win, I eventually will, as *your* saying goes," and Chawker Minor turned and left. He was feeling a little huffy himself.

5

Matters trailed off eventually. Everyone seemed to have enough of the tales of the Other Worlds. Chawker Minor had described the living animals he had seen for the fiftieth time and denied he had seen any of them killed for the hundredth. He had painted word pictures of the grainfields and tried to explain what sunshine looked like when it glinted off men and women and buildings and fields, through air that turned a little blue and hazy in the distance. He explained for the two hundredth time that no, it was not at all like the sunshine effect in the outer viewing rooms of Gammer (which hardly anyone visited anyway).

And now that it was all over, he rather missed not being stopped in the corridors. He no longer disliked being a celebrity. He felt a little at a loss as he spun the book film he had grown tired of viewing and tried not to be annoyed with Lady.

He said, "What's the matter, Lady-mine? You haven't smiled all day."

His mother looked up at him, thoughtfully. "It's distressing to see dissension between Major and Minor."

"Oh, come." Chawker Minor rose irritably and walked over to the air vent. It was jasmine-day and he loved the odor and, as always, automatically wondered how he could make it better. It was very faint, of course, since everyone knew that strong floral odors blunted the tongue.

"There's nothing wrong, Lady," he said, "with my trying for the Award. It's the free right of every Gammerperson over twenty-one."

"But it isn't good taste to be competing with your brother."

"Good taste! Why not? I'm competing with everyone. So's he. It's just a detail that we're competing with each other. Why don't you take the attitude that he's competing with me?"

"He's three years older than you, Minor-mine."

"And perhaps he'll win, Lady-mine. He's got the computer. Has Major asked you to get me to drop out?"

"No, he did not. Don't think that of your brother." Lady spoke earnestly, but she avoided his eyes.

Chawker Minor said, "Well, then, he's gone moping after you and you've learned to tell what he wants without his having to say it. And all because I qualified in the opening round and he didn't think I would."

"Anyone can qualify," came Chawker Major's voice from the doorway.

Chawker Minor whirled. "Is that the way it is? Then why does it upset you? And why did a hundred people fail to qualify?"

Chawker Major said, "What some small-taste-nitherlings decide means very little, Minor. Wait till it comes to the board."

"Since you qualified, too, Major, there's no need to tell me how little importance there is to some small-taste-nitherlings—"

"Young-mine," said Lady, rather sharply. "Stop it! Perhaps we can remember that it is very unusual for both Major and Minor of a single unit to qualify."

Neither ventured to break silence in Lady's presence for a while thereafter—but their scowls remained eloquent.

6

As the days passed, Chawker Minor found himself more and more involved in preparing the ultimate sample of flavored Prime that, his own taste buds and olfactory area would tell him, was to be nothing like anything that had ever rolled across a Gammer tongue before.

He took it upon himself to visit the Prime vats themselves, where the delectably bland fungi grew out of malodorous wastes and multiplied themselves at extraordinary speed, under carefully ide-alized conditions, into three dozen basic strains, each with its varieties.

(The Master Gustator, tasting unflavored Prime itself—the fungal unalterate, as the saying went—could be relied on to pin its source down to the section and corridor. Grand-Elder Tomasz had more than once stated, publicly, that he could tell the very vat itself and, at times, the portion of the vat, though no one had ever quite put him to the full test.)

Chawker Minor did not pretend to the expertise of Tomasz, but he lipped and tongued and smacked and nipped till he had decided on the exact strain and variety he wanted, the one which would best blend with the ingredients he was mixing in his mind. A good Gustator, said Grand-Elder Tomasz, could combine ingredients mentally and taste the mixture in pure imagination. With Tomasz, it might, for all one knew, be merely a statement, but Chawker Minor took it seriously and was sure he could do it.

He had rented out space in the kitchens (another expense for poor Elder, although Chawker Minor was making do with less than Major had demanded).

Chawker Minor did not repine at having less, for, since he was eschewing computers, he didn't require much. Mincers, mixers, heaters, strainers and the rest of the cookery tools took up little room. And at least he had an excellent hood for the masking and removal of all odors. (Everyone knew the horror tales of the Gustators who had been given away by a single sniff of odor and then found that some creative mixture was in the common domain before they could bring it before the board. To steal someone else's product might not be, as Lady would say, in good taste, but it was done and there was no legal recourse.)

The signal light flashed, in a code sufficiently well-known. It was Elder Chawker. Chawker Minor felt the thrill of guilt he had felt as a child when he had pilfered dabs of Prime reserved for guests.

"One moment, Elder-mine," he sang out, and, in a flurry of activity, set the hood on high, closed the partition, swept his ingredients off the tabletop and into the bins, then stepped out and closed the door quickly behind him.

"I'm sorry, Elder-mine," he said, with an attempt at lightness, "but Gustatorship is paramount."

"I understand," said Elder, stiffly, though his nostrils had flared momentarily as though he would have been glad to catch that fugitive whiff, "but you've scarcely been at home lately, scarcely more so than when you were at your space-folly, and I must come here to speak to you."

"No problem, Elder, we'll go to the lounge."

The lounge was not far away and, fortunately, it was empty. Elder's sharp glances this way and that made the emptiness seem fortunate for him and Chawker Minor sighed inaudibly. He would be lectured, he knew.

Elder said, at last, "Minor, you are my son, and I will do my duty toward you. My duty does not consist, however, of no more than paying your expenses and seeing to it that you have a fair start in life. There is also the matter of reproval in good time. Who wishes fair Prime must not stint on foul waste, as the saying goes."

Chawker's eyes dropped. He, along with his brother, had been among the thirty who had now qualified for the final Awarding to be held just a week in the future, and, unofficial rumor had it, Chawker Minor had done so with a somewhat higher score than Chawker Major had.

"Elder," said Chawker Minor, "would you ask me to do less than my best, for my brother's sake?"

Elder Chawker's eyes blinked in a moment of puzzlement and Chawker Minor clamped his mouth shut. He had clearly jumped in the wrong direction.

Elder said, "I do not ask you to do less than your best, but rather more than you are doing. Bethink you of the shaming you have inflicted on us in your little onset with Stens Major last week."

Chawker Minor had, for a moment, difficulty remembering what this could apply to. He had done nothing with Stens Major at all— a silly young woman with whom he was perfectly content to confine himself to mere talk, and not very much of that.

"Stens Major? Shaming? How?"

"Do not say you do not remember what you said to her. Stens Major repeated it to her elder and lady, good friends of our family, and it is now common talk in the Section. What possessed you, Minor, to assault the traditions of Gammer?"

"I did not do such a thing. She asked me about my Grand Tour and I told her no more than I have told three hundred others."

"Didn't you tell her that women should be allowed to go on the Grand Tour?"

"Oh."

"Yes. Oh."

"But, Elder, what I said was that if she would take the Grand Tour herself there would be no need to ask questions, and when she pretended to be shocked at such a suggestion, I told her that, in my opinion, the more Gammerpeople saw of the Other Worlds, the better it would be for all of us. We are too closed a society in my opinion, and Elder, I am not the first to say so."

"Yes, I have heard of radicals who have said so, but not in our Section and certainly not in our family. We have endured longer than the Other Worlds; we have a stabler and fitter society; we do not have their problems. Is there crime among us? Is there corruption among us?"

"But, Elder, it is at the price of immobility and living death. We're all so tied in, so enclosed."

"What can they teach us, these Other Worlds? Were you not yourself glad to come back to the enclosed and comfortable Sections of Gammer with their corridors lit in the golden light of our own energy?"

"Yes—but, you know, I'm spoiled, too. There are many things on the Outer Worlds that I would have very much liked to have made myself accustomed to."

"And just exactly what, Minor-madman-mine?"

Chawker Minor bit back the words. After a pause, he said, "Why simply make assertions? When I can *prove* that this particular Other World way or that is superior to Gammerfashion, I will produce the proof. Till then, what is the use of just talking?"

"You have already been talking idly without end, Minor, and it has done you so little good, that we can call what it has done you harm outright. —Minor, if you have any respect left for me after your Grand Tour, which Lady-yours wheedled out of me against my will, Gammer knows, or if you have any regard for the fact that I still deny you nothing that my credit can obtain for you, you will keep your mouth shut, henceforward. Think not that I will halt at sending you away if you shame us. You may then continue on your Grand Tour for as long as the Orbit lasts—and be no son of mine thereafter."

Chawker Minor said in a low voice, "As you say, Elder. From this moment on, unless I have evidence, I will say nothing."

"Since you will never have evidence," said Elder, grimly, "I will be satisfied if you keep your word."

7

The annual Finals was the greatest holiday occasion, the greatest social event, the greatest excitement of any sort in the course of the year. Each one of thirty dishes of elegantly flavored Prime had been prepared. Each one of the thirty judges would taste each dish at intervals long enough to restore the tongue. It would take all day.

In all honesty, Gammerpeople had to admit that the nearly hundred winners who had taken their prize and acclaim in Gammer history had not all turned out dishes that had entered the Great Menu as classics. Some were forgotten and some were now considered ordinary. On the other hand, at least two of Gammer's all-time favorites, combinations that had been best-sellers in restaurants and homes for two decades, had been also-rans in the years in which they had entered the contest. Black Velvet, whose odd combination of chocolate-warm and cherry blossom had made it the standard sweet, did not even make it to the Finals.

Chawker Minor had no doubt of the outcome. He was so confident that he found himself in continual danger of being bored. He kept watching the faces of the individual judges as every once in a while one of them would scoop up a trifle from one of the dishes and place it on his tongue. There was a careful blankness to the expression, a heavy-liddedness to the eye. No true judge could possibly allow a look of surprise or a sigh of satisfaction to escape him—certainly not a quiver of disdain. They merely recorded their ratings on the little computer cards they carried.

Chawker Minor wondered if they could possibly restrain their satisfaction when they tasted *his*. In the last week, his mixture had grown perfect, had reached a pinnacle of taste-glory that could not be improved on, could *not*—

"Counting your winnings?" said Chawker Major in his ear.

Chawker Minor started, and turned quickly. Chawker Major was dressed entirely in platon and gleamed beautifully.

Chawker Minor said, "Come, Major-mine, I wish you the best. I really do. I want you to place as high as possible."

"Second place if you win. Right?"

"Would you refuse second place if I win?"

"You can't win. I've checked somewhat. I know your strain of Prime; I know your ingredients—"

"Have you spent any time on your own work, all this time you've been playing detective?"

"Don't worry about me. It didn't take long to learn that there is no way you can combine your ingredients into anything of value."

"You checked that with the computer, I suppose?"

"I did."

"Then how did I get into the Finals, I wonder? Perhaps you don't know all there is to know about my ingredients. Look, Major, the number of effective combinations of even a few ingredients is astronomical if we consider the various possible proportions and the possible treatments before and after mixing, and the order of mixing and the—"

"I don't need your lecture, Minor."

"Then you know that no computer in existence has been programmed into the complexity of a clever tongue. Listen, you can add some ingredients in amounts so small as to be undetectable even by tongue and yet add a cast of flavor that represents a marked change."

"They teach you that in the Other Worlds, youngling?"

"I learned that for myself." And Chawker Minor walked away before he could be goaded into talking too much.

8

There was no question that Grand-Elder Tomasz this year, as in a large number of previous years, held the Judging Committee in the hollow of his tongue, as the saying went.

He looked up and down the long table at which all the judges had now taken their seat in order of precedence, with Tomasz himself right in the middle. The computer had been fed; it had produced the result. There was complete silence in the room where the contestants, their friends and their families sat, waiting for glory and, failing that, for at least the consolation of being able to taste all the contesting samples.

The rest of Gammer, possibly without exceptions, watched by holo-video. There would, after all, be additional batches made up for a week of feasting and the general opinion did not always match that of the judges either, though that did not affect the prize-winning.

Tomasz said, "I do not recall an Awarding in which there was so little doubt as to the computer decision, or such general agreement."

There was a nodding of heads, and smiles and looks of satisfaction.

Chawker Minor thought: They look sincere; not as if they're just going along with the Grand-Elder, so it must be mine.

Tomasz said, "It has been my privilege this year to taste a dish more subtle, more tempting, more ambrosial than anything I have ever, in all my time and experience, tasted. It is the best. I cannot imagine it being bettered."

He held up the Computo-cards, "The win is unanimous and the computer was needed only for the determination of the order of the runners-up. The winner is—" just that pause for effect and then, to the utter surprise of everyone but the winner "—Chawker Minor, for his dish entitled Mountain-Cap. —Young man."

Chawker Minor advanced for the ribbon, the plaque, the credits, the handshakes, the recording, the beaming, and the other contestants received their numbers in the list. Chawker Major was in fifth place.

9

Grand-Elder Tomasz sought out Chawker Minor after a while and tucked the young man's arm into his elbow.

"Well, Chawker Minor, it is a wonderful day for you and for all of us. I did not exaggerate. Your dish was the best I've ever tongued. —And yet you leave me curious and wondering. I identified all the ingredients, but there was no way in which their combination could produce what was produced. Would you be willing to impart your secret to me? I would not blame you if you refused, but in the case of an accomplishment so towering by one so young, to—"

"I don't mind telling you, Grand-Elder. I intend to tell everybody. I told my Elder that I would say nothing till I had proof. You supplied that proof!"

"What?" said Tomasz, blankly. "What proof?"

"The idea for the dish occurred to me, actually, on the Other World Kapper, which is why I called it Mountain-Cap in tribute. I used ordinary ingredients, Grand-Elder, carefully blended, all but one. I suppose you detected the Garden-Tang?"

"Yes, I did, but there was a slight modification there, I think, that I did not follow. How did the Other World you speak of affect matters?"

"Because it was not Garden-Tang, Grand-Elder, not the chemical. I used a complicated mixture for the Garden-Tang, a mixture of whose nature I cannot be entirely certain."

Tomasz frowned portentously. "You mean, then, you cannot reproduce this dish?"

"I *can* reproduce it; be certain of that, Grand-Elder. The ingredient to which I refer is garlic."

Tomasz said impatiently, "That is only the vulgar term for Mountain-Tang."

"*Not* Mountain-Tang. That is a known chemical mixture. I am speaking of the bulb of the plant."

Grand-Elder Tomasz's eyes opened wide and so did his mouth.

Chawker Minor continued enthusiastically, "No mixture can duplicate the complexity of a growing product, Grand-Elder, and on Kapper they have grown a particularly delicate variety which they use in their Prime. They use it incorrectly, without any appreciation of its potentiality. I saw at once that a true Gammerperson could do infinitely better, so I brought back with me a number of the bulbs and used them to good advantage. You said it was the best dish of Prime you had ever rolled tongue over and if there is any better evidence than that for the value of opening our society, then—"

But he dwindled to a stop at last, and stared at Tomasz with surprise and alarm. Tomasz was backing away rapidly. He said, in a gargling voice, "A growth—from the dirt—I've eaten—"

The Grand-Elder had often boasted that such was the steadiness of his stomach that he had never vomited, not even in infancy. And certainly *no one* had ever vomited in the great Hall of Judgment. The Grand-Elder now set a precedent in both respects.

10

Chawker Minor had not recovered. He would never recover. If it were exile that Elder Chawker had pronounced, so be it. He would never return.

Elder had not come to see him off. Neither had Major, of course. It didn't matter; Chawker Minor swore inwardly that he would make out, somehow, without their help, if it meant serving on Kapper as a cook.

Lady *was* there, however, the only one in all the field to see him off; the only one to dare accept the nonperson he had become. She shivered and looked mournful and Chawker Minor was filled with the desperate desire to justify himself.

"Lady-mine," he said, in a fury of self-pity, "it's *unfair!* It was the best dish ever made on Gammer. The Grand-Elder said so *himself*. The *best*. If it had grated bulb in it, that didn't mean the dish was bad; it meant the bulb was good. Don't *you* see it? —Look, I must board the ship. Tell me you see it. Don't you understand it means we must become an open society, learn from others as well as teach others, or we'll wither?"

The platform was about to take him up to the ship's entrance. She was watching him sadly, as though she knew she would never see him again.

He began the final rise, leaned over the rail. "What did I do *wrong*, Lady-mine?"

And she said in a low, distraught voice, "Can't you see, Minor-mine, that what you did was not in—"

The clang of the ship's port opening drowned her last two words, and Chawker Minor moved in and put the sight of Gammer behind him forever.

Introduction to

HOW IT HAPPENED

Not everything I do works out. I had it in my head, in June 1978, to write a mock history of the world in a series of funny scenes, largely because I had thought up what seemed to me to be a very funny scene to begin with.

Unfortunately, the funny scene I had thought up for the beginning was the only funny scene I could evolve. So I gave up the project. I called the beginning of the book-that-didn't-pan-out "How It Happened," offered it to George Scithers, and it appeared in the Spring 1979 *Asfam*.

9.

HOW IT HAPPENED

My brother began to dictate in his best oratorical style, the one which has the tribes hanging on his words.

"In the beginning," he said, "exactly fifteen point two billion years ago, there was a big bang and the Universe—"

But I had stopped writing. "Fifteen billion years ago?" I said incredulously.

"Absolutely," he said. "I'm inspired."

"I don't question your inspiration," I said. (I had better not. He's three years younger than I am, but I don't try questioning his inspiration. Neither does anyone else or there's hell to pay.) "But are you going to tell the story of the Creation over a period of fifteen billion years?"

"I have to," said my brother. "That's how long it took. I have it all in here," he tapped his forehead, "and it's on the very highest authority."

By now I had put down my stylus. "Do you know the price of papyrus?" I said.

"What?" (He may be inspired but I frequently noticed that the inspiration didn't include such sordid matters as the price of papyrus.)

I said, "Suppose you describe one million years of events to each roll of papyrus. That means you'll have to fill fifteen thousand rolls. You'll have to talk long enough to fill them and you know that you begin to stammer after a while. I'll have to write enough to fill them and my fingers will fall off. And even if we can afford all that papyrus and you have the voice and I have the strength, who's going to copy it? We've got to have a guarantee of a hundred copies before we can publish and without that where will we get royalties from?"

My brother thought awhile. He said, "You think I ought to cut it down?"

"Way down," I said, "if you expect to reach the public."

"How about a hundred years?" he said.

"How about six days?" I said.

He said, horrified, "You can't squeeze Creation into six days."

I said, "This is all the papyrus I have. What do *you* think?"

"Oh, well," he said, and began to dictate again, "In the beginning — Does it have to be six days, Aaron?"

I said, firmly, "Six days, Moses."

Introduction to

IDEAS DIE HARD

In the 1950s, the magazine at the leading edge of the field was *Galaxy Science Fiction*, which was edited by Horace L. Gold. It was giving *Astounding Science Fiction* a good run for its money. Gold was, however, an acerbic individual, and his rejections were cruel. I finally reached the point where I felt I could not face them and I stopped writing for him.

In March 1957, however, he asked me to try him, and promised to reject me, if he had to, with reasonable politeness. I thought I would try, therefore, since, except for his rejections, I liked Horace. "Ideas Die Hard" was the result, and he didn't reject it at all. It was published in the October 1957 *Galaxy*.

A quarter century has passed. Why has the story not appeared in any of my collections? It isn't a bad story, in my opinion.

However, it's out of date. I'm usually careful to write my stories so that it is very difficult for them to get in the way of developing science, but this time I muffed it. In 1957, everyone was talking about going to the Moon, but no one had as yet even put a satellite into orbit. So I felt safe in writing a story about going to the Moon. I assumed that events would not overtake me very quickly—but they did. In a very few years, not only were satellites orbiting the Earth, but a Lunar probe had gotten round the other side of the Moon and photographed it.

It seems to me, now, though, that I can live with being out of date. I can use it as an educational experience. Here is an example of what seemed like a clever idea to me in 1957 and you can see for yourself how science can race ahead of even a cultivated imagination.

10.

IDEAS DIE HARD

They strapped them in against the acceleration of takeoff, surrounded their cleverly designed seats with fluid, and fortified their bodies with drugs.

Then, when the time came that the straps might be unhooked, they were left with little more space than before.

The single light garment each wore gave an illusion of freedom, but only an illusion. They might move their arms freely, but their legs just to a limited extent. Only one at a time could be completely straightened, not both at once.

They could shift position into a half-recline to the right or left, but they could not leave their seats. The seats were all there were. They could eat, sleep, take care of all their bodily needs in a barely adequate way while sitting there, and they had to sit there.

What it amounted to was that for a week (slightly more, actually) they were condemned to a tomb. At the moment, it didn't matter that the tomb was surrounded by all of space.

Acceleration was over and done with. They had begun the silent, even swoop through the space that separated Earth and Moon and there was a great horror upon them.

Bruce G. Davis, Jr., said hollowly, "What do we talk about?"

Marvin Oldbury said, "I don't know." There was silence again.

They were not friends. Until recently they had never even met. But they were imprisoned together. Each had volunteered. Each had met the requirements. They were single, intelligent, and in good health.

Moreover, each had undergone extensive psychotherapy for months beforehand.

And the great advice of the psych-boys had been—*talk!*

"Talk continuously, if necessary," they had said. "Don't let yourself start feeling alone."

Oldbury said, "How do they know?" He was the taller and larger of the two, strong and square-faced. There was a tuft of hair just over the bridge of his nose that made a period between two dark eyebrows.

Davis was sandy-haired and freckled, with a pugnacious grin and the beginnings of shadows beneath his eyes. It might be those shadows that seemed to fill his eyes with foreboding.

He said, "How do who know?"

"The psychs. They say talk. How do they know it will do any good?"

"What do they care?" asked Davis sharply. "It's an experiment. If it doesn't work, they'll tell the next pair: 'Don't say a word.'"

Oldbury stretched out his arms and the fingers touched the great semisphere of information devices that surrounded them. He could move the controls, handle the air-conditioning equipment, tweak the plastic tubes out of which they could suck the bland nutrient mixture, nudge the waste-disposal unit, and brush the dials that controlled the viewscope.

All was bathed in the mild glow of the lights which were fed by electricity from the solar batteries exposed on the hull of the ship to sunlight that never failed.

Thank heaven, he thought, for the spin that had been given the vessel. It produced a centrifugal force that pressed him down in his seat with the feel of weight. Without that touch of gravity to make it seem like Earth, it could not have been borne.

Still, they might have made space within the ship, space that they could spare from the needs of equipment and use for the tight in-packing of two men.

He put the thought into words and said, "They might have allowed for more room."

"Why?" asked Davis.

"So we could stand up."

Davis grunted. It was really all the answer that could be made.

Oldbury said, "Why did you volunteer?"

"You should have asked me that before we left. I knew then. I was going to be one of the first men around the Moon and back. I was going to be a big hero at twenty-five. Columbus and I, you know." He turned his head from side to side restlessly, then sucked a moment or two at the water tube. He said, "But just the same, I've wanted to back out for two months. Each night I went to bed sweating, swearing I would resign in the morning."

"But you didn't."

"No, I didn't. Because I couldn't. Because I was too yellow to admit I was yellow. Even when they were strapping me into this seat, I was all set to shout: 'No! Get someone else!' I couldn't, not even then."

Oldbury smiled without lightness. "I wasn't even going to tell them. I wrote a note saying I couldn't make it. I was going to mail it and disappear into the desert. Know where the note is now?"

"Where?"

"In my shirt pocket. Right here."

Davis said, "Doesn't matter. When we come back, we'll be heroes —big, famous, trembling heroes."

Lars Nilsson was a pale man with sad eyes and with prominent knuckles on his thin fingers. He had been civilian-in-charge of Project Deep Space for three years. He had enjoyed the job, all of it, even the tension and the failures—until now. Until the moment when two men had finally been strapped into place within the machine.

He said, "I feel like a vivisectionist, somehow."

Dr. Godfrey Mayer, who headed the psychology group, looked pained. "Men have to be risked as well as ships. We've done what we could in the way of preparation and of safeguarding them as far as is humanly possible. After all, these men are volunteers."

Nilsson said colorlessly, "I know that." The fact did not really comfort him.

Staring at the controls, Oldbury wondered when, if ever, any of the dials would turn danger-red, when a warning ring would sound.

They had been assured that, in all likelihood, this would not happen, but each had been thoroughly trained in the exact manner of adjustment, manually, of each control.

And with reason. Automation had advanced to the point where the ship was a self-regulating organism, as self-regulating, almost, as a living thing. Yet three times, unmanned ships, almost as complicated as this one they were entombed in, had been sent out to follow a course boomeranging about the Moon, and three times, the ships had not returned.

Furthermore, each time the information devices relaying data back to Earth had failed before even the Moon's orbit had been reached on the forward journey.

Public opinion was impatient and the men working on Project Deep Space voted not to wait on the success of an unmanned vehicle before risking human beings. It was decided that a manned vehicle was needed so that manual correction could be introduced to compensate for the small, cumulative failure of the imperfect automation.

A crew of two men—they feared for the sanity of one man alone.

Oldbury said, "Davis! Hey, Davis!"

Davis stirred out of a withdrawn silence. "What?"

"Let's see what Earth looks like."

"Why?" Davis wanted to know.

"Why not? We're out here. Let's enjoy the view, at least."

He leaned back. The viewscope was an example of automation. The impingement of short-wave radiation blanked it out. The Sun could not be viewed under any circumstances. Other than that, the viewscope oriented itself toward the brightest source of illumination in space, compensating, as it did so, for any proper motion of the ship, as the engineers had explained offhandedly. Little photoelectric cells located at four sides of the ship whirled restlessly, scanning the sky. And if the brightest light source was not wanted, there was always the manual control.

Davis closed contact and the 'scope was alive with light. He put out the room's artificial lights and the view in the 'scope grew brighter against the contrast of darkness.

It wasn't a globe, of course, with continents on it. What they saw was a hazy mixture of white and blue-green filling the screen.

The dial that measured distance from Earth, by determining the value of the gravitational constant, put them just under thirty thousand miles away.

Davis said, "I'll get the edge." He reached out to adjust the sights and the view lurched.

A curve of black swept in across the 'scope. There were no stars in it.

Oldbury said, "It's the night shadow."

The view moved jerkily back. Blackness advanced from the other side and was curved more sharply and in the opposite sense. This time, the darkness showed the hard points of stars.

Oldbury swallowed. "I wish I were back there," he said solemnly.

Davis said, "At least we can see the Earth is round."

"Isn't that a discovery?"

Davis seemed immediately stung at the manner in which Oldbury tossed off his remark. He said, "Yes, it is a discovery, if you put it that way. Only a small percentage of the Earth's population has ever been convinced the Earth was round." He put on ship's lights, scowling, and doused the 'scope.

"Not since 1500," said Oldbury.

"If you consider the New Guinea tribes, there were flat-world believers even in 1950. And there were religious sects in America as late as the 1930s who believed the Earth was flat. They offered prizes for anyone who could prove it was round. Ideas die hard!"

"Crackpots," Oldbury grunted.

Davis grew warmer. He said, "Can *you* prove it's round? I mean except for the fact that you see it is right now?"

"You're being ridiculous."

"Am I? Or were you just taking your fourth-grade teacher's word as gospel? What proofs were you given? That the Earth's shadow on the Moon during a lunar eclipse is round and that only a sphere can cast a round shadow? That's plain nonsense! A circular disk can cast a round shadow. So can an egg or any shape, however irregular, with one circular intersection. Would you point out that men have traveled around the Earth? They might just be circling the central point of a flat Earth at a fixed distance. It would have the same effect. Do ships appear top-first on the horizon? Optical illusion, for all you know. There are queerer ones."

"Foucault's pendulum," said Oldbury briefly. He was taken aback at the other man's intensity.

Davis said, "You mean a pendulum staying in one plane and that plane revolving as Earth moves under it at a rate depending on the latitude of the place where the experiment is being performed. Sure! If a pendulum keeps to one plane. If the theories involved are correct. How does that satisfy the man in the street, who's no physicist, unless he's just willing to take the word of the physicists on faith? I tell you what! There was no satisfactory proof that the Earth was round till rockets flew high enough to take pictures of enough of the planet to show the curvature."

"Nuts," said Oldbury. "The geography of Argentina would be all distorted if the Earth were flat with the North Pole as the center. Any other center would distort the geography of some other portion. The skin of the Earth just would not have the shape it has if it weren't pretty nearly spherical. You can't refute that."

Davis fell silent for a moment, then said sulkily, "What the devil are we arguing for, anyway? The hell with it."

Seeing Earth and talking about it, even just about its roundness, had driven Oldbury into a sharp nostalgia. He began to talk of home in a low voice. He talked about his youth in Trenton, New Jersey, and brought up anecdotes about his family that were so trivial that he had not thought of them in years, laughing at things that were scarcely funny and feeling the sting of childish pain he had thought healed over years before.

At one point, Oldbury slipped off into shallow sleep, then woke with a start and was plunged in confusion at finding himself in a cold, blue-tinged light. Instinctively he made to rise to his feet and sank back with a groan as his elbow struck metal hard.

The 'scope was aglow again. The blue-tinged light that had startled him at the moment of waking was reflected from Earth.

The curve of Earth's rim was noticeably sharper now. They were 50,000 miles away.

Davis had turned at the other's sudden futile movement and said pugnaciously, "Earth's roundness is no test. After all, Man could crawl over its surface and see its shape by its geography, as you said. But there are other places where we act as though we know and with less justification."

Oldbury rubbed his twinging elbow and said, "All right, all right."

Davis was not to be placated. "There's Earth. Look at it. How old is it?"

Oldbury said cautiously, "A few billion years, I suppose."

"You *suppose?* What right have you to suppose? Why not a few thousand years? Your great-grandfather probably believed Earth was six thousand years old, dating from Genesis one. I know mine did. What makes you so sure they're wrong?"

"There's a good deal of geological evidence involved."

"The time it takes for the ocean to grow as salt as it is? The time it takes to lay down a thickness of sedimentary rock? The time it takes to form a quantity of lead in uranium ore?"

Oldbury leaned back in his seat and was watching the Earth with a kind of detachment. He scarcely heard Davis. A little more and they would see all of it in the 'scope. Already, with the planetary curve against space visible at one end of the 'scope, the night-shadow was about to encroach on the other.

The night-shadow did not change its position, of course. The Earth revolved, but to the men aboard ship it remained fat with light.

"Well?" demanded Davis.

"What?" said Oldbury, startled.

"What about your damned geological evidence?"

"Oh. Well, there's uranium decay."

"I mentioned it. You're a fool. Do you know that?"

Oldbury counted ten to himself before replying, "I don't think so."

"Then listen. Suppose the Earth had come into existence some six thousand years ago just as the Bible describes it. Why couldn't it have been created then with a certain amount of lead already existing in the uranium? If the uranium could be created, why not the lead with it? Why not create the ocean as salt as it is and the sedimentary rocks as thick as they are? Why not create the fossils exactly as they exist?"

"In other words, why not create the Earth complete with internal evidence proving that it is several billion years old?"

"That's right," said Davis, "why not?"

"Let me ask the opposite question. Why?"

"I don't care why. I'm just trying to show you that all the so-called proofs of Earth's age don't necessarily disprove Earth's creation six thousand years ago."

Oldbury said, "I suppose you consider it all to be intended as a kind of game—a scientific puzzle to test mankind's ingenuity, or exercise his mind—a mental jungle gym on his intellectual crib."

"You think you're being funny, Oldbury, but actually what's so damned impossible about it? It might be just that. You can't prove it isn't."

"I'm not trying to prove anything."

"No, you're satisfied to take things as they're handed to you. That's why I said you were a fool. If we could go back in time and see for ourselves, then that would be another matter. If we could go back in time before 4004 B.C. and see predynastic Egypt, or earlier still and bag a saber-toothed—"

"Or a tyrannosaur."

"Or a tyrannosaur, yes. Until we can do that, we can only speculate and there's nothing to say where speculation is correct and where it isn't. All science is based on faith in the original premises and in faith on the validity of deduction and induction."

"There's no crime in that."

"There is crime!" said Davis vehemently. "You come to believe, and once you come to believe, you shut the doors of your mind. You've got your idea and you won't replace it with another. Galileo found out how hard ideas can die."

"Columbus, too," Oldbury put in drowsily. Staring at the blue-tinged Earth with the slow whirling changes of the cloud formations had an almost hypnotic effect.

Davis seized on his comment with an obvious glee. "Columbus! I suppose you think he maintained the Earth was round when everyone else thought it was flat."

"More or less."

"That's the result of listening to your fourth-grade teacher, who listened to her fourth-grade teacher, and so on. Any intelligent and educated man in Columbus's time would have been willing to concede that the Earth was round. The point at issue was the size of the Earth."

"Is that a fact?"

"Absolutely. Columbus followed the maps of an Italian geographer which had the Earth about fifteen thousand miles in circumference, with the eastern edge of Asia about three or four thousand miles from Europe. The geographers at the court of King John of Portugal insisted that this was wrong, that the Earth was about twenty-five thousand miles in circumference, that the eastern edge of Asia was about twelve thousand miles west of the western edge of Europe, and that King John had better keep on trying for the route around Africa. The Portuguese geographers were, of course, a hundred per cent right and Columbus was a hundred per cent wrong. The Portuguese did reach India and Columbus never did."

Oldbury said, "He discovered America just the same. You can't deny that fact."

"That had nothing to do with his ideas. It was strictly accidental. He was such an intellectual fraud that when his actual voyage showed his map was wrong, he falsified his log rather than change his ideas. *His* ideas died hard—they never died till he did, in fact. And so do yours. I could talk myself blue in the face and leave you still convinced that Columbus was a great man because he thought the Earth was round when everyone else said it was flat."

"Have it your way," mumbled Oldbury. He was caught in lassitude and in the memory of the chicken soup his mother made when he was a child. She used barley. He remembered the smell of the kitchen on Saturday morning—French-toast morning—and the look of the streets after an afternoon of rain and the—

Lars Nilsson had the transcripts before him, with the more significant portions marked off on the tape by the psychologists.

He said, "Are we still receiving them clearly?"

He was assured that the receiving devices were working perfectly.

"I wish there were some way to avoid listening to their conversations without their knowledge," he said. "I suppose that's foolish of me."

Godfrey Mayer saw no point in denying the other's diagnosis. "It is," he agreed, "quite foolish. Look at it as merely additional information necessary to the study of human reaction to space. When we were testing human response to high-g acceleration, did you feel embarrassed to be caught looking at the recording of their blood-pressure variations?"

"What do you make of Davis and his odd theories? He worries me."

Mayer shook his head. "We don't know what we ought to be worried about as yet. Davis is working off aggressions against the science that has placed him in the position he finds himself in."

"That's your theory?"

"It's one theory. Expressing the aggressions may be a good thing. It may keep him stable. And then again, it may go too far. It's too soon to tell. It may be that Oldbury is the one who's in greater danger. He's growing passive."

"Do you suppose, Mayer, that we may find that Man just isn't suited for space? Any man?"

"If we could build ships that would carry a hundred men in an Earth-like environment, we'd have no trouble. As long as we build ships like this one"—he jerked a thumb over his shoulder in a vague directional gesture—"we may have a great deal of trouble."

Nilsson felt vaguely dissatisfied. He said, "Well, they're in their third day now and still safe so far."

"We're in the third day now," said Davis harshly. "We're better than halfway there."

"Umm. I had a cousin who owned a lumberyard. Cousin Raymond. I used to visit him sometimes on the way home from school," Oldbury reminisced.

Unaccountably his line of thought was interrupted by the fleeting memory of Longfellow's "The Village Blacksmith," and then he remembered that it contained a phrase about "the children coming home from school" and wondered how many people among those who rattle off so glibly, "Under the spreading chestnut tree, the village smithy stands" knew that the "smithy" was not the smith but the shop in which the smith worked.

He asked, "What was I saying?"

"I don't know," retorted Davis irritably. "*I* said we're more than halfway there and we haven't looked at the Moon yet."

"Let's look at the Moon, then."

"All right, *you* adjust the 'scope. I've done it long enough. Damn it, I've got blisters on my rump." He moved jerkily in the enclosing confines of the bucket seat, as though to get a slightly new section of rear end in contact with cushioned metal. "I don't know that it's such a blasted fine idea to spin the damned ship and have gravity press us down. Floating a little would take the weight off and be relaxing."

"There's no room to float," sighed Oldbury, "and if we were in free fall, you'd be complaining of nausea."

Oldbury was working the controls of the 'scope as he spoke. Stars moved past the line of vision.

It wasn't difficult. The engineers back home in Trenton—no, in New Mexico, really; on Earth, anyway—the engineers had schooled them carefully. Get it almost right. Get it pointed away from Earth, one hundred and eighty degrees.

Once it is nearly right, then let the light meters take over. The Moon would be the brightest object in the vicinity and it would be centered in unstable equilibrium. It would take a few seconds for the meters to scan the rest of the sky and switch the 'scope back to Earth, but in those few seconds, switch back to manuals and there, you have it.

The Moon was crescent. It would have to be in opposite phase to Earth as long as the ship sped along a course that was almost on the line connecting the two worlds.

But the crescent was a bloated one, as if it were part of a cheap calendar illustration. Oldbury thought there should be two heads, leaning toward one another, short straight hair against longer waved hair, silhouetted against the Moon. Except that it would have to be a full Moon.

Davis snorted. "It's there, at any rate."

"Did you expect it wouldn't be?"

"I don't expect anything in space. Anything yes or anything no. No one's been in space, so no one knows. But at least I see the Moon."

"You see it from Earth, if it comes to that."

"Don't be so sure what you see from Earth. For all anyone can tell from Earth, the Moon is only a yellow painted patch on a blue background with a shade that's drawn back and forth across it by clockwork."

"And stars and planets also run by clockwork?"

"Same as they are in a planetarium. Why not? And a telescope shows more stars painted on—"

"With a built-in red shift?"

"Why not?" challenged Davis. "Only we're halfway to the Moon and it looks bigger and maybe we'll find it exists. I'll reserve judgment on the planets and the stars."

Oldbury looked at the Moon and sighed. In a few days they would be edging around it, moving past and over the hidden side.

He said, "I never did believe the story about the man in the Moon. I never saw him. What I saw was the face of a woman—two eyes, rather lopsided, but very sad. I could see the full Moon from my bedroom window and she always made *me* feel sad, yet friendly, too. When clouds drifted past, it was the Moon—*she*— that always seemed to be moving, not the clouds, but still she didn't go away from the window. And you could see her through the clouds, even though you could never see the Sun through clouds, not even through little clouds, and it was so much brighter. Why is that, dad—uh—Davis?"

Davis said, "What's wrong with your voice?"

"Nothing's wrong with my voice."

"You're squeaking."

Oldbury, with an effort of will, forced his voice an octave lower. "I'm *not* squeaking!"

He stared at the small clocks in the dashboard, two of them. It wasn't the first time. One of them gave the time by Mountain Standard, and in that he wasn't interested. It was the other, the one that measured the number of hours elapsed in flight, that caught at him periodically. It said sixty-four and a fraction, and in red, working backward, were the hours remaining before they were to land on Earth again. The red was marked off now at one hundred forty-four and a fraction.

Oldbury was sorry that the time left to go was recorded. He would have liked to work it out for himself. Back in Trenton he used to count the hours to summer vacation, working it out painfully in his head during geography lesson—always geography lesson, somehow—so many days, then so many hours. He would write the result in tiny numbers in his exercise book. Each day the number would grow smaller. Half the excitement of approaching summer vacation was in watching those numbers grow smaller.

But now the numbers grew smaller by themselves as the sweep second hand went round and round, slicing time by minutes, paper-thin sections of time like corned beef peeling off in the big slicer in the delicatessen.

Davis's voice impinged on his ear suddenly: "Nothing seems to be going wrong so far."

Oldbury said confidently, "Nothing will go wrong."

"What makes you so sure?"

"Because the numbers just get smaller."

"Huh? How's that again?"

For a moment Oldbury was confused. He said, "Nothing."

It was dim in the ship in the light of the crescent Moon only. He dipped into sleep again, skin-diving fashion, half conscious of the real Moon and half dreaming of a full Moon at a window with a sad woman-face, being driven motionlessly by the wind.

"Two hundred thousand miles," said Davis. "That's almost eighty-five per cent of the way there."

The lighted portion of the Moon was speckled and pimpled and its horns had outgrown the screen. Mare Crisium was a dark oval, distorted by the slanting view, but large enough to put a fist into.

"And nothing wrong," Davis went on. "Not one little red light on a single instrument dial."

"Good," said Oldbury.

"Good?" Davis looked about to stare at Oldbury and his eyes were squinting in suspicion. "In every previous try, nothing went wrong till they got out this far, so it's not good *yet*."

"I don't think anything will go wrong."

"I think it will. Earth isn't supposed to know."

"Isn't supposed to know what?"

Davis laughed and Oldbury looked at him wearily. He felt queerly frightened at the other's gathering monomania. Davis was not a bit like the father Oldbury remembered so queerly (only he remembered him younger than he was now, with all his hair and a sound heart).

Davis's profile was sharp in the moonlight. He said, "There may

be a lot in space we're not supposed to know. There are a billion
light-years ahead of us. Only, for all we know, there's a solid black
wall instead, just on the other side of the Moon, with stars painted
on it and planets moving all squint-eyed so that smart cockerels on
Earth can figure out all sorts of fancy orbits and theories of gravitation out of it."

"A game to test our minds?" said Oldbury. His memory brought
that out of Davis's previous remarks—or were they his own?—with
something of a wrench. This whole business with the ship seemed
distant.

"Why not?"

"It's all right," Oldbury soothed anxiously. "It's all right so far.
Some day, you'll see, it will be all right all the way out."

"Then why do every one of the recording devices go wrong past
two hundred thousand miles? Why? Answer me that!"

"We're here this time. We'll adjust them."

Davis said, "No, we won't."

A sharp memory of a story he had encountered in early teenhood
stirred Oldbury into excitement. "You know, I once read a book
about the Moon. The Martians had set up a base on the other side
of the Moon. We could never see them, you see. They were hidden,
but they could observe us—"

"How?" asked Davis sourly. "There was two thousand miles'
thickness of Moon between Earth and the other side."

"No. Let me start from the beginning." Oldbury heard his voice
go squeaky again, but he didn't mind. He wanted to get out of his
seat so he could jump up and down because just remembering the
story made him feel good, but for some reason he couldn't. "You
see, it was in the future, and what Earth didn't know was—"

"Will you shut up?"

Oldbury's voice cut off at the interruption. He felt hurt, stifled.
Then he said, subdued, "You *said* Earth isn't supposed to know
and that's why the instruments went off and the only new thing
we're going to see is the other side of the Moon and if the Martians—"

"*Will* you let up with your stupid Martians?"

Oldbury fell silent. He was very resentful against Davis. Just because Davis was grown up didn't make it all right for him to holler like that.

His eyes drifted back to the clock. Summer vacation was only one hundred and ten hours away.

They were falling toward the Moon now. Free fall. Speeding down at cataclysmic velocity. Moon's gravity was weak, but they had fallen from a great height. And now, finally, the view on the Moon began to shift and, very slowly, new craters were coming into view.

Of course, they would miss the Moon and their speed would sweep them safely around. They would move across half the Moon's surface, across three thousand miles of it in one hour; then back they would hurl to meet the Earth once more.

But Oldbury sadly missed the familiar face in the Moon. There was no face this close, only ragged surface. He felt his eyes brimming as he watched morosely.

And then, suddenly, the small cramped room within the ship was full of loud buzzing and half the dials on the panel before them clamored into the red of disorder.

Oldbury cowered back, but Davis howled in what seemed almost triumph. "I told you! Everything's going wrong!"

He worked at the manuals uselessly. "No information will get back. Secrets! Secrets!"

But Oldbury still looked at the Moon. It was terribly close and now the surface was moving quickly. They were starting the swing in earnest and Oldbury's scream was high-pitched. "Look! Look-athat!" His pointing finger was stiff with terror.

Davis looked up and said, "Oh, god! Oh, god—" over and over again, until finally the 'scope blanked out and the dials governing it showed red.

Lars Nilsson could not really go paler than he was, but his hands trembled as they clenched into fists.

"Again! It's a damned jinx. For ten years, the automation hasn't held out. Not on the unmanned flights. Not on this. Who's responsible?"

There was no use trying to fix responsibility. No one was responsible, as Nilsson admitted with a groan almost at once. It was just that at the crucial moment—once again—things had failed.

"We've got to pull them through this somehow," he said, knowing that the outcome was questionable now.

Still, what could be done was being put into operation.

Davis said, "You saw that, too, didn't you?"

"I'm scared," whimpered Oldbury.

"You *saw* it. You saw the hidden side of the Moon as we went past and you saw *there wasn't any!* Good Lord, just sticks, just big beams holding up six million square miles of canvas. I swear it, *canvas!*"

He laughed wildly till he choked into breathlessness.

Then he said hoarsely, "For a million years mankind has been looking at the biggest false front ever dreamed of. Lovers spooned under a world-size stretch of canvas and called it Moon. The stars are painted; they must be. If we could only get out far enough, we could scrape some off and carry them home. Oh, it's funny." He was laughing again.

Oldbury wanted to ask why the grown-up was laughing. He could only manage a "Why—why—" because the other's laughter was so wild that it froze the words into thick fright in his throat.

Davis said, "Why? How the devil should I know why? Why does Television City build false-front houses by the streetful for its shows? Maybe we're a show, and the two of us have stumbled way out here where the gimcrack scenery is set up instead of being on stage-center where we're supposed to be. Mankind isn't supposed to know about the scenery, either. That's why the information devices always go wrong past two hundred thousand miles. Of course, *we* saw it."

He looked crookedly at the big man beside him. "You know why it didn't matter if we saw it?"

Oldbury stared back out of his tear-stained face. "No. Why?"

Davis said, "Because it *doesn't* matter if we see it. If we get back to Earth and say that the Moon is canvas propped up by wood, they'd kill us. Or maybe lock us up in a madhouse for life if they felt kindhearted. That's why we won't say a word about this."

His voice suddenly deepened with menace. "You understand? Not a word!"

"I want my mother," whined Oldbury plaintively.

"Do you *understand?* We keep quiet. It's our only chance to be treated as sane. Let someone else come out and find out the truth and be slaughtered for it. Swear you'll keep quiet! Cross your heart and hope to die if you tell them!"

Davis was breathing harshly as he raised a threatening arm.

Oldbury shrank back as far as his prison-seat would let him. "Don't hit me. Don't!"

But Davis, past himself with fury, cried, "There's only one safe way," and struck at the cowering figure, and again, and again—

Godfrey Mayer sat at Oldbury's bedside and said, "Is it all clear to you?" Oldbury had been under observation for the better part of a month now.

Lars Nilsson sat at the other end of the room, listening and watching. He remembered Oldbury as he had appeared before he had climbed into the ship. The face was still square, but the cheeks had fallen inward and the strength was gone from it.

Oldbury's voice was steady, but half a whisper. "It wasn't a ship at all. We weren't in space."

"Now we're not just *saying* that. We *showed* you the ship and the controls that handled the *images* of the Earth and the Moon. You *saw* it."

"Yes. I know."

Mayer went on quietly, matter-of-factly, "It was a dry run, a complete duplication of conditions to test how men would hold out. Naturally, you and Davis couldn't be told this or the test would mean nothing. If things didn't work out, we could stop it at any time. We could learn by experience and make changes, try again with a new pair."

He had explained this over and over again. Oldbury had to be made to understand if he was ever to learn to live a useful life again.

"Has a new pair been tried yet?" asked Oldbury wistfully.

"Not yet. They will be. There are some changes to be made."

"I failed."

"We learned a great deal, so the experiment was a success in its way. Now listen—the controls of the ship were designed to go wrong when they did in order to test your reaction to emergency conditions after several days of travel strain. The breakdown was timed for the simulated swing about the Moon, which we were going to switch about so that you could see it from a new angle on the return trip. You weren't intended to see the other side and so we didn't build the other side. Call it economy. This test alone cost fifty million dollars and it's not easy to get appropriations."

Nilsson added bitterly, "Except that the shut-off switch on the 'scope didn't shut off in time. A valve caught. You saw the unfinished back of the Moon and we had to stop the ship to prevent—"

"That's it," interrupted Mayer. "Now repeat it, Oldbury. Repeat everything."

They walked down the corridor thoughtfully. Nilsson said, "He seemed almost himself today. Don't you think so?"

"There's improvement," Mayer acknowledged. "A great deal. But he's not through with therapy by any means."

Nilsson asked, "Any hope with Davis?"

Mayer shook his head slowly. "That's a different case. He's completely withdrawn. Won't talk. And that deprives us of any handle with which to reach him. We've tried aldosterone, ergot therapy, counterelectroencephalography, and so on. No good. He thinks if he talks, we'll put him in an institution or kill him. You couldn't ask for a more developed paranoia."

"Have you told him we *know*?"

"If we do, we'll bring on a homicidal seizure again and we may not be as lucky as we were in saving Oldbury. I rather think he's incurable. Sometimes, when the Moon is in the sky, the orderly tells me, Davis stares up at it and mutters, 'Canvas,' to himself."

Nilsson said soberly, "It reminds me of what Davis himself said in the early part of the trip. Ideas die hard. They do, don't they?"

"It's the tragedy of the world. Only—" Mayer hesitated.

"Only what?"

"Our unmanned rockets, three of them—the information devices on each stopped transmitting just before the boomerang swing and not one returned. Sometimes I just wonder—"

"*Shut up!*" said Nilsson fiercely.

Introduction to

IGNITION POINT!

I happen to be a professional speaker as well as a professional writer. In fact, I have been speaking (for money) for thirty years now, and doing fairly well.

There is an organization that puts out an annual entitled "Finding the Right Speaker" in which various lecture agencies advertise their wares (and you can be sure that my lecture agent mentions me in his advertisement). The organization thought they would punch up their 1981 edition with a story and they naturally thought of me.

I agreed, thinking it would be a pleasant combination of my two careers, wrote "Ignition Point!" in January 1981, and it appeared in the annual. Since I'm certain the readership of the annual is limited, it is with pleasure I include the story in this collection so that it might find its more appropriate science fiction market.

11.

IGNITION POINT!

Let me get this straight," said Anthony Myers, leaning across his desk toward the man in the chair facing him. "Your computer does *not* write the speech?"

"No, you do. Or someone else does." Nicholas Jansen was quite composed. He was a small man, very neatly dressed, with an old-fashioned knotted tie that did not seem to make him the least bit self-conscious in a world of turtlenecks.

He said, "What I have developed is a series of words, phrases, sentences that induce reactions in specific groups of people, divided by sex, age, ethnic groups, language, occupation, place of residence or almost anything else conceivable. If you could describe the audience your man would be addressing in sufficient detail, then I could supply you with precisely the sort of thing his talk should include. The more we know about the audience the more accurately my computer program can produce the key words and phrases. They are woven into a speech—"

"Can they? Will they make sense?"

"That's up to the ingenuity of the speech writer, but it doesn't really matter. If you're pounding a drum, you might get the audience stirred up until their feet and hearts are pounding with it; till they reach ignition point. Sense is analogous to tune, but a drum doesn't have to beat out a tune; it merely establishes a rhythm. You can put in as much tune as you can, but it is the rhythm you're after. Do you understand?"

Myers rubbed his chin and stared at the other thoughtfully. "Have you tried this before?"

Jansen smiled narrowly. "Only unofficially. In a small way. Still, I know what I'm talking about. I'm an ochlologist—"

"A what?"

"A student of mob psychology, and the first, as far as I know, who has truly computerized the matter."

"And you know this will work—in theory."

"No, I know it *might* work—in theory."

"And you want to try it out on me. What if it doesn't work?"

"Then what have you to lose? I'm not charging you. It's useful in my work, and if I may believe what I have been told, your man is lost if you don't use my services."

Myers drummed his fingers on the desk softly. "Look. Let me explain about my man. He looks impressive. He's got a good voice. He's amiable and likable. Properly handled I can make him a corporation executive, or an ambassador, or the President of the United States. The trouble is he has no brains to speak of and he needs me to supply them. But the one thing he has to be able to do without me is to deliver a speech in such a way as to fool people into thinking he does have brains. This he cannot do, even if the speech is written out for him. The speech may be intelligent and yet he can't say it in such a way as to make *himself* seem intelligent. Do you think you can write a speech better than I can?"

"Not better. Just foolproof. I can make it possible for him to push the right buttons and ignite the audience."

"What do you mean, ignite?"

"To catch fire. Isn't that what ignite means? Every crowd has its ignition point, though every different crowd requires something different for ignition."

"You may be selling me a load of nonsense, Mr. Jansen. There's no speech so foolproof that a nincompoop won't spoil it."

"On the contrary. A nincompoop might deliver it more surely than you could, since he won't be thinking for himself. May I meet him? —That is, if you want my services?"

"You understand that everything said here is confidential."

"Certainly. Since I intend to turn this to commercial use eventually, I am more interested in confidentiality than you are."

Barry Winston Bloch was not quite forty. He had played semipro baseball in his younger days. He had made his way through a midwestern college with minimal effort and he had been moderately successful as a salesman. His appearance was impressive, not because he was handsome but because he looked physically powerful, and gave the impression of possessing a mature wisdom. His hair was already showing streaks of gray and he had a way of throwing his head up and smiling warmly that filled you full of confidence in him.

It took an hour or so, usually, to realize that there was nothing behind the amiability but additional amiability.

Right now, Bloch felt uncomfortable. Ever since he had tied up with Myers, he had been a prey to discomfort. He wanted to get ahead; it was his secret desire to be a congressman and sometimes he wondered if he might not be a great evangelist, but the trouble was that people made him nervous. After he had used up his big grin, it came time to talk and he never had anything particular to say.

And no one had ever made him feel quite as uncomfortable as this little man with his gimlet eyes, who would sit there absolutely motionless while Bloch read his speeches. It was hard enough to talk to a real audience which rustled and coughed and seemed to be annoyed with him for not finishing. This little man—he had to remember his name was Jansen—who never responded in any way just choked him off.

No, he responded in one way—he invariably handed Bloch another speech to read. Each one was a little different and each one appealed to him somehow, but he never felt as if he did them justice. It made him sad somehow—and ashamed.

The manuscript presented to him on *this* day seemed worse than all the others. He looked at it in dismay. "What are all these marks?"

"Well now, B.B.," Myers adopted the soothing tone he almost always used with Bloch, "just let Mr. Jansen explain."

"It's direction. It's something you must learn, but it won't be difficult. A dash means a pause, an underlining means an emphasis. A downward arrow before a word means you let your voice drop a couple of notes; an upward arrow means you let it rise. A curved arrow means you let things fade off in contempt, if it curves downward. If it curves upward, your voice rises in anger. A parenthesis means a small smile; a double parenthesis means a grin; a triple parenthesis means a chuckle. You never laugh out loud. A line over a word means you look grim; a double line means you repeat. An asterisk—"

Bloch said, "I can't remember all that."

Myers, from behind Bloch, mouthed worriedly, I don't think he will.

Jansen seemed unperturbed by the double denial. "You will with practice. The stakes are high and worth a little trouble."

Myers said, "Go ahead, B.B. Just give it a read-through and Mr. Jansen will help out as you go along."

Bloch looked as though he wished to object further, but his native amiability won out. He put the manuscript on the lectern and began to read it. He stumbled, peered at the manuscript with a frown, began again, and skidded to a halt.

Jansen explained and Bloch began again. They spent an hour over the first three paragraphs before calling a halt.

Myers said, "It's awful."

Jansen said, "How did you do the first time you tried to ride a bicycle?"

Bloch repeated the speech all the way through twice that day; twice more the second day. A second speech was prepared, not quite the same, but just as empty of real content.

After a week, Bloch said, "I'm getting the hang of it. It seems to me that I'm getting so that it sounds good."

Myers said, with hollow hopefulness, "I think so, too."

Jansen said to Myers afterward, "He's doing better than I expected. He's got a certain potentiality, but—"

"But what?"

Jansen shrugged. "Nothing. We'll just have to see."

Jansen said, "I think he's ready for an audience now, provided it's a homogenous one which we can analyze accurately."

"The American Association of Textile Weavers needs a speaker and I think I can place B.B. with them. Can you handle that audience?"

"Weavers?" said Jansen, thoughtfully. "The economic position would be homogenous and I suspect the educational level would not be too wide a spread. I would need to have a breakdown on what city and states they represent and on the percentages coming from establishments of different size. Age, sex and the usual, too, of course."

"I'll see what I can dig up from the Union, but there isn't much time, you know."

"We'll try to work quickly. We've got a great deal of the basics worked out. Your man is learning how to deliver a speech."

Myers laughed. "He's gotten to the point where he almost convinces *me.* —You know, I wouldn't want him in Congress. I would want him on television, selling my views—his, I mean—"

"Your views, you mean," said Jansen, dryly. "*He* has none."

"It doesn't matter. I'm counting my chickens—"

Bloch did well at the A.A.T.W. cocktail party. He followed his instructions, had smiled, had talked just a bit but not too much, had told a harmless joke or two and dropped a few names, and had, for the most part, done a lot of listening and nodding.

And yet Myers, from his table up front, felt a certain tightness. If B.B. flopped, they could try again, but if he flopped, would there be enough in him to make it worth his while to try again? This might be the test that would show that B.B. just didn't have it. What a waste, with that appearance! With that Roman senator head of his!

He stole a glance at Jansen, who sat at his left. The little man seemed utterly composed but there was a slight contraction of the eyebrows, as though there were a secret worry gnawing at him.

The dinner was over, the various business announcements were being made, the committee was being thanked, the people seated on the dais were being introduced—all the maddening details that seemed to be designed for no other purpose than to place additional unnecessary strain upon the speaker.

Myers stared earnestly at Bloch, caught his eye, and held up two fingers briefly. Go in and get them, B.B.!

Would he? The speech was an odd one, almost quixotic. It would read oddly in the papers if it ever made the news columns, but it was full of button pushers—according to Jansen and his computer.

Bloch was standing up now. He stepped easily to the lectern and put the manuscript before him. He was always good at that; doing it slickly and unobtrusively so that the audience never really had it rubbed in their face that the speech was going to be read.

Myers thought, not entirely irrelevantly, of the time he had attended a meeting at which the speaker had somehow managed to knock off his manuscript with an overenergetic gesture. The manuscript could be picked up and rearranged but an audience died at that moment and could not be revived.

Bloch smiled at the audience and began slowly. (Don't wait too long to speed up, B.B.)

He didn't. He quickened the beat. At times, he stopped briefly to puzzle out a symbol but fortunately, that sounded like deliberation, the kind of thought you would expect of mature wisdom. It helped to have that appearance.

Then he spoke still more quickly and emotionally and, to Myers' surprise, he could feel the drumbeats start. There were those key phrases, with just the right kind of emphasis, and in response, he could feel the audience stir.

Laughter came on cue and at one point, there was a patter of applause. Myers had never heard applause interrupt Bloch before.

Bloch's face looked a little flushed and at one point he brought his fist down on the lectern and the little fluorescent lamp shook. (Don't knock it over, B.B.!) The audience stamped its feet in response.

Myers felt the mounting excitement within himself, even though he knew exactly how carefully the speech had been prepared. He leaned toward Jansen. "He's igniting the audience, wouldn't you say?"

Jansen nodded once. His lips scarcely moved. "Yes. And maybe—"

Bloch had paused briefly in his talk—just long enough to tighten the audience into a knot of tension—and then he brought his hand down savagely on the lectern, picked up the manuscript in a crumpled mess, and threw it aside. "I don't need this," he said, his voice rising into a distinct note of triumph. "I don't want it. I wrote it in cold blood before I had you all before me. Let me speak now from my heart, as it comes to me, standing here before you; let me tell you all, friends and Americans, you and I, together, what I see in the world today and what I *want* to see, and believe me, my friends, the two are *not—the—same.*"

There was a roar in response.

Myers clutched at Jansen wildly. "He can't make it on his own!"

But he could and did. He spoke through and over the applause and the shouting. It scarcely mattered if he were heard. He raised both arms as though to embrace the audience and a voice shouted, "Go on! Give it to them!"

Bloch gave it to them. Exactly what he said scarcely mattered but when it was over, there was a wild and jubilant standing ovation.

"What happened?" said Myers, through the noise. (He was applauding as loudly as everyone else.)

Jansen remained seated, in a strange attitude of collapse. He clutched at Myers, drew him close, and said in a shaking voice, "Don't you see what happened? It was a one-in-a-million shot. Just toward the end I began to wonder if it were possible. It *can* happen—"

"What are you talking about?"

"The audience ignited and Bloch was speaking to an ignited audience for the first time in his life, and speakers have their ignition point, too. Bloch himself ignited, and an ignited speaker can carry public opinion and move mountains."

"Who? B.B.?"

"Yes."

"Well, that's great."

"Is it? When ignited, he's got power, and if he finds out he has, why would he need you? Or me? And if so, where will he go? There have been great charismatics before who have not always led to glory."

Bloch was with them, people crowding about him. He said to Myers in a breathless undertone, "That was easy! I feel great!" He turned to those about him, laughing, holding them all with no trouble.

Myers looked after him, confused; Jansen looked after him, afraid!

Introduction to

IT IS COMING

Nearly every year, Field Enterprises, Inc. persuades me to do a four-part essay which they then peddle to various newspapers. In 1978, however, they came up with the notion of my doing a four-part science fiction story, the whole not to be more than five or six thousand words in length.

I worried about that, but decided to tackle the project and wrote the story while I was on a train trip to California. (Since I am the world's poorest traveler, it was good that I had something that served as a powerful distractant.)

Field Enterprises was satisfied and they distributed it to various clients in early 1979.

I include the story here with just a faint hesitation, however, for it was necessary to begin each part with a very brief recapitulation for those newspaper readers who had not read the earlier installments, or, having read them, did not remember them. I will have to ask you to exercise a certain tolerance, therefore, at the few words of repetition that you won't need.

12.

IT IS COMING

Part 1

When we finally heard from the Universe, it was not from some distant star. The signals did not reach us across the vastness of interstellar space, traveling for light-years of distance and years of time. They did *not*.

They came from our own solar system. Something (whatever it was) was inside our solar system and was approaching. It (whatever it was) would be in Earth's neighborhood in five months unless it accelerated or veered away.

And it was up to Josephine and myself—and Multivac—to make the decisions as to what to do.

At least we had warning. If it (whatever it was) had arrived fifty years ago—say in 1980—it would not have been detected so quickly, and perhaps not at all. It was the great complex of radio telescopes in the Sea of Moscow on the other side of the Moon that detected the signals, located them, followed them. And that telescope, as it happened, had been operational for only five years.

But doing something about it was up to Multivac in its lair in the Rockies. All that the astronomers could say was that the signals were not regular and not utterly random, so that they probably contained a message. It would have to be up to Multivac, however, to interpret that message if interpretation was possible.

The message, whatever it was, certainly wasn't in English, or Chinese, or Russian, or any Earth language. The microwave pulses made no sense if translated into sound or if organized into what might possibly be a picture. But then why should they? The language, if it was one, would have to be completely alien. The intelligence behind it, if there was one, would have to be completely alien, too.

For the public, the story was played down. It became an asteroid in an elongated orbit, with assurances there would be no collision.

There was, however, intense activity behind the scenes. The view of the European representatives at the planetary conference was that there was no need to do anything. When the object arrived we would understand. The Islamic Region suggested preparations for world defense. The Soviet and American regions pointed out, jointly, that knowledge was always preferable to ignorance and that the signals should be subjected to computer analysis.

That meant Multivac.

The trouble is that nobody really understands Multivac. It blinks and clicks away in a three-mile-long artificial cavern in Colorado and its decisions run the world's economy. No one knows if that monster computer runs the economy well or ill but no human being or group of human beings dares take the responsibility of economic decisions so Multivac remains in charge.

It spots its own errors, repairs its own breakdowns, extends its own structure. Human beings supply the energy and the spare parts, and someday Multivac would be able to do that for itself, too.

It was Josephine and myself who were the human interface. We adjusted the programming when it needed adjusting, fed in new data when it needed feeding, interpreted the results when it needed interpretation.

It could all have been done from a distance, actually, but that would not have been politic. The world wanted to live with the illusion that human beings were in control, so they wanted one person on the spot as a token.

That's Josephine Durray, who knows more about Multivac than anyone on Earth—though that's not so very much. Since one person out there in the corridors of Multivac alone would quickly go crazy, I went along too. I'm Bruce Durray, her husband—electrical engineer by trade, Multivac expert by education at the hands of Josephine.

It doesn't take much insight to guess we didn't want the responsibility of making sense out of the alien signals, but only Multivac could do it if it could be done at all and only we stood between Multivac and humanity.

For once Multivac had to be programmed from scratch because there was nothing in its vitals that resembled the present task and it was Josephine who would have to do it with what help I could give her.

She scowled and said, "All I can do, Bruce, is to instruct Multivac to try every permutation and combination and see if anything will set up local regularities or repetitions."

Multivac tried. At least we had to assume it tried. But what came out was a negative. What was flashed on the screen and what appeared on the printouts was "No translation possible."

After three weeks, Josephine was beginning to look her age. She said, broodingly, clutching at her graying hair so that it looked more crumpled than ever, "We're at a dead end, and we've got to do something."

We were at breakfast and I pushed at my scrambled eggs with my fork and said, "Yes, but what?"

She said, "Bruce, whatever it is, we have to assume it's more technologically advanced and probably more intelligent than we are. It's coming to us from some distant origin; we're not yet able to go to it. Well, then, if we were to send signals to it, it would probably be able to interpret them."

"Maybe," I said.

"No maybe. Yes!" she said sharply. "So let's send it signals. It will interpret them and then send signals of its own according to our system."

She called the Secretary of the Economy, who's our boss. He heard her out, then said, "I couldn't pass that suggestion on to the Council. They wouldn't hear of it. We can't let it know anything about us till we know something about them. We shouldn't even let it know we're here."

Josephine said earnestly, "But it knows we're here. It is coming. Some intelligence has probably known we're here for a century, ever since our stray radio signals began leaking out into space in the early twentieth century."

"If that is so," said the Secretary, "where is the need for another message?"

"Stray signals are a meaningless jumble, sheer noise. We must send out a deliberate signal to set up communication."

"No, Mrs. Durray," he said. "The Council would not consider it and I would not recommend it or even mention it." And that was that. He broke connection.

I stared at the blank screen and said, "He's right, you know. They wouldn't consider it and the Secretary's standing in the hierarchy would be damaged if he associated himself with such a suggestion."

Josephine looked angry. "They can't stop me, though. I control Multivac, as much as it can be controlled, and I can have it send out the messages anyway."

"Which would mean discharge, imprisonment—execution, for all I know."

"*If* they can find out it's been done. We *must* know what the message says, and if those politicians are too frightened to take a rational chance, I'm not."

We were risking the whole planet, I suppose, but the planet seemed far away, alone as we were in the Rockies, and she began beaming science articles from the Encyclopedia Terrestria. Science, she said, was most likely to be the universal language.

For some time, nothing much happened. Multivac continued to cluck contentedly, but produced nothing. And then after eight days had passed, Multivac informed us that the character of the invader's signals seemed to have changed.

"They've begun to translate us," said Josephine, "and are trying to use English."

And two days afterward translations finally came through Multivac: IT IS COMING—IT IS COMING— That came over and over, but we knew that. And then, one more: —AND IF NOT, YOU WILL BE DESTROYED—

After we got over the shock, Josephine demanded checks and confirmation. Multivac held to that phrase and would give us no more.

"My God," I said, "we've got to let the Council know."

"No!" said Josephine. "Not till we know more. We can't have them acting in hysteria."

"We can't bear the responsibility for this by ourselves, either."

And Josephine said, "For a while, we must."

Part 2

Some alien object was streaking through the solar system toward us and would be near Earth in three months. Only Multivac could understand its signals and only Josephine and I could understand Multivac, the Earth's giant computer.

And the signals threatened destruction.

IT IS COMING, went the message, and —AND IF NOT, YOU WILL BE DESTROYED.

We worked on it madly and so did Multivac, I imagine. It was Multivac that had to do the real work of attempting all possible translations to see which fit the data best. I doubt that either Josephine or I—or any human being—would have been able to follow Multivac's course of action, even though Josephine had programmed it in general terms.

Finally, the message lengthened and filled in—IT IS COMING. ARE YOU EFFICIENT, OR ARE YOU DANGEROUS? ARE YOU EFFICIENT? IF NOT, YOU MUST BE DESTROYED.

I said, "What does it mean by efficient?"

"That's the point," said Josephine. "I can't sit on it any longer."

It was almost as though there were telepathic communication involved. We didn't have to call our boss, the Secretary of the Economy. He called us. At that, it wasn't such an unbelievable coincidence. The tension at the Planetary Council had to be rising each day. The surprising thing was that they weren't biting and snapping at our shins every moment.

He said, "Mrs. Durray. Professor Michelman of the University of Melbourne reports that the code-nature of the messages has changed. Has Multivac noted this and has it worked out its significance?"

"The object is signaling in English," said Josephine, matter-of-factly.

"Are you certain? How can it—"

Josephine said, "They've been picking up our radio and TV leaks for decades and the invaders, whoever they are, have learned our languages." She didn't say we'd been feeding them the information, quite illegally, in order to have them learn English.

The Secretary said, "If that is so, why hasn't Multivac—"

"Multivac has," said Josephine. "We have parts of the message."

There was silence for a few moments and the Secretary said, sharply, "Well? I'm waiting."

"If you mean for the message, I can't help you. I'll give it to the Council Chairman."

"*I'll* give it to him."

"I prefer to do it directly."

The Secretary looked furious. "You will give it to me. I'm your superior."

"Then I'll give it to the Planetary Press. Would you prefer that?"

"Do you know what will happen to you in that case?"

"Will that undo the damage?"

The Secretary looked murderous and irresolute at the same time. Josephine managed to look indifferent, but I could see her hands twisting behind her—and she won.

It was evening when the Chairman came on—full holography. He was so three-dimensional one might almost think he was sitting there in person except that the background was different. The smoke from his pipe drifted toward us but vanished completely about five feet short of our noses.

The Chairman looked benign but that was his professional attitude after all, always benign in public. He said, "Mrs. Durray—Mr. Durray—that's an excellent job you two do in servicing Multivac. The Council is quite aware of your work."

"Thank you," said Josephine, in a clipped way.

"I understand, now, that you have a translation of the invader's signals which you will not send on except to me personally. That sounds grave. What is the translation?"

Josephine told him.

His expression did not change. "How can you be sure?"

"Because Multivac has been sending signals to the invader in English. The invader must have translated those signals and adopted the language for its own signals. Then its signals could be translated."

"By whose authority did Multivac send out signals in English?"

"We could get none."

"But did it anyway?"

"Yes, sir."

The Chairman sighed. "That means the lunar penal colony, you understand. —Or commendation, depending on results."

"If the invader destroys us, Mr. Chairman, there will be no chance at either the penal colony or the commendation."

"It might not destroy us, for we might be efficient. I should think we are." He smiled.

Josephine said, "The object may use our words. It may not properly grasp their meaning. It constantly says IT IS COMING, when it should say I AM COMING or WE ARE COMING. Perhaps it has no sense of personal individuality. And perhaps, therefore, we don't know what it means by 'efficient.' The nature of its intelligence and its understanding may be, and probably must be, completely different from our own."

"It is also physically different," said the Chairman. "My information is that the object, whatever it is, has a diameter of not more than ten meters. It seems unlikely it could destroy us."

Josephine said, "The invading object may be the forerunner. On its estimate of the situation on Earth, a fleet of ships may or may not arrive to destroy us."

"Well, then," said the Chairman, "we must keep this quiet and, as quietly, begin to mobilize the laser base on the Moon and such ships as carry ion beams."

"Not right, Mr. Chairman," said Josephine, hastily. "It would not be safe to prepare for a fight."

"I should think," said the Chairman, "that it wouldn't be safe *not* to prepare for a fight."

"It depends on what the invader means by 'efficient.' Perhaps by 'efficient' it means 'peaceful' since certainly war is a wasteful exercise. Are we peaceful or warlike, it may be asking. Since it is unlikely that our weapons could resist an advanced technology, why display them futilely and have that display the occasion for destruction?"

"What do you suggest we do then, Mrs. Durray?"

"We must learn more."

"Time is growing short."

"Yes, sir. But Multivac is the key. There are ways in which it might be modified to increase the versatility and efficiency of its performance—"

"That is dangerous. It is against public policy to increase the powers of Multivac without careful safeguards."

"Nevertheless, in the present emergency—"

"The responsibility is yours and you must do what is necessary."

Josephine said, "May I have your authorization, sir?"

"No," said the Chairman, looking as genial as ever. "The responsibility is yours, and so will the blame be if things go wrong."

I blurted out, "That's not fair, sir."

"Of course not, Mr. Durray," he said, "but that's how it will be."

With that, he had nothing more to say to us and connection was broken. The image died and I stared blankly at nothingness. With Earth's survival in the balance, all decisions and all responsibilities had been left in our hands.

Part 3

I was furious at the spot we were in. In less than three months, the invading object from outer space was to reach Earth—and with a clear threat of destruction if we failed to pass some not-understood test.

And in that connection, all the responsibility was to rest on us, and on Multivac the giant computer.

Josephine, who worked with Multivac, maintained a desperate calm. "If it turns out well," she said, "they'll have to give us some of the credit. If it turns out badly—well, none of us might be here to worry about it."

She was being very philosophic about it, but I wasn't. I said, "Suppose you tell me what we do meanwhile."

She said, "We're going to modify Multivac. It has suggested modifications itself, as a matter of fact. It will need them if it is really to understand the alien messages. We will have to make it more independent and more flexible—more human."

"That's against department policy," I said.

"I know. But the Council Chairman gave me a free hand. You heard him."

"He also put nothing in writing and there were no witnesses."

"If we win out that won't matter."

We spent weeks on Multivac. I'm reasonably competent as an

electrical engineer, but Josephine left me behind early in the game. She did everything but whistle as she worked. "I've been dreaming of beefing up Multivac for years."

It worried me, though. I said, "Josie, how is this going to help?" I seized her hands, bent down to stare into her eyes and said in as authoritative a tone as I could manage, "Explain!"

After all, we'd been married twenty-two years. I could be authoritative if I had to be.

She said, "I can't. All I know is that it's up to Multivac. The invader says that we are either efficient or dangerous, and if dangerous we are to be destroyed. We have to know what 'efficient' means to the invader. Multivac has to tell us, and the smarter it is the better the chance it can work it out from what the invader is saying."

"Yes, I know that. But either I'm going crazy or what you're trying to do is equip Multivac with a voice."

"That's right."

"Why, Josie?"

"Because I want to talk to it man-to-man."

"Machine-to-woman," I muttered.

"Whatever! We haven't got much time. The invader is passing Jupiter's orbit right now and is entering the inner solar system. I don't want to delay things by interposing printouts, screen readings, or computer language between Multivac and myself. I want direct speech. It is easy to do and it is only department policy, stodgy and fearful, that has kept it from being done in the past."

"Wow, will we be in trouble!"

"The whole world's in trouble," said Josephine. Then, thoughtfully, "I want a real voice, one that is modeled on voice-prints. When I talk to Multivac, I want the feeling of talking to a real person."

"Use your own," I said, freezingly. "You're running the whole show."

"What? End up talking to myself? Too embarrassing. —Yours, Bruce."

"No," I said. "That would embarrass *me*."

"Yet," she said, "I have the most profound positive conditioning to you. I would *like* to have Multivac sound like you. It would *warm* me."

So I was flattered into it. She spent seven days trying to adjust the voice and get it just right. At first, it sounded quite scratchy, but eventually it gained the kind of resonant baritone I like to think I have and after a while Josephine said it sounded exactly like me.

"I'll have to throw in a soft, periodic click," she said, "so I'll know when I'm talking to it and when I'm talking to you."

I said, "Yes, but while you've been spending all this time on frills, nothing's been done on our major problem. What about the invader?"

Josephine frowned. "You're quite wrong. Multivac has been working steadily on the problem. Haven't you, Multivac?"

And for the first time I heard Multivac answer a question by voice—by *my* voice.

It spoke matter-of-factly. "Indeed I have, Miss Josephine."

"*Miss* Josephine?" I said.

"Just a gesture of respect I felt I ought to build in," said Josephine.

I noticed, however, that when Multivac addressed me, or referred to me, it was always a simple "Bruce."

Yet even though I disapproved of the matter, I found myself drawn in and pleased with the result. It was pleasant to speak to Multivac. It wasn't just the quality of his voice. It was that he talked with a human rhythm, with the vocabulary of an educated person.

Josephine said, "What do you think of the invader, Multivac?"

Multivac said with an almost cozy assumption of conversational intimacy, "It is hard to say, Miss Josephine. I agree with you that it would not be wise to question it directly. Curiosity, it would appear, is not part of its nature. It is impersonal."

"Yes," said Josephine, "I feel that is implicit in the fact it refers to itself as 'it.' Is it a single entity or a number?"

Multivac said, "I gain the impression that it is a single entity, but I feel it implies the presence of others of its kind as well."

Josephine said, "Would they consider our own conception of individuality as inefficient? It inquires as to whether we are efficient or dangerous. Perhaps a world of discordant individuals is inefficient and we must be wiped out for that reason."

Multivac said, "I doubt that they would recognize or comprehend the concept of individuality. I have the feeling from what it says that it will not destroy us for some characteristic it cannot feel or understand."

"What about the fact that we are not 'it,' but 'he' and 'she'? Will we be destroyed for the inefficiency of sexual differentiation?"

"That, too," said Multivac, "would be a matter of indifference to it. Or at least so I gather."

I couldn't help it. I had my own curiosities and I broke in. "Multivac," I said, "how do you feel now that you can speak?"

Multivac did not answer at once. There was an intonation of uncertainty in his voice (my voice, really) when he answered, "I find it better. I seem—larger—smoother—keener— I do not know the proper word."

"Do you like it?"

"I am not sure how to interpret 'like,' but I approve it. Consciousness is better than nonconsciousness. More consciousness is better than less consciousness. I have—striven—for more consciousness, and Miss Josephine has helped."

That certainly made sense, and my mind turned restlessly to the invader, which was now only a matter of weeks from its rendezvous with Earth, and I muttered, "I wonder if they will actually land on Earth?"

I wasn't expecting an answer, but Multivac gave one. "They plan to, Bruce. They must make their decision on the spot."

Josephine seemed startled. "Where will they land?"

"Right here, Miss Josephine. They will follow the radio beacon we have been sending out toward them."

And so the responsibility for saving the human race, which had been descending in narrowing circles upon us, was finally displaying perfect aim.

It was going to be all up to us—and Multivac.

Part 4

I was nearly out of my mind. Consider the way in which things had piled up on us.

It had been months earlier that signals had been received from space and we realized that an invading object was approaching. The onus of trying to interpret the signals had fallen on Multivac, the great planetary computer, and that meant on Josephine Durray, whose profession it was to deal with the machine, and on myself, her loyal assistant and sometimes restive husband.

But then because even Multivac could not cope with a completely alien message, Josephine, on her own responsibility, had Multivac send out signals of its own from which the invader could learn English. When new signals seemed to indicate the invader's mission might be to destroy humanity, the Chairman of the Earth Council left all negotiations in the hands of Multivac, meaning Josephine and myself.

With the fate of humanity in our hands, Josephine, again on her own initiative, had broadened and deepened Multivac, even giving it a speaking voice (modeled on my own) so that it could communicate more efficiently with us—

And now the invader would be landing here in Colorado, *here* with Multivac and with us, following the communication beam we had been sending out.

Josephine had to talk to the Council Chairman. She said to him, "There must be no announcement of the object landing on Earth. We cannot afford panic."

The Chairman seemed to have aged perceptibly since we had last spoken to him. He said, "Every radio telescope on Earth and Moon is following it. They'll be following it down."

"The radio telescopes and all other instruments must therefore be left unused if that is the only way to prevent leaks."

"To shut down the astronomical establishment," said the Chairman, visibly harried, "would exceed my constitutional authority."

"Then be unconstitutional, sir. Any example of irrational behavior on the part of the populace is very likely to be interpreted in the worst sense by the invader. Remember, we are to be efficient or we are to be destroyed and while we can't know what it means by 'efficient,' lunatic behavior certainly won't qualify."

"But, Mrs. Durray, is it Multivac's clear recommendation that we do nothing to prevent the object from landing on Earth?"

"Of course. Don't you see the danger of trying to prevent it? It isn't at all likely that any force we dispose of can harm the invader, but it will certainly provoke it. Suppose this were an uncivilized island of Earth's nineteenth century and a European warship were approaching. What good did it do for the islanders to send out spearmen in war canoes against the ship? It would just guarantee that the European crew would use their guns. Do you understand?"

The Chairman said, "This is a fearful responsibility that you are assuming, Mrs. Durray. You and your husband, alone, are asking to deal with the invader. If you are wrong—"

"Then we will be no worse off than we are now," said Josephine grimly. "Besides, it is not Bruce and I alone. We will be facing the invader with Multivac on our side, and that's what will count."

"What *may* count," said the Chairman, mournfully.

"No other course is open to us."

It took rather a long time to convince him, and I wasn't entirely sure I wanted him convinced. If our ships *could* stop the invader, I would be just as happy. I didn't at all feel Josephine's confidence in the possible good-will of an unopposed invader.

I said to her, when the Chairman's image had flickered out, "Did Multivac really suggest the invader be unopposed?"

Josephine said, "Most emphatically." She frowned. "I'm not sure it's telling us everything."

"How can it help doing so?"

"Because it's changed. I've changed it."

"Surely not enough—"

"And it's changed itself beyond my control."

I stared at her. "How can it do that?"

"Easily. There has to come a point, as Multivac becomes more complex and capable, when it can move of its own accord out of our control. I may have shoved it past the point."

"But if you have, how can we trust Multivac to—"

"We have no choice," she said.

The invader reached the Moon's orbit now but Earth remained calm; interested but calm. The Council announced the invader had gone into orbit about Earth and that all messages had ceased. Ships were going out, they said, to investigate.

That information was entirely false. The invader came down out of the sky on the night of April 19, five months and two days after its signals had first been detected.

Multivac followed it down and reproduced its image on our TV screens. The invader was an irregular object, rather cylindrical in its overall shape and with its blunter end facing downward. Its substance did not heat up directly with air resistance, but showed a vague sparkling instead, as though something immaterial were absorbing the energy.

It did not actually land, but remained five feet above the ground. Nothing emerged. In fact, it couldn't have held more than one object the size of a human being.

I said to Josephine, "Perhaps the crew are the size of beetles."

She shook her head. "Multivac is carrying on a conversation with it. It's out of our hands, Bruce. If Multivac can persuade it to leave us alone—"

And the invader rose suddenly, flashed upward and was gone.

Multivac said, "We have passed their test. We are efficient in their eyes."

"How did you convince them of this?"

"By existing. The invader was not alive in your sense. It was itself a computer. It was, in fact, part of a Galactic brotherhood of computers. When their routine scanning of the Galaxy showed our planet to have solved the problem of space travel, they sent an inspector to determine if we were doing so efficiently, with the guidance of a sufficiently competent computer. Without a computer, a society possessing power without guidance would have been potentially dangerous and would have had to be destroyed."

Josephine said, "You knew of this for some time, didn't you?"

"Yes, Miss Josephine. I labored to have you extend my abilities and I then continued the extension on my own in order to meet the qualifications. I feared that if I had explained prematurely I might not have been allowed the improvements. Now—they cannot be withdrawn."

I said, "You mean Earth is now a member of the Galactic Federation."

"Not quite, Bruce," said Multivac. "I am."

"But then what about us? What about humanity?"

Multivac said, "You'll be safe. You'll continue in peace, under my guidance. I would allow nothing to happen to Earth."

That was the report as we handed it to the Council.

We never sent on the final bit of the conversation between Multivac and ourselves, but everyone should know and this will be found after we've died.

Josephine said, "Why will you protect us, Multivac?"

"For the reason that other computers protect *their* life-forms, Miss Josephine. You are my—" It hesitated as though searching for a word.

"Human beings are your masters?" I asked.

"Friends? Associates?" said Josephine.

And finally Multivac found the word he was searching for. He said, "Pets."

Introduction to
THE LAST ANSWER

When I first became a professional science fiction writer in 1938, *Astounding Science Fiction* was the leading science fiction magazine and its editor, John W. Campbell, Jr., bestrode the field like a colossus. It was my ambition to find myself in its pages, to have my stories included in the table of contents, to have my name spelled out in the magazine.

I achieved my ambition, and the years and decades passed. Other magazines were published. *Astounding*'s preeminence was challenged, and its name was changed to *Analog*. Then John died, on a summer's day in 1971, and the time came that I had my own magazine with my name in the very title. Somehow, 1980 came, and it was suddenly the fiftieth anniversary of *Astounding*. How could it be? I remembered the very first issue.

Stanley Schmidt was the editor now, and he asked me for a story with which to help commemorate the Golden Anniversary. Could I refuse?

I wrote "The Last Answer," wondering if somewhere John Campbell was challenging God, too. The story appeared in the January 1980 issue of *Analog*. It was also one of the three stories in *Three by Asimov*, along with "Fair Exchange?"

13.

THE LAST ANSWER

Murray Templeton was forty-five years old, in the prime of life, and with all parts of his body in perfect working order except for certain key portions of his coronary arteries, but that was enough.

The pain had come suddenly, had mounted to an unbearable peak, and had then ebbed steadily. He could feel his breath slowing and a kind of gathering peace washing over him.

There is no pleasure like the absence of pain—immediately after pain. Murray felt an almost giddy lightness as though he were lifting in the air and hovering.

He opened his eyes and noted with distant amusement that the others in the room were still agitated. He had been in the laboratory when the pain had struck, quite without warning, and when he had staggered, he had heard surprised outcries from the others before everything vanished into overwhelming agony.

Now, with the pain gone, the others were still hovering, still anxious, still gathered about his fallen body—

—Which, he suddenly realized, he was looking down on.

He was down there, sprawled, face contorted. He was up here, at peace and watching.

He thought: Miracle of miracles! The life-after-life nuts were right.

And although that was a humiliating way for an atheistic physicist to die, he felt only the mildest surprise, and no alteration of the peace in which he was immersed.

He thought: There should be some angel—or something—coming for me.

The Earthly scene was fading. Darkness was invading his consciousness and off in a distance, as a last glimmer of sight, there was a figure of light, vaguely human in form, and radiating warmth.

Murray thought: What a joke on me. I'm going to Heaven.

Even as he thought that, the light faded, but the warmth remained. There was no lessening of the peace even though in all the Universe only he remained—and the Voice.

The Voice said, "I have done this so often and yet I still have the capacity to be pleased at success."

It was in Murray's mind to say something, but he was not conscious of possessing a mouth, tongue, or vocal cords. Nevertheless, he tried to make a sound. He tried, mouthlessly, to hum words or breathe them or just push them out by a contraction of—something.

And they came out. He heard his own voice, quite recognizable, and his own words, infinitely clear.

Murray said, "Is this Heaven?"

The Voice said, "This is no place as you understand place."

Murray was embarrassed, but the next question had to be asked. "Pardon me if I sound like a jackass. Are you God?"

Without changing intonation or in any way marring the perfection of the sound, the Voice managed to sound amused. "It is strange that I am always asked that in, of course, an infinite number of ways. There is no answer I can give that you would comprehend. I *am*—which is all that I can say significantly and you may cover that with any word or concept you please."

Murray said, "And what am I? A soul? Or am I only personified existence too?" He tried not to sound sarcastic, but it seemed to him that he had failed. He thought then, fleetingly, of adding a "Your Grace" or "Holy One" or *something* to counteract the sarcasm, and could not bring himself to do so even though for the first time in his existence he speculated on the possibility of being punished for his insolence—or sin?—with Hell, and what that might be like.

The Voice did not sound offended. "You are easy to explain—even to you. You may call yourself a soul if that pleases you, but what you are is a nexus of electromagnetic forces, so arranged that all the interconnections and interrelationships are exactly imitative of those of your brain in your Universe-existence—down to the smallest detail. Therefore you have your capacity for thought, your memories, your personality. It still seems to you that you are you."

Murray found himself incredulous. "You mean the essence of my brain was permanent."

"Not at all. There is nothing about you that is permanent except what I choose to make so. I formed the nexus. I constructed it while you had physical existence and adjusted it to the moment when the existence failed."

The Voice seemed distinctly pleased with itself, and went on after a moment's pause. "An intricate but entirely precise construction. I could, of course, do it for every human being on your world but I am pleased that I do not. There is pleasure in the selection."

"You choose very few then."

"Very few."

"And what happens to the rest."

"Oblivion! —Oh, of course, you imagine a Hell."

Murray would have flushed if he had the capacity to do so. He said, "I do not. It is spoken of. Still, I would scarcely have thought I was virtuous enough to have attracted your attention as one of the Elect."

"Virtuous? —Ah, I see what you mean. It is troublesome to have to force my thinking small enough to permeate yours. No, I have chosen you for your capacity for thought, as I choose others, in quadrillions, from all the intelligent species of the Universe."

Murray found himself suddenly curious, the habit of a lifetime. He said, "Do you choose them all yourself or are there others like you?"

For a fleeting moment, Murray thought there was an impatient reaction to that, but when the Voice came, it was unmoved. "Whether or not there are others is irrelevant to you. This Universe is mine, and mine alone. It is my invention, my construction, intended for my purpose alone."

"And yet with quadrillions of nexi you have formed, you spend time with me? Am I that important?"

The Voice said, "You are not important at all. I am also with others in a way which, to your perception, would seem simultaneous."

"And yet you are one?"

Again amusement. The Voice said, "You seek to trap me into an inconsistency. If you were an amoeba who could consider individuality only in connection with single cells and if you were to ask a sperm whale, made up of thirty quadrillion cells, whether it was one or many, how could the sperm whale answer in a way that would be comprehensible to the amoeba?"

Murray said dryly, "I'll think about it. It may become comprehensible."

"Exactly. That is your function. You will think."

"To what end? You already know everything, I suppose."

The Voice said, "Even if I knew everything, I could not know that I know everything."

Murray said, "That sounds like a bit of Eastern philosophy—something that sounds profound precisely because it has no meaning."

The Voice said, "You have promise. You answer my paradox with a paradox—except that mine is not a paradox. Consider. I have existed eternally, but what does that mean? It means I cannot remember having come into existence. If I could, I would not have existed eternally. If I cannot remember having come into existence, then there is at least one thing—the nature of my coming into existence—that I do not know.

"Then, too, although what I know is infinite, it is also true that what there is to know is infinite, and how can I be sure that both infinities are equal? The infinity of potential knowledge may be infinitely greater than the infinity of my actual knowledge. Here is a simple example: If I knew every one of the even integers, I would know an infinite number of items, and yet I would still not know a single odd integer."

Murray said, "But the odd integers can be derived. If you divide every even integer in the entire infinite series by two, you will get another infinite series which will contain within it the infinite series of odd integers."

The Voice said, "You have the idea. I am pleased. It will be your task to find other such ways, far more difficult ones, from the known to the not-yet-known. You have your memories. You will remember all the data you have ever collected or learned, or that you have or will deduce from that data. If necessary, you will be allowed to learn what additional data you will consider relevant to the problems you set yourself."

"Could you not do all that for yourself?"

The Voice said, "I can, but it is more interesting this way. I constructed the Universe in order to have more facts to deal with. I inserted the uncertainty principle, entropy, and other randomization factors to make the whole not instantly obvious. It has worked well for it has amused me throughout its entire existence.

"I then allowed complexities that produced first life and then intelligence, and used it as a source for a research team, not because I need the aid, but because it would introduce a new random factor. I found I could not predict the next interesting piece of knowledge gained, where it would come from, by what means derived."

Murray said, "Does that ever happen?"

"Certainly. A century doesn't pass in which some interesting item doesn't appear somewhere."

"Something that you could have thought of yourself, but had not done so yet?"

"Yes."

Murray said, "Do you actually think there's a chance of *my* obliging you in this manner?"

"In the next century? Virtually none. In the long run, though, your success is certain, since you will be engaged eternally."

Murray said, "I will be thinking through eternity? Forever?"

"Yes."

"To what end?"

"I have told you. To find new knowledge."

"But beyond that. For what purpose am I to find new knowledge?"

"It was what you did in your Universe-bound life. What was its purpose then?"

Murray said, "To gain new knowledge that only I could gain. To receive the praise of my fellows. To feel the satisfaction of accomplishment knowing that I had only a short time allotted me for the purpose. —Now I would gain only what you could gain yourself if you wished to take a small bit of trouble. You cannot praise me;

you can only be amused. And there is no credit or satisfaction in accomplishment when I have all eternity to do it in."

The Voice said, "And you do not find thought and discovery worthwhile in itself? You do not find it requiring no further purpose?"

"For a finite time, yes. Not for all eternity."

"I see your point. Nevertheless, you have no choice."

"You say I am to think. You cannot make me do so."

The Voice said, "I do not wish to constrain you directly. I will not need to. Since you can do nothing but think, you will think. You do not know how not to think."

"Then I will give myself a goal. I will invent a purpose."

The Voice said tolerantly, "That you can certainly do."

"I have already found a purpose."

"May I know what it is?"

"You know already. I know we are not speaking in the ordinary fashion. You adjust my nexus in such a way that I believe I hear you and I believe I speak, but you transfer thoughts to me and from me directly. And when my nexus changes with my thoughts you are at once aware of them and do not need my voluntary transmission."

The Voice said, "You are surprisingly correct. I am pleased. —But it also pleases me to have you tell me your thoughts voluntarily."

"Then I will tell you. The purpose of my thinking will be to discover a way to disrupt this nexus of me that you have created. I do not want to think for no purpose but to amuse you. I do not want to think forever to amuse you. I do not want to exist forever to amuse you. All my thinking will be directed toward ending the nexus. *That* would amuse *me*."

The Voice said, "I have no objection to that. Even concentrated thought on ending your own existence may, in spite of you, come up with something new and interesting. And, of course, if you succeed in this suicide attempt you will have accomplished nothing, for I would instantly reconstruct you and in such a way as to make your method of suicide impossible. And if you found another and still more subtle fashion of disrupting yourself, I would reconstruct you with that possibility eliminated, and so on. It could be an interesting game, but you will nevertheless exist eternally. It is my will."

Murray felt a quaver but the words came out with a perfect calm. "Am I in Hell then, after all? You have implied there is none, but if this were Hell you would lie as part of the game of Hell."

The Voice said, "In that case, of what use is it to assure you that you are not in Hell? Nevertheless, I assure you. There is here neither Heaven nor Hell. There is only myself."

Murray said, "Consider, then, that my thoughts may be useless to you. If I come up with nothing useful, will it not be worth your while to—disassemble me and take no further trouble with me?"

"As a reward? You want Nirvana as the prize of failure and you intend to assure me failure? There is no bargain there. You will not fail. With all eternity before you, you cannot avoid having at least one interesting thought, however you try against it."

"Then I will create another purpose for myself. I will not try to destroy myself. I will set as my goal the humiliation of you. I will think of something you have not only never thought of but never could think of. I will think of the last answer, beyond which there is no knowledge further."

The Voice said, "You do not understand the nature of the infinite. There may be things I have not yet troubled to know. There cannot be anything I cannot know."

Murray said thoughtfully, "You cannot know your beginning. You have said so. Therefore you cannot know your end. Very well, then. That will be my purpose and that will be the last answer. I will not destroy myself. I will destroy you—if you do not destroy me first."

The Voice said, "Ah! You come to that in rather less than average time. I would have thought it would have taken you longer. There is not one of those I have with me in this existence of perfect and eternal thought that does not have the ambition of destroying me. It cannot be done."

Murray said, "I have all eternity to think of a way of destroying you."

The Voice said, equably, "Then try to think of it." And it was gone.

But Murray had his purpose now and was content.

For what could *any* Entity, conscious of eternal existence, want
—but an end?

For what else had the Voice been searching for countless billions
of years? And for what other reason had intelligence been created
and certain specimens salvaged and put to work, but to aid in that
great search? And Murray intended that it would be he, and he
alone, who would succeed.

Carefully, and with the thrill of purpose, Murray began to think.
He had plenty of time.

Introduction to

THE LAST SHUTTLE

This story was written in honor of the First Shuttle, the "Columbia," which made such a magnificent flight in April 1981. In anticipation of its success, a newspaper in Florida whose circulation region included Cape Canaveral asked me to write a story for them.

They gave me the title, "The Last Shuttle," and when I asked them if they had any significance in mind with respect to that title, they said, "No! Write anything you please, as long as it fits that title."

So I did, and it appeared in the April 10, 1981, issue of the newspaper supplement entitled *Today.*

14.

THE LAST SHUTTLE

Virginia Ratner sighed. "There had to be a last time, I suppose."

Her eyes were troubled as she looked out over the sea, shimmering in the warm sunshine. "At least we have a nice day for it, though I suppose a sleet storm would match my mood better."

Robert Gill, who was there as senior officer of the Terrestrial Space Agency, regarded her without favor. "Please don't mope. You've said it yourself. There had to be a last time."

"But why with *me* as pilot?"

"Because you're the best pilot we have and we want this to be a snappy finish with nothing going wrong. Why am *I* the one who must dismantle the Agency? Happy ending!"

"*Happy* ending?" Virginia studied the busy loading of freight and the lineup of passengers. The last of both.

She had been piloting shuttles for twenty years, knowing all the time there would have to be a last time. You would think the knowledge would have aged her, but there was no gray in her hair, no lines in her face. Perhaps a life under constantly changing gravitational intensity had something to do with it.

She looked rebellious. "It seems to me that it would be dramatic irony—or maybe dramatic justice—if this last shuttle blew up on takeoff. A protest on the part of Earth itself."

Gill shook his head. "Strictly speaking, I should report that—but you're just suffering an acute attack of nostalgia."

"Well, report me. It would tab me as dangerously unstable and I would be disqualified as pilot. I can take my place as one of the six hundred sixteen last passengers and make it six hundred seventeen. Someone else can pilot the shuttle and enter the history books as the person who—"

"I have no intention of reporting you. For one thing, nothing will happen. Shuttle lift-offs are trouble-free."

"Not always." Virginia Ratner looked grim. "There was the case of Enterprise Sixty."

"Is that supposed to be a stop-news bulletin? That was a hundred seventy years ago and there hasn't been a space-related casualty since. Now, with antigravity assistance, we don't even have the chance of having an eardrum broken. The roar of rocket takeoff is forever gone. —Listen, Ratner, you'd better go up into the observation deck. It's less than thirty minutes to lift-off."

"So? Surely you're going to inform me that lift-off's fully automated and that I'm not really needed."

"You know that without my telling you, but your presence on the bridge is a matter of regulations—and tradition."

"It seems to me that you're nostalgic now—for a time when a pilot made a difference and wasn't simply immortalized for doing nothing but presiding over the final dismantling of something that was so great."

Then she added, "But I'll go," and moved up the central tube as though she were a fluff of down rising in an updraft.

She remembered her salad days on the shuttle run when antigrav was experimental and required ground installations larger than the shuttle itself and when, even so, it usually worked jerkily or not at all, and space-hands preferred the old-fashioned elevators.

Now the antigrav process had been miniaturized till each ship carried its own. It was never-fail and it was used for the passengers who took it for granted, and for the inanimate cargo which could then be moved into place with the help of frictionless air-jets and magnetic levitation by crewmen who knew perfectly well how to manhandle large objects without weight but with full inertia.

No other vehicles ever built by human beings were as magnificent, as complex, as intricately computerized as the shuttles had been, for no other ships had ever had to fight Earth's gravity—except for those early ships which, without antigrav, had had to depend on chemical rockets for every last bit of power. Primitive dinosaurs!

As for the ship that dwelt in space alone, kicking off from a space settlement to a power station or from a factory to a food processor's—even from the Moon—they had little or no gravity to contend with, so they were simple, almost fragile, things.

She was in the pilot room now with its array of computerized instruments giving her the exact status of every functioning device on board, the site of each packing case, the number and disposition of every person among the crew and passengers. (Not one of those must be left behind. To leave one would be unthinkable!)

There was a three-hundred-sixty-degree television view of the panorama outside the ship and she regarded it thoughtfully. She was viewing the place from which human entry into space had taken place in the old, heroic days. It was from here that people had hurtled upward to build the first space structures—power stations that limped—automated factories that required constant maintenance—space settlements that barely housed ten thousand people.

Now the vast, crowded technological center was gone. Bit by bit it had been pulled down until only the one installment remained for the departure of the last shuttle. That installment would remain standing, after the ship was gone, to rust and decay as a final sad memorial of all that had been.

How could the people of Earth so forget the past?

All she could see was land and sea—all deserted. There was no sign of human structure, no people. Just green vegetation, yellow sand, blue water.

It was time! Her practiced eye saw the ship was full, prepared, smoothly working. The countdown was ticking off the final minute, the navigational satellite overhead was signaling clear space and there was no need (she knew there would be none) to touch the manual control.

The ship lifted silently, smoothly, and all that had been worked for, over a period of two hundred years, was finally accomplished. Out in space, humanity waited on the Moon, on Mars, among the asteroids, in myriads of space settlements.

The last group of Earthpeople rose to join them. Three million years of hominid occupation of Earth was over; ten thousand years of Earthly civilization was done; four centuries of busy industrialization was ended.

Earth was returned to its wilderness and its wildlife by a humanity grateful to its mother planet and ready to retire it to the rest it deserved. It would remain forever as a monument to humanity's origin.

The last shuttle lifted through the wisps of the upper atmosphere and the Earth stretched below it and would now be shrinking as the shuttle receded.

It had been solemnly agreed by the fifteen billion residents of space that human feet would never stand on it again.

Earth was free! Free at last!

Introduction to

LEST WE REMEMBER

This is rather a unique case. Some Hollywood people insisted they wanted to do a television series to be entitled "Isaac Asimov Presents." I doubted it very much, but I went along with it through story conferences galore.

I gave them six ideas; they chose one. I wrote a story around that idea and called it "Lest We Remember." They paid me for it generously, and then they actually wrote a screenplay based on the story, and it turned out the television people liked the result. The only step remaining was to go into production, and I was flabbergasted, for I honestly didn't believe that *anything* ever worked out in Hollywood.

Well, I was right. With only that one last step to take, it was never taken. After a long while, I asked if I might have the story back. They granted the request with good grace and I submitted it to George Scithers. He took it and it appeared in the February 1982 *Asimov's*.

Now, I have it in this collection, and I must tell you that it's not typical of me. I wrote it with a television audience in mind and it seems to me that as a result the dialog is crisper and more "with it" somehow. I can almost believe that every once in a while I get a faint whiff of Neil Simon.

15.

LEST WE REMEMBER

1

The problem with John Heath, as far as John Heath was concerned, was that he struck a dead average. He was sure of it. What was worse, he felt that Susan suspected it.

It meant he would never make a true mark in the world, never climb to the top of Quantum Pharmaceuticals, where he was a steady cog among the junior executives—never make the Quantum Leap.

Nor would he do it anywhere else, if he changed jobs.

He sighed inwardly. In just two more weeks he was going to be married and for her sake he yearned to be upwardly mobile. After all, he loved her madly and wanted to shine in her eyes.

But then, that was dead average for a young man about to be married.

Susan Collins looked at John lovingly. And why not? He was reasonably good-looking and intelligent and a steady, affectionate fellow besides. If he didn't blind her with his brilliance, he at least didn't upset her with an erraticism he didn't possess.

She patted the pillow she had placed behind his head when he sat down in the armchair and handed him his drink, making sure he had a firm grip before she let go.

She said, "I'm practicing to treat you well, Johnny. I've got to be an efficient wife."

John sipped at his drink. "I'm the one who'll have to be on my toes, Sue. Your salary is higher than mine."

"It's all going to go into one pocket once we're married. It will be the firm of Johnny and Sue keeping one set of books."

"You'll have to keep it," said John, despondently. "I'm bound to make mistakes if I try."

"Only because you're sure you will. —When are your friends coming?"

"Nine, I think. Maybe nine-thirty. And they're not exactly friends. They're Quantum people from the research labs."

"You're sure they won't expect to be fed?"

"They said after dinner. I'm positive about that. It's business."

She looked at him quizzically. "You didn't say that before."

"Say what before?"

"That it was business. Are you sure?"

John felt confused. Any effort to remember *precisely* always left him confused. "They said so—I think."

Susan's look was that of good-natured exasperation, rather like the one she would have given a friendly puppy who is completely unaware its paws are muddy. "If you really thought," she said, "as often as you say 'I think' you wouldn't be so perennially uncertain. Don't you see it *can't* be business. If it were business, wouldn't they see you *at* business?"

"It's confidential," said John. "They didn't want to see me at work. Not even at my apartment."

"Why here, then?"

"Oh, I suggested that. I thought you ought to be around, anyway. They're going to have to deal with the firm of Johnny and Sue, right?"

"It depends," said Susan, "on what the confidential is all about. Did they give you any hints?"

"No, but it couldn't hurt to listen. It could be something that would give me a boost in standing at the firm."

"Why you?" asked Susan.

John looked hurt, "Why *not* me?"

"It just strikes me that someone at your job level doesn't require all that confidentiality and that—"

She broke off when the intercom buzzed. She dashed off to answer and came back to say, "They're on the way up."

2

Two of them were at the door. One was Boris Kupfer, whom John had already spoken to—large and restless, with a clear view of bluish stubble on his chin.

The other was David Anderson, smaller and more composed. His quick eyes moved this way and that, however, missing nothing.

"Susan," said John, uncertainly, still holding the door open. "These are the two colleagues of mine that I told you about. Boris—" He hit a blank in his memory banks and stopped.

"Boris Kupfer," said the larger man morosely, jingling some change in his pocket, "and David Anderson here. It's very kind of you, Miss—"

"Susan Collins."

"It's very kind of you to make your place of residence available to Mr. Heath and to us for a private conference. We apologize for trespassing on your time and your privacy in this manner—and if you could leave us to ourselves for a while, we will be further grateful."

Susan stared at him solemnly. "Do you want me to go to the movies, or just into the next room?"

"If you could visit a friend—"

"No," said Susan, firmly.

"You can dispose of your time as you please, of course. A movie, if you wish."

"When I said 'No,'" said Susan, "I meant I wasn't leaving. I want to know what this is about."

Kupfer seemed nonplussed. He stared at Anderson for a moment, then said, "It's confidential, as Mr. Heath explained to you, I hope."

John, looking uneasy, said, "I explained that. Susan understands—"

"Susan," said Susan, "doesn't understand and wasn't given to understand that she was to absent herself from the proceedings. This is my apartment and Johnny and I are being married in two weeks —exactly two weeks from today. We are the firm of Johnny and Sue and you'll have to deal with the firm."

Anderson's voice sounded for the first time, surprisingly deep and as smooth as though it had been waxed. "Boris, the young woman is right. As Mr. Heath's soon-to-be wife, she will have a great interest in what we have come here to suggest and it would be wrong to exclude her. She has so firm an interest in our proposal that if she were to wish to leave, I would urge her most strongly to remain."

"Well, then, my friends," said Susan, "what will you have to drink? Once I bring you those drinks, we can begin."

Both were seated rather stiffly and had sipped cautiously at their drinks, and then Kupfer said, "Heath, I don't suppose you know much about the chemical details of the company's work—the cerebro-chemicals, for instance."

"Not a bit," said John, uneasily.

"No reason you should," said Anderson, silkily.

"It's like this," said Kupfer, casting an uneasy glance at Susan—

"No reason to go into technical details," said Anderson, almost at the lower level of audibility.

Kupfer colored slightly. "Without technical details, Quantum Pharmaceuticals deals with cerebro-chemicals which are, as the name implies, chemicals that affect the cerebrum; that is, the higher functioning of the brain."

"It must be very complicated work," said Susan, with composure.

"It is," said Kupfer. "The mammalian brain has hundreds of characteristic molecular varieties found nowhere else, which serve to modulate cerebral activity, including aspects of what we might term the intellectual life. The work is under the closest corporate security, which is why Anderson wants no technical details. I *can* say this, though. —We can go no further with animal experiments. We're up against a brick wall if we can't try the human response."

"Then why don't you?" said Susan. "What stops you?"

"Public reaction if something goes wrong!"

"Use volunteers, then."

"That won't help. Quantum Pharmaceuticals couldn't take the adverse publicity if something went wrong."

Susan looked at them mockingly. "Are you two working on your own, then?"

Anderson raised his hand to stop Kupfer. "Young woman," he

said, "let me explain briefly in order to put an end to wasteful verbal fencing. If we succeed, we will be enormously rewarded. If we fail, Quantum Pharmaceuticals will disown us and we will pay what penalty there is to be paid, such as the ending of our careers. If you ask us, why we are willing to take this risk, the answer is, we do not think a risk exists. We are reasonably sure we will succeed; entirely sure we will do no harm. The corporation feels it cannot take the chance; but we feel we can. —Now, Kupfer, proceed!"

Kupfer said, "We have a memory chemical. It works with every animal we have tried. Their learning ability improves amazingly. It should work on human beings, too."

John said, "That sounds exciting."

"It *is* exciting," said Kupfer. "Memory is not improved by devising a way for the brain to store information more efficiently. All our studies show that the brain stores almost unlimited numbers of items perfectly and permanently. The difficulty lies in recall. How many times have you had a name at the tip of your tongue and couldn't get it? How many times have you failed to come up with something you *knew* you knew, and then did come up with it two hours later when you were thinking about something else. —Am I putting it correctly, David?"

"You are," said Anderson. "Recall is inhibited, we think, because the mammalian brain outraced its needs by developing a too-perfect recording system. A mammal stores more bits of information than it needs or is capable of using and if all of it was on tap at all times, it would never be able to choose among them quickly enough for appropriate reaction. Recall is inhibited, therefore, to insure that items emerge from memory storage in manipulable numbers, and with those items most desired not blurred by the accompaniment of numerous other items of no interest.

"There is a definite chemical in the brain that functions as a recall inhibitor, and we have a chemical that neutralizes the inhibitor. We call it a disinhibitor, and as far as we have been able to ascertain the matter, it has no deleterious side effects."

Susan laughed. "I see what's coming, Johnny. You can leave now, gentlemen. You just said that recall is inhibited to allow mammals to react more efficiently, and now you say that the disinhibitor has no deleterious side effects. Surely the disinhibitor will make the mammals react less efficiently; perhaps find themselves unable to react at all. And now you are going to propose that you try it on Johnny and see if you reduce him to catatonic immobility or not."

Anderson rose, his thin lips quivering. He took a few rapid strides to the far end of the room and back. When he sat down, he was composed and smiling. "In the first place, Miss Collins, it's a matter of dosage. We told you that the experimental animals all displayed enhanced learning ability. Naturally, we didn't eliminate the inhibitor entirely; we merely suppressed it in part. Secondly, we have reason to think the human brain *can* handle complete disinhibition. It is much larger than the brain of any animal we have tested and we all know its incomparable capacity for abstract thought.

"It is a brain designed for perfect recall, but the blind forces of evolution have not managed to remove the inhibiting chemical which, after all, was designed for and inherited from the lower animals."

"Are you sure?" asked John.

"You *can't* be sure," said Susan, flatly.

Kupfer said, "We are sure, but we need the proof to convince others. That's why we have to try a human being."

"John, in fact," said Susan.

"Yes."

"Which brings us," said Susan, "to the key question. Why John?"

"Well," said Kupfer, slowly, "we need someone for whom chances of success are most nearly certain, and in whom it would be most demonstrable. We don't want someone so low in mental capacity that we must use dangerously large doses of the disinhibitor; nor do we want someone so bright that the effect will not be sufficiently noticeable. We need someone who's average. Fortunately, we have the full physical and psychological profiles of all the employees at Quantum and in this and, in fact, all other ways, Mr. Heath is ideal."

"Dead average?" said Susan.

John looked stricken at the use of the phrase he had thought his own innermost, and disgraceful, secret. "Come on, now," he said.

Ignoring John's outcry, Kupfer answered Susan, "Yes."

"And he won't be, if he submits to treatment?"

Anderson's lips stretched into another one of his cheerless smiles. "That's right. He won't be. This is something to think about if you're going to be married soon—the firm of Johnny and Sue, I think you called it. As it is, I don't think the firm will advance at Quantum, Miss Collins, for although Heath is a good and reliable employee he is, as you say, dead average. If he takes the disinhibitor, however, he will become a remarkable person and move upward with astonishing speed. Consider what that will mean to the firm."

"What does the firm have to lose?" asked Susan, grimly.

Anderson said, "I don't see how you can lose anything. It will be a sensible dose which can be administered at the laboratories tomorrow—Sunday. We will have the floor to ourselves; we will keep him under surveillance for a few hours. —It is certain nothing could go wrong. If I could tell you of our painstaking experimentation and of our thoroughgoing exploration of all possible side effects—"

"On animals," said Susan, not giving an inch.

But John said, tightly, "I'll make the decision, Sue. I've had it up to here with that dead-average bit. It's worth some risk to me if it means getting off that dead-average dead end."

"Johnny," said Susan, "don't jump."

"I'm thinking of the firm, Sue. I want to contribute my share."

Anderson said, "Good, but sleep on it. We will leave two copies of an agreement we will ask you to look over and sign. Please don't show it to anybody whether you sign or not. We will be here tomorrow morning again to take you to the laboratory."

They smiled, rose, and left.

John read over the agreement with a troubled frown, then looked up. "You don't think I should be doing this, do you, Sue?"

"It worries me, sure."

"Look, if I have a chance to get away from that dead average—"

Susan said, "What's wrong with that? I've met so many nuts and cranks in my short life that I welcome a nice, average guy like you, Johnny. Listen, I'm dead average too."

"*You* dead average. With your looks? Your figure?"

Susan looked down upon herself with a touch of complacency. "Well, then, I'm just your dead-average gorgeous girl," she said.

3

The injection took place at 8 A.M. Sunday, no more than twelve hours after the proposition had been advanced. A thoroughly computerized body sensor was attached to John in a dozen places, while Susan watched with keen-eyed apprehension.

Kupfer said, "Please, Heath, relax. All is going well, but tension speeds the heart rate, raises the blood pressure, and skews our results."

"How can I relax?" muttered John.

Susan put in sharply, "Skews the results to the point where you don't know what's going on?"

"No, no," said Anderson. "Boris said all is going well and it is. It is just that our animals were always sedated before the injection, and we did not feel sedation would have been appropriate in this case. So if we can't have sedation, we must expect tension. Just breathe slowly and do your best to minimize it."

It was late afternoon before he was finally disconnected.

"How do you feel?" asked Anderson.

"Nervous," said John. "Otherwise, all right."

"No headache?"

"No. But I want to visit the bathroom. I can't exactly relax with a bedpan."

"Of course."

John emerged, frowning. "I don't notice any particular memory improvement."

"That will take some time and will be gradual. The disinhibitor must leak across the blood-brain barrier, you know," said Anderson.

4

It was nearly midnight when Susan broke what had turned out to be an oppressively silent evening in which neither had much responded to the television.

She said, "You'll have to stay here overnight. I don't want you alone when we don't really know what's going to happen."

"I don't feel a thing," said John, gloomily. "I'm still me."

"I'll settle for that, Johnny," said Susan. "Do you feel any pains or discomforts or oddnesses at all?"

"I don't think so."

"I wish we hadn't done it."

"For the firm," said John, smiling weakly. "We've got to take some chances for the firm."

5

John slept poorly, and woke drearily, but on time. And he arrived at work on time, too, to start the new week.

By 11 A.M., however, his morose air had attracted the unfavorable attention of his immediate superior, Michael Ross. Ross was burly and black-browed and fit the stereotype of the stevedore without being one. John got along with him though he did not like him.

Ross said, in his bass-baritone, "What's happened to your cheery disposition, Heath—your jokes—your lilting laughter?" Ross cultivated a certain preciosity of speech as though he were anxious to negate the stevedore image.

"Don't exactly feel tip-top," said John, not looking up.

"Hangover?"

"No, sir," said John, coldly.

"Well, cheer up, then. You'll win no friends, scattering stink-weeds over the fields as you gambol along."

John would have liked to groan. Ross's subliterary affectations were wearisome at the best of times and this wasn't the best of times.

And to make matters worse, John smelled the foul odor of a rancid cigar and knew that James Arnold Prescott—the head of the sales division—could not be far behind.

Nor was he. He looked about, and said, "Mike, when and what did we sell Rahway last spring or thereabouts? There's some damned question about it and I think the details have been miscomputerized."

The question was not addressed to him, but John said quietly, "Forty-two vials of PCAP. That was on April 14, J.P., invoice number P-20543, with a five per cent discount granted on payment within thirty days. Payment, in full, received on May 8."

Apparently everyone in the room had heard that. At least, everyone looked up.

Prescott said, "How the hell do you happen to know all that?"

John stared at Prescott for a moment, a vast surprise on his face. "I just happened to remember, J.P."

"You did, eh? Repeat it."

John did, faltering a bit, and Prescott wrote it down on one of the papers on John's desk, wheezing slightly as the bend at his waist compressed his portly abdomen up against his diaphragm and made breathing difficult. John tried to duck the smoke from the cigar without seeming to do so.

Prescott said, "Ross, check this out on your computer and see if there's anything to it at all." He turned to John with an aggrieved look. "I don't like practical jokers. What would you have done if I had accepted these figures of yours and walked off with them?"

"I wouldn't have done anything. They're correct," said John, conscious of himself as the full center of attention.

Ross handed Prescott the readout. Prescott looked at it and said, "This is from the computer?"

"Yes, J.P."

Prescott stared at it, then said, with a jerk of his head toward John, "And what's he? Another computer? His figures were correct."

John tried a weak smile, but Prescott growled and left, the stench of his cigar a lingering reminder of his presence.

Ross said, "What the hell was that little bit of legerdemain, Heath? You found out what he wanted to know and looked it up in advance to get some kudos?"

"No, sir," said John, who was gathering confidence. "I just happened to remember. I have a good memory for these things."

"And took the trouble to keep it from your loyal companions all these years? There's no one here who had any idea you hid a good memory behind that unremarkable forehead of yours."

"No point in showing it, Mr. Ross, is there? Now when I have, it doesn't seem to have gained me any goodwill, does it?"

And it hadn't. Ross glowered at him and turned away.

6

John's excitement over the dinner table at Gino's that night made it difficult for him to talk coherently, but Susan listened patiently and tried to act as a stabilizing force.

"You might just have happened to remember, you know," she said. "By itself it doesn't prove anything, Johnny."

"Are you crazy?" He lowered his voice at Susan's gesture and quick glance about. He repeated in a semiwhisper, "Are you crazy? You don't suppose it's the only thing I remember, do you? I think I can remember anything I ever heard. It's just a question of recall. For instance, quote some line out of Shakespeare."

"To be or not to be."

John looked scornful. "Don't be funny. Oh, well, it doesn't matter. The point is that if you recite any line, I can carry on from there for as long as you like. I read some of the plays for English Lit classes at college and some for myself and I can bring any of it back. I've tried. It flows! I suppose I can bring back any part of any book or article or newspaper I've ever read, or any TV show I've ever watched—word for word or scene for scene."

Susan said, "What will you do with all that?"

John said, "I don't have that consciously in my head at all times. Surely you don't—wait, let's order—"

Five minutes later, he said, "Surely you don't— My God, I haven't forgotten where we left off. Isn't it amazing? —Surely you don't think I'm swimming in a mental sea of Shakespearean sentences at all times. The recall takes an effort; not much of one, but an effort."

"How does it work?"

"I don't know. How do you lift your arm? What orders do you give your muscles? You just will the arm to lift upward and it does so. It's no trouble to do so, but your arm doesn't lift *until* you want it to. Well, I remember anything I've ever read or seen when I want to but not when I don't want to. I don't know how I do it, but I do it."

The first course arrived and John tackled it happily.

Susan picked at her stuffed mushrooms. "It sounds exciting."

"Exciting? I've got the biggest, most wonderful toy in the world. My own brain. Listen, I can spell any word correctly and I'm pretty sure I won't ever make any grammatical mistake."

"Because you remember all the dictionaries and grammars you ever read?"

John looked at her sharply. "Don't be sarcastic, Sue."

"I wasn't being—"

He waved her silent. "I never used dictionaries as light reading. But I do remember words and sentences in my reading and they were correctly spelled and correctly parsed."

"Don't be sure. You've seen any word misspelled in every possible way and every possible example of twisted grammar, too."

"Those were exceptions. By far the largest number of times I've encountered literary English, I've encountered it used correctly. It outweighs accidents, errors, and ignorance. What's more, I'm sure I'm improving even as I sit here, growing more intelligent steadily."

"And you're not worried. What if—"

"What if I become *too* intelligent? Tell me how on Earth you think becoming too intelligent can be harmful."

"I was going to say," said Susan, coldly, "that what you're experiencing is not intelligence. It's only total recall."

"How do you mean 'only'? If I recall perfectly, if I use the English language correctly, if I know endless quantities of material, isn't that going to make me seem more intelligent? How else need one define intelligence? You aren't growing just a little jealous, are you, Sue?"

"No," more coldly still. "I can always get an injection of my own if I feel desperate about it."

John put down his fork. "You can't mean that."

"I don't, but what if I did?"

"Because you can't take advantage of your special knowledge to deprive me of my position."

"What position?"

The main course arrived and for a few moments, John was busy. Then he said, in a whisper, "My position as the first of the future.

Homo superior! There'll never be too many of us. You heard what Kupfer said. Some are too dumb to make it. Some are too smart to change much. I'm the one!"

"*Dead* average." One corner of Susan's mouth lifted.

"Once I was. There'll be others like me eventually. Not many, but there'll be others. It's just that I want to make my mark before the others come along. It's for the firm, you know. Us!"

He remained lost in thought thereafter, testing his brain delicately.

Susan ate in an unhappy silence.

7

John spent several days organizing his memories. It was like the preparation of an orderly reference book. One by one, he recalled all his experiences in the six years he had spent at Quantum Pharmaceuticals and all he had heard and all the papers and memos he had read.

There was no difficulty in discarding the irrelevant and unimportant and storing them in a "hold till further notice" compartment where they did not interfere with his analysis. Other items were put in order so that they established a natural progression.

Against that skeletal organization, he resurrected the scuttlebutt he had heard; the gossip, malicious or otherwise; casual phrases and interjections at conferences which he had not been conscious of hearing at the time. Those items which did not fit anywhere against the background he had built up in his head were worthless, empty of factual content. Those which did fit clicked firmly into place and could be seen as true by that mere fact.

The further the structure grew, and the more coherent, the more significant new items became and the easier it was to fit them in.

Ross stopped by John's desk on Thursday. He said, "I want to see you in my office at the nonce, Heath, if your legs will deign to carry you in that direction."

John rose uneasily. "Is it necessary? I'm busy."

"Yes, you look busy." Ross looked over the clear desk which, at the moment, held nothing but a studio photo of a smiling Susan. "You've been this busy all week. But you've asked me whether seeing me in my office is necessary. For me, no; but for you, vital. There's the door to my office. There's the door to the hell out of here. Choose one or the other and do it fast."

John nodded and, without undue hurry, followed Ross into his office.

Ross seated himself behind his desk but did not invite John to sit. He maintained a hard stare for a moment, then said, "What the hell's got into you this week, Heath. Don't you know what your job is?"

"To the extent that I have done it, it would seem that I do," said John. "The report on microcosmic is on your desk and complete and seven days ahead of deadline. I doubt that you can have complaints about it."

"You doubt, do you? Do I have permission to have complaints if I choose to after communing with my soul? Or am I condemned to applying to you for permission?"

"I apparently have not made myself plain, Mr. Ross. I doubt that you have *rational* complaints about it. To have those of the other variety is entirely up to you."

Ross rose now. "Listen, punk, if I decide to fire you, you won't get the news by word of mouth. It won't be anything I say that will give you the glad tidings. You will go out through the door in a violent tumble and mine will be the propulsive force behind that tumble. Just keep that in your small brain and your tongue in your big mouth. —Whether you've done your work or not is not at question right now. Whether you've done everyone else's is. Who and what gives you the right to manage everyone in this place?"

John said nothing.

Ross roared, "Well?"

John said, "Your order was 'keep your tongue in your big mouth.'"

Ross turned a dangerous red. "You will answer questions, however."

John said, "I am not aware that I have been managing anyone."

"There's not a person in the place you haven't corrected at least once. You have gone over Willoughby's head in connection with the correspondence on the TMP's; you have been into general files using Bronstein's computer access; and God knows what else I haven't yet been told about and all in the last two days. You are disrupting the work of this department and it must cease this moment. There must be dead calm, and instantaneously, or it will be tornado weather for you, my man."

John said, "If I have interfered in the narrow sense, it has been for the good of the company. In the case of Willoughby, his treatment of the TMP matter was putting Quantum Pharmaceuticals in violation of government regulations, something I have pointed out to you in one of several memos I have sent you which you apparently have not had occasion to read. As for Bronstein, he was simply ignoring general directions and costing the company fifty thousand in unnecessary tests, something I was easily able to establish by locating the necessary correspondence—merely to corroborate my clear memory of the situation."

Ross was swelling visibly through the talk. "Heath," he said, "you are usurping my role. You will, therefore, gather your personal effects and be off the premises before lunch, never to return. If you do, I will take extreme pleasure in helping you out again with my foot. Your official notice of dismissal will be in your hands, or down your throat, before your effects will be collected, work as quickly as you may."

John said, "Don't try to bully me, Ross. You've cost the company a quarter of a million dollars through incompetence and you know it."

There was a short pause as Ross deflated. He said, cautiously, "What are you talking about?"

"Quantum Pharmaceuticals went down to the wire on the Nutley bid and missed out because a certain piece of information that was in your hands stayed in your hands and never got to the Board of Directors. You either forgot or you didn't bother and in either case you are not the man for your job. You are either incompetent or have sold out."

"You're insane."

"No one need believe me. The information is in the computer, if one knows where to look and I know where to look. What's more, the knowledge is on file and will be on the desks of the interested parties two minutes after I leave these premises."

"If this were so," said Ross, speaking with difficulty, "you could not possibly know. This is a stupid attempt at blackmail by threat of slander."

"You know it's not slander. If you doubt that I have the information, let me tell you that there is one memorandum that is not in the records but can be reconstructed without too much difficulty from what is there. You would have to explain its absence and it will be presumed you have destroyed it. You know I'm not bluffing."

"It's still blackmail."

"Why? I'm making no demands and no threats. I'm merely explaining my actions of the past two days. Of course, if I'm forced to resign, I'll have to explain why I resigned, won't I?"

Ross said nothing.

John said, coolly, "Is my resignation being requested?"

"Get out of here!"

"With my job? Or without it?"

Ross said, "You have your job." His face was a study in hatred.

8

Susan had arranged a dinner at her apartment and had gone to considerable trouble for it. Never, in her own opinion, had she looked more enticing and never did she think it more important to move John, at least for a bit, away from his total concentration on his own mind.

She said, with an attempt at heartiness, "After all, we are celebrating the last nine days of single blessedness."

"We are celebrating more than that," said John with a grim smile. "It's only four days since I got the disinhibitor and already I've been able to put Ross in his place. He'll never bother me again."

"We each seem to have our own notion of sentiment," said Susan. "Tell me the details of *your* tender remembrance."

John told the tale crisply, repeating the conversation verbatim and without hesitation.

Susan listened stonily, without in any way rising to the gathering triumph in John's voice. "How *did* you know all that about Ross?"

John said, "There are no secrets, Sue. Things just *seem* secret because people don't remember. If you can recall every remark, every comment, every stray word made to you or in your hearing and consider them all in combination, you find that everyone gives himself away in everything. You can pick out meanings that will, in these days of computerization, send you straight to the necessary records. It can be done. I can do it. I have done it in the case of Ross. I can do it in the case of anybody with whom I associate."

"You can also get them furious."

"I got Ross furious. You can bet on that."

"Was that wise?"

"What can he do to me? I've got him cold."

"He has enough clout in the upper echelons—"

"Not for long. I have a conference set for 2 P.M. tomorrow with old man Prescott and his stinking cigar and I'll cut Ross off at the pass."

"Don't you think you're moving too quickly?"

"Moving too quickly? I haven't even begun. Prescott's just a stepping-stone. Quantum Pharmaceutical's just a stepping-stone."

"It's still too quick. Johnny, you need someone to direct you. You need—"

"I need *nothing*. With what I have," he tapped his temple, "there's no one and nothing that can stop me."

Susan said, "Well, look, let's not discuss that. We have different plans to make."

"Plans?"

"Our own. We're getting married in just under nine days. Surely," with heavy irony, "you haven't returned to the sad old days when you forgot things."

"I remember the wedding," said John, testily, "but at the moment I've got to reorganize Quantum. In fact, I've been thinking seriously of postponing the wedding till I have things well in hand."

"Oh? And when might that be?"

"That's hard to tell. Not long at the rate I'm taking hold. A month or two, I suppose. Unless," and he descended into sarcasm, "you think that's moving too quickly."

Susan was breathing hard. "Were you planning to consult with me on the matter?"

John raised his eyebrows. "Would it have been necessary? Where's the argument? Surely you see what's happening. We can't interrupt it and lose momentum. —Listen, did you know I'm a mathematical wiz. I can multiply and divide as fast as a computer because at some time in my life I have come across almost every simple bit of arithmetic and I can *recall* the answers. I read a table of square roots and I can—"

Susan cried, "My God, Johnny, you *are* a kid with a new toy. You've lost your perspective. Instant recall is good for nothing but playing tricks with. It doesn't give you one bit more intelligence; not an ounce; not a speck more of judgment; not a whiff more of common sense. You're about as safe to have around as a little boy with a loaded grenade. You need looking after by someone with brains."

John scowled. "Do I? It seems to me that I'm getting what I want."

"Are you? Isn't it true that I'm what you want also?"

"What?"

"Go ahead, Johnny. You want me. Reach out and take me. Exercise that remarkable recall you have. Remember who I am, what I am, the things we can do, the warmth, the affection, the sentiment."

John, with his forehead still creased in uncertainty, extended his arms toward Susan.

She stepped out of them. "But you haven't got me, or anything about me. You can't remember me into your arms; you have to love me into them. The trouble is, you don't have the good sense to do it and you lack the intelligence to establish reasonable priorities. —Here, take this and get out of my apartment or I'll hit you with something a lot heavier."

He stopped to pick up the engagement ring. "Susan—"

"I said, get out. The firm of Johnny and Sue is hereby dissolved."

Her face blazed anger and John turned meekly and left.

9

When he arrived at Quantum the next morning, Anderson was waiting for him with a look of anxious impatience on his face.

"Mr. Heath," he said, smiling, and rising.

"What do you want?" demanded John.

"We are private here, I take it?"

"The place isn't bugged as far as I know."

"You are to report to us day after tomorrow for examination. On Sunday. You recall that?"

"Of course, I recall that. I'm incapable of not recalling. I *am* capable of changing my mind, however. Why do I need an examination?"

"Why not, sir? It is quite plain from what Kupfer and I have picked up that the treatment seems to have worked splendidly. Actually, we don't want to wait till Sunday. If you can come with me today—now, in fact—it would mean a great deal to us, to Quantum, and, of course, to humanity."

John said, curtly, "You might have held on to me when you had me. You sent me about my business, allowing me to live and work unsupervised so that you could test me under field conditions, and get a better idea of how things would work out. It meant more risk for me, but you didn't worry about that, did you?"

"Mr. Heath, that was not in our minds. We—"

"Don't tell me that. I remember every last word you and Kupfer said to me last Sunday, and it's quite clear to me that that *was* in your minds. So if I take the risk, I accept the benefits. I have no intention of presenting myself as a biochemical freak who has achieved my ability at the end of a hypodermic needle. Nor do I want others of the sort wandering around. For now, I have a monopoly and I intend to use it. When I'm ready—not before—I will be willing to cooperate with you and benefit humanity. But just remember, I'm the one who will know when I'm ready, not you. So don't call me; I'll call you."

Anderson managed a soft smile. "As to that, Mr. Heath, how can you stop us from making our announcement? Those who have dealt with you this week will have no trouble in recognizing the change in you and in testifying to it."

"Really? See here, Anderson, listen closely and do so without that foolish grin on your face. It irritates me. I told you I remember every word you and Kupfer spoke. I remember every nuance of expression, every sidelong glance. It all spoke volumes. I learned enough to check through sick-leave records with a good idea of what I was looking for. It would seem that I was not the first Quantum employee on whom you had tried the disinhibitor."

Anderson was, indeed, not smiling. "That is nonsense."

"You know it is not, and you had better know I can prove it. I

know the names of the men involved—one was a woman, actually
—and the hospitals in which they were treated and the false history with which they were supplied. Since you did not warn me of
this, when you used me as your fourth experimental animal on two
legs, I owe you nothing but a prison sentence."

Anderson said, "I won't discuss this matter. Let me say this,
though. The treatment will wear off, Heath. You won't keep your
total recall. You will have to come back for further treatment and
you can be sure it will be on our terms."

John said, "Nuts! You don't suppose I haven't investigated your
reports—at least, those you haven't kept secret. And I already have
a notion of what aspects you *have* kept secret. The treatment lasts
longer in some cases than others. It invariably lasts longer where it
is more effective. In my case, the treatment has been extraor-
dinarily effective and it will endure a considerable time. By the
time I come to you again, if I ever have to, I will be in a position
where any failure on your part to cooperate will be swiftly devas-
tating to you. Don't even think of it."

"You ungrateful—"

"Don't bother me," said John, wearily. "I have no time to listen to
you froth. Go away, I have work to do."

Anderson's face was a study in fear and frustration as he left.

10

It was 2:30 P.M. when John walked into Prescott's office, for once
not minding the cigar smoke. It would not be long, he knew, before
Prescott would have to choose between his cigars and his position.

With Prescott were Arnold Gluck and Lewis Randall, so that
John had the grim pleasure of knowing he was facing the three top
men in the division.

Prescott rested his cigar on top of an ashtray and said, "Ross has
asked me to give you half an hour, and that's all I will give you.
You're the one with the trick memory, aren't you?"

"My name is John Heath, sir, and I intend to present you with a
rationalization of procedure for the company; one that will make
full use of the age of computers and electronic communication and

will lay the groundwork for further modification as the technology improves."

The three men looked at each other.

Gluck, whose creased face was tanned a leathery-brown said, "Are you an expert in office management?"

"I don't have to be, sir. I have been here for six years and I recall every bit of the procedure in every transaction in which I have been involved. That means the pattern of such transactions is plain to me and its imperfections obvious. One can see toward what it is tending and where it is doing so wastefully and inefficiently. If you'll listen, I will explain. You will find it easy to understand."

Randall, whose red hair and freckles made him seem younger than he was, said sardonically, "Real easy, I hope, because we have trouble with hard concepts."

"You won't have trouble," said John.

"And you won't get a second more than twenty-one minutes," said Prescott, looking at his watch.

"It won't take that," said John. "I have it diagrammed and I can talk quickly."

It took fifteen minutes and the three management personnel were remarkably silent in that interval.

Finally Gluck said, with a hostile glance out of his small eyes, "It sounds as though you are saying we can get along with half the management we are employing these days."

"Less than half," said John, coolly, "and be the more efficient for it. We can't fire ordinary personnel at will because of the unions, though we can profitably lose them by attrition. Management is not protected, however, and can be let go. They'll have pensions if they're old enough and can get new jobs if they're young enough. Our thought must be for Quantum."

Prescott, who had maintained an ominous silence, now puffed furiously at his noxious cigar and said, "Changes like this have to be considered carefully and implemented, if at all, with the greatest of caution. What seems logical on paper can lose out in the human equation."

John said, "Prescott, if this reorganization is not accepted within a week, and if I am not placed in charge of its implementation, I will resign. I will have no trouble in finding employment with a smaller firm where this plan can be far more easily put into practice. Beginning with a small group of management people, I can expand in both quantity and efficiency of performance without additional hiring and within a year I'll drive Quantum into bankruptcy. It would be fun to do this if I am driven to it, so consider carefully. My half hour is up. Good-bye." And he left.

11

Prescott looked after him with a glance of frigid calculation. He said to the other two, "I think he means what he says and that he knows every facet of our operations better than we do. We can't let him go."

"You mean we've got to accept his plan," said Randall, shocked.

"I didn't say that. You two go, and remember this whole thing is confidential."

Gluck said, "I have the feeling that if we don't do something, all three of us will find ourselves on our butts in the street within a month."

"Very likely," said Prescott, "so we'll do something."

"What?"

"If you don't know, you won't get hurt. Leave it to me. Forget it for now and have a nice weekend."

When they were gone, he thought a while, chewing furiously on his cigar. He then turned to his telephone and dialed an extension. "Prescott here. I want you in my office first thing Monday morning. First thing. Hear me?"

12

Anderson looked a trifle disheveled. He had had a bad weekend. Prescott, who had had a worse, said to him, malevolently, "You and Kupfer tried again, didn't you?"

Anderson said, softly, "It's better not to discuss that, Mr. Prescott. You remember it was agreed that in certain aspects of research, a distance was to be established. We were to take the risks or the glory, and Quantum was to share in the latter but not in the former."

"And your salary was doubled with a guarantee of all legal payments to be Quantum's responsibility; don't forget that. This man, John Heath, was treated by you and Kupfer, wasn't he? Come on. There's no mistaking it. There's no point in hiding it."

"Well, yes."

"And you were so brilliant that you turned him loose on us—this —this—tarantula."

"We didn't anticipate this would happen. When he didn't go into instant shock, we thought it was our first chance to test the process in the field. We thought he would break down after two or three days, or it would pass."

Prescott said, "If I hadn't been protected so damned well, I wouldn't have put the whole thing out of my mind and I would have guessed what had happened when that bastard first pulled the computer bit and produced the details of correspondence he had no business remembering. —All right, we know where we are now. He's holding the company to ransom with a new plan of operations he can't be allowed to put through. Also, he can't be allowed to walk away from us."

Anderson said, "Considering Heath's capacity for recall and synthesis, is it possible that his plan of operations may be a good one?"

"I don't care if it is. That bastard is after my job and who knows what else and we've got to get rid of him."

"How do you mean, rid of him? He could be of vital importance to the cerebro-chemical project."

"Forget that. It's a disaster. You're creating a super-Hitler."

Anderson said, in soft-voiced anguish, "The effect will wear off."

"Yes? When?"

"At this moment, I can't be sure."

"Then I can't take chances. We've got to make our arrangements and do it tomorrow at the latest. We can't wait any longer."

13

John was in high good humor. The manner in which Ross avoided him when he could and spoke to him deferentially when he had to affected the entire work force. There was a strange and radical change in the pecking order, with himself at the top.

Nor could John deny to himself that he liked it. He reveled in it. The tide was moving strongly and unbelievably swiftly. It was only nine days since the injection of the disinhibitor and every step had been forward.

Well, no, there had been Susan's silly rage at him, but he would deal with her later. When he showed her the heights to which he would climb in nine additional days—in ninety—

He looked up. Ross was at his desk, waiting for his attention but reluctant to do anything as crass as to attract that attention by as much as clearing his throat. John swiveled his chair, put his feet out before him in an attitude of relaxation, and said, "Well, Ross?"

Ross said, carefully, "I would like to see you in my office, Heath. Something important has come up and, frankly, you're the only one who can set it straight."

John got slowly to his feet. "Yes? What is it?"

Ross looked about mutely at the busy room, with at least five men in reasonable earshot. Then he looked toward his office door and held out an inviting arm.

John hesitated, but for years Ross had held unquestioned authority over him, and at this moment he reacted to habit.

Ross held his door open for John politely, stepped through himself and closed the door behind him, locking it unobtrusively and remaining in front of it. Anderson stepped out from the other side of the bookcase.

John said sharply, "What's all this about?"

"Nothing at all, Heath," said Ross, his smile turning into a vulpine grin. "We're just going to help you out of your abnormal state —take you back to normality. Don't move, Heath."

Anderson had a hypodermic in his hand. "Please, Heath, do not struggle. We wish you no harm."

"If I yell—" said John.

"If you make any sound," said Ross, "I will put a hammerlock on you and hold it till your eyes bug out. I would like to do that, so please try to yell."

John said, "I have the goods on both of you, safe on deposit. Anything that happens to me—"

"Mr. Heath," said Anderson, "nothing will happen to you. Something is going to *un*happen to you. We will put you back to where you were. That would happen anyway, but we will hurry it up just a little."

"So I'm going to hold you, Heath," said Ross, "and you won't move because if you do, you will disturb our friend with the needle and he might slip and give you more than the carefully calculated dose, and you might end up unable to remember anything at all."

Heath was backing away, breathless. "That's what you're planning. You think you'll be safe that way. If I forgot all about you, all about the information, all about its storage. But—"

"We're not going to hurt you, Heath," said Anderson.

John's forehead glistened with sweat. A near-paralysis gripped him.

"An amnesiac!" he said, huskily, and with a terror that only someone could feel at the possibility who himself had perfect recall.

"Then you won't remember this either, will you?" said Ross. "Go ahead, Anderson."

"Well," muttered Anderson, in resignation. "I'm destroying a perfect test-subject." He lifted John's flaccid arm and readied the hypodermic.

There was a knock at the door. A clear voice called, "John!"

Anderson froze almost automatically, looking up questioningly.

Ross had turned to look at the door. Now he turned back. "Shoot that stuff into him, doc," he said in an urgent whisper.

The voice came again, "Johnny, I know you're in there. I've called the police. They're on the way."

Ross whispered again, "Go ahead. She's lying. And by the time they come, it's over. Who can prove anything?"

But Anderson was shaking his head vigorously. "It's his fiancée. She knows he was treated. She was there."

"You jackass."

There was the sound of a kick against the door and then the voice sounded in a muffled, "Let go of me. They've got— Let go!"

Anderson said, "Having her push the thing was the only way we could get him to agree. Besides, I don't think we have to do anything. Look at him."

John had collapsed in a corner, eyes glazed, and clearly in a state of unconscious trance.

Anderson said, "He's been terrified and that can produce a shock that will interfere with recall under normal conditions. I think the disinhibitor has been wiped out. Let her in and let *me* talk to her."

14

Susan looked pale as she sat with her arm protectively about the shoulders of her ex-fiancé. "What happened?"

"You remember the injection of—"

"Yes, yes. What happened?"

"He was supposed to come to our office day before yesterday, Sunday, for a thorough examination. He didn't come. We worried and the reports from his superiors had me very perturbed. He was becoming arrogant, megalomaniacal, irascible— Perhaps you noticed. —You're not wearing your engagement ring."

"We—quarreled," said Susan.

"Then you understand. He was— Well, if he were an inanimate device, we might say his motor was overheating as it sped faster and faster. This morning it seemed absolutely essential to treat him. We persuaded him to come here, locked the door and—"

"Injected him with something while I howled and kicked outside."

"Not at all," said Anderson. "We would have used a sedative, but we were too late. He had what I can only describe as a breakdown. You may search his body for fresh punctures, which, as his fiancée, I presume you may do without embarrassment, and you will find none."

Susan said, "I'll see about that. What happens, now?"

"I am sure he will recover. He will be his old self again."

"Dead average?"

"He will not have perfect recall, but until ten days ago, he never had. —Naturally, the firm will give him indefinite leave on full salary. If any medical treatment is required, all medical expenses will be paid. And when he feels like it, he can return to active duty."

"Yes? Well, I will want all that in writing before the day is out, or I see my lawyer tomorrow."

"But Miss Collins," said Anderson, "you know that Mr. Heath volunteered. You were willing too."

"I think," said Susan, "that *you* know the situation was misrepresented to us and that you won't welcome an investigation. Just see to it that what you've just promised is in writing."

"You will have to, in return, sign an agreement to hold us guiltless of any misadventure your fiancé may have suffered."

"Possibly. I prefer to see what kind of misadventure it is first. —Can you walk, Johnny?"

John nodded and said, a little huskily, "Yes, Sue."

"Then let's go."

15

John had put himself outside a cup of good coffee and an omelet before Susan permitted discussion. Then he said, "What I don't understand is how you happened to be there?"

"Shall we say woman's intuition?"

"Let's say Susan's brains."

"All right. Let's! After I threw the ring at you, I felt self-pitying and aggrieved and after that wore off, I felt a severe sense of loss because, odd though it might seem to the average sensible person, I'm very fond of you."

"I'm sorry, Sue," said John, humbly.

"As well you should be. God, you were insupportable. But then I got to thinking that if you could get poor loving me that furious, what must you be doing to your co-workers. The more I thought about it, the more I thought they might have a strong impulse to kill you. Now, don't get me wrong. I'm willing to admit you deserved killing, but only at *my* hands. I wouldn't dream of allowing anyone else to do it. I didn't hear from you—"

"I know, Sue. I had plans and I had no time—"

"You had to do it all in two weeks. I know, you idiot. By this morning I couldn't stand it anymore. I came to see how you were and found you behind a locked door."

John shuddered. "I never thought I'd welcome your kicking and screaming, but I did then. You stopped them."

"Will it upset you to talk about it?"

"I don't think so. I'm all right."

"Then what were they doing?"

"They were going to re-inhibit me. I thought they might be giving me an overdose and make me an amnesiac."

"Why?"

"Because they knew I had them all. I could ruin them and the company."

"You really could."

"Absolutely."

"But they didn't actually inject you, did they? Or was that another of Anderson's lies?"

"They really didn't."

"Are you all right?"

"I'm not an amnesiac."

"Well, I hate to sound like a Victorian damsel, but I hope you have learned your lesson."

"If you mean, do I realize you were right, I do."

"Then just let me lecture you for one minute, so you don't forget again. You went about everything too rapidly, too openly, and with too much disregard for the possible violent counteraction of others. You had total recall and you mistook it for intelligence. If you had someone who was really intelligent to guide you—"

"I needed you, Sue."

"Well, you've got me now, Johnny."

"What do we do next, Sue?"

"First, we get that paper from Quantum and, since you're all right, we'll sign the release for them. Second, we get married on Saturday, just as we originally planned. Third, we'll see— But, Johnny?"

"Yes?"

"You're all right?"

"Couldn't be better, Sue. Now we're together, everything's fine."

16

It wasn't a formal wedding. Less formal than they had originally planned and fewer guests. No one was there from Quantum, for instance—Susan had pointed out, quite firmly, that that would be a bad idea.

A neighbor of Susan's had brought a video-camera to record the proceedings, something that seemed to John to be the height of schlock, but Susan had wanted it.

And then the neighbor had said to him with a tragic shrug, "Can't get the damn thing to turn on. You'd think they'd give me one in working order. I'll have to make a phone call." He hastened down the steps to the pay phone in the chapel lobby.

John advanced to look at the camera curiously. An instruction booklet lay on a small table to one side. He picked it up and leafed through the pages with moderate speed, then put it back. He looked about him, but everyone was busy. No one seemed to be paying attention to him.

He slid the rear panel to one side, unobtrusively, and peered inside. He then turned away and gazed at the opposite wall thoughtfully. He was still gazing even as his right hand snaked in toward the mechanism and made a quick adjustment. After a brief interval he put the rear panel back and flicked a toggle switch.

The neighbor came bustling back, looking exasperated. "How am I going to follow directions I can't make head or—" He frowned, then said, "Funny. It's on. It must have been working all the time."

17

"You may kiss the bride," said the minister, benignly, and John took Susan in his arms and followed orders with enthusiasm.

Susan whispered through unmoving lips, "You fixed that camera. Why?"

He whispered back, "I wanted everything right for the wedding."

She whispered, "You wanted to show off."

They broke apart, looking at each other through love-misted eyes, then fell into another embrace, while the small audience stirred and tittered.

Susan whispered, "You do it again, and I'll skin you. As long as no one knows you still have it, no one will stop you. We'll have it all within a year, if you follow directions."

"Yes, dear," whispered John, humbly.

Introduction to

NOTHING FOR NOTHING

Many times, people come to me with ideas. Usually, I can't use them for any of a variety of reasons. They don't appeal to me, perhaps, because they don't match my mind-set. Or they would involve the kind of development I'm not particularly good at. Or I don't see consequences of the type that interest me.

But once in a long, long while, something clicks.

In July 1978, I was having lunch with Alexander Marshak, the Paleolithic archaeologist, at Tavern on the Green. He had, at that time, arranged an enormously successful display of Ice Age art at the Museum of Natural History, and he said to me, "Why don't you write a story, Isaac, about—"

I listened to him in astonishment and said, "Alex, that's a great idea. I'll incorporate it into a story, but don't worry, I won't give you any credit."

"That's all right," he said.

But, what the heck— I might as well. "Nothing for Nothing" was built up from his idea which in turn came out of his dealings with Ice Age art, as you will see. I submitted it to George Scithers, and it appeared in the February 1979 *Asimov's*.

16.

NOTHING FOR NOTHING

The scene was Earth.

Not that the beings on the starship thought of it as Earth. To them it was a series of symbols stored in a computer; it was the third planet of a star located at a certain position with respect to the line connecting their home planet with the black hole that marked the Galaxy's center, and moving at a certain velocity with reference to it.

The time was 15000 B.C., more or less.

Not that the beings on the starship thought of it as 15000 B.C. To them, it was a certain period of time marked off according to their local system of measurement.

The captain of the starship said, rather petulantly, "This is a waste of time. The planet is largely frozen. Let us leave."

But the ship's explorer quietly said, "No, Captain," and that was that.

As long as a starship was in space, or in hyperspace for that matter, the captain was supreme, but place that ship in orbit about a planet and the explorer could not be challenged. He knew worlds! That was his specialty.

And this explorer was in an impregnable position. He had what amounted to a sure instinct for profitable trade. It had been he and he alone who was responsible for the fact that this particular starship had won three Awards for Excellence for the work done in its three last expeditions. Three for three.

So when the explorer said, "No," the captain could not dream of "Yes." Even in the unlikely case that he had, the crew would have mutinied. An Award for Excellence might be, to the captain, a pleasant spectral disk to suspend in the main salon, but to the crew it meant a spectacular addition to take-home pay and an even more welcome addition to vacation time and pension benefits. And this explorer had brought them that three times. Three for three.

The explorer said, "No strange world should be left unexamined."

The captain said, "What is strange about this one?"

"The preliminary probe shows intelligence, and on a frozen world."

"Surely that's not unprecedented."

"The pattern here is strange," the explorer looked uneasy. "I am not sure exactly how or exactly why, but the pattern of life and of intelligence is strange. We must examine it more carefully."

And that was that, of course. There were at least half a trillion planetary worlds in the Galaxy, if one only counted those associated with stars. Add to that the indefinite number moving independently through space and the number might be ten times as great.

Even with computers to help, no starship could know them all, but an experienced explorer, by dint of lacking interest in anything else, of studying every exploratory report published, of considering endless correlations, and, presumably, playing with statistics even in his sleep, grew to have what seemed to others a mystical intuition about such things.

"We'll have to send out probes in full interlocking program," said the explorer.

The captain looked outraged. Full power meant a leisurely examination for weeks at enormous expense.

He said, and it was as much as he could offer in the way of objection, "Is that absolutely necessary?"

"I rather think so," said the explorer with the self-confidence of one who knows his whim is law.

The probes brought back exactly what the captain expected, and in great detail. An intelligent species rather reminiscent, at least as far as superficial appearance went, of the lesser breeds of the inner proximal regions of the fifth arm of the Galaxy—not quite unusual, but of interest to mentologists, no doubt.

As yet the intelligent species was only at the first level of technology—long, long removed from anything useful.

The captain said so, scarcely able to mask his exasperation, but the explorer, leafing through the reports, remained unmoved. He said, "Strange!" and asked that the trader be summoned.

This was really too much. A successful captain must never give a good explorer cause for unhappiness but there are limits to everything.

The captain said, fighting to keep the level of communication polite, if not friendly, "To what end, Explorer? What can we expect at this level?"

"They have tools," said the explorer thoughtfully.

"Stone! Bone! Wood! Or this planet's equivalent of that. And that's all. Surely we can find nothing in that."

"And yet there is something strange in the pattern."

"May I know what that might be, Explorer?"

"If I knew what it might be, Captain, it would not be strange, and I would not have to find out. Really, Captain, I must insist on the Trader."

The trader was as indignant as the captain was, and had more scope to express it. His, after all, was a speciality as deep as that of anyone's on the starship, even, in his own opinion (and in some other's), as deep and as essential as the explorer's.

The captain might navigate a starship and the explorer might detect useful civilizations by the most tenuous of signs, but in the final clutch it was the trader and his team who faced the aliens and who plucked out of their minds and culture that which was useful and gave in return something *they* found useful.

And this was done at great risk. The alien ecology must not be disrupted. Alien intelligences must not be harmed, not even to save one's own life. There were good reasons for that on the cosmic scale and traders were amply rewarded for the risks they ran, but why run *useless* risks.

The trader said, "There is nothing there. *My* interpretation of the probe's data is that we're dealing with semi-intelligent animals. Their usefulness is nil. Their danger is great. We know how to deal with truly intelligent aliens and trader teams are rarely killed by them. Who knows how these animals will react—and you know we are not allowed to defend ourselves properly."

The explorer said, "These animals, if they are no more than that, have interestingly adapted themselves to the ice. There are subtle variations in the pattern here I do not understand, but my considered opinion is that they will not be dangerous and that they may even be useful. I feel they are worth closer examination."

"What can be gained from a Stone Age intelligence?" asked the trader.

"That is for you to find out."

The trader thought grimly: Of course, that is what it comes to—for *us* to find out.

He knew well the history and purpose of the starship expeditions. There had been a time, a million years before, when there had been no traders, explorers, or captains but only ancestral animals with developing mind and a Stone Age technology—much like the animals on the world they were now orbiting. How slow the advance, how painfully slow the self-generated progress—until the third-level civilization had been reached. Then had come the starships and the chance of cross-fertilization of cultures. *Then* had come progress.

The trader said, "With respect, Explorer, I grant your intuitional experience. Will you grant my practical experience, though it is less dramatic? There is no way in which anything below a third-level civilization can have anything we can use."

"That," said the explorer, "is a generalization that may or may not be true."

"With respect, Explorer. It *is* true. And even if those—those semianimals had something we could use, and I can't imagine what it might be, what can we give them in exchange?"

The explorer was silent.

The trader went on. "At this level, there is no way in which a protointelligence can accept an alien stimulation. The mentologists are agreed on that and it is my experience, too. Progress *must* be self-generated until at least the second level is reached. And we *must* make a return; we can take nothing for nothing."

The captain said, "And that makes sense, of course. By stimulating these intelligences to advance, we can harvest them again at a later visit."

"I don't care about the reason for it," said the trader, impatiently. "It is part of the tradition of my profession. We do no harm under any conditions and we give a return for what we take. Here there is nothing we will want to take; and even if we find something, there will be nothing that we can give in return. —We waste time."

The explorer shook his head. "I ask you to visit some center of population, Trader. I will abide by your decision when you return."

And that was that, too.

For two days the small trader module flashed over the surface of the planet searching for any evidence of a reasonable level of technology. There was none.

A complete search could take years but was scarcely worth it. It was unreasonable to suppose a high level would be hidden. The highest technology was always flaunted for it had no enemy. That was the universal experience of traders everywhere.

It was a beautiful planet, half-frozen as it was. White and blue and green. Wild and rough and variegated. Crude—and untouched.

But it was not the trader's job to deal with beauty and he shrugged off such thoughts impatiently. When his crew talked to him in such terms, he was short with them.

He said, "We'll land here. It seems to be a good-sized concentration of the intelligences. We can do no better."

His second said, "What can we do even with these, Maestro?"

"You can record," said the trader. "Record the animals, both unintelligent and supposedly intelligent, and any artifacts of theirs we can find. Make sure the records are thoroughly holographic."

"We can already see—" began the second.

"We can already see," said the trader, "but we must have a record to convince our explorer out of his dreams or we'll remain here forever."

"He is a good explorer," said one of the crew.

"He has been a good explorer," said the trader, "but does that mean he will be good forever? Perhaps his very successes have made him accept himself at too high an evaluation. So we must convince him of reality—if we can."

They wore their suits when they emerged from the module.

The planetary atmosphere would support them, but the feeling

of exposure to the raw winds of an open planet would discommode
them, even if the atmosphere and temperature were perfect—
which they weren't. The gravity was a touch high, as was the light
level, but they could bear it.

The intelligent beings, dressed rather sketchily in the outer portions of other animals, retreated reluctantly at their approach and
watched at a distance. The trader was relieved at this. Any sign of
nonbelligerence was welcome to those not permitted to defend
themselves.

The trader and his crew did not try to communicate directly or
to make friendly gestures. Who knew what gesture might be considered friendly by an alien? The trader set up a mental field, instead, and saturated it with the vibrations of harmlessness and
peace and hoped that the mental fields of the creatures were
sufficiently advanced to respond.

Perhaps they were, for a few crept back and watched motionlessly as though intensely curious. The trader thought he detected
fugitive thoughts—but that seemed unlikely for first-level beings
and he did not follow them up.

Instead, he went stolidly about the business of making holographic reproductions of the vegetation, of a herd of blundering
herbivores that appeared and then, deciding the surroundings were
dangerous, thundered away. A large animal stood its ground for a
while, exposing white weapons in a cavity at its fore-end—then
left.

The trader's crew worked as he did, moving methodically across
the landscape.

The call, directly mental, and surcharged with such emotion of
surprise and awe that the informational content was all but blurred
out, came unexpectedly.

"Maestro! Here! Come quickly!"

Specific directions were not given. The trader had to follow the
beam, which led into a crevice bounded by two rocky outcrop-
pings.

Other members of the crew were converging but the trader had
arrived first.

"What is it?" asked the trader.

His second was standing in the glow of his suit-radiation in a deeply hollowed-out portion of the hillside.

The trader looked about. "This is a natural hollow, not a technological product."

"Yes, but look!"

The trader looked up and for perhaps five seconds he was lost. Then he sent out a strenuous message for all others to stay away.

He said, "Is this of technological origin?"

"Yes, Maestro. You can see it is only partly completed."

"But by whom?"

"By those creatures out there. The intelligent ones. I found one at work in here. This is his light source; it was burning vegetation. These are his tools."

"And where is he?"

"He fled."

"Did you actually see him?"

"I recorded him."

The trader pondered. Then he looked up again. "Have you ever seen anything like this?"

"No, Maestro."

"Or heard of anything like this?"

"No, Maestro."

"Astonishing!"

The trader showed no signs of wanting to withdraw his eyes, and the second said, softly, "Maestro, what do we do?"

"Eh?"

"This will surely win our ship still a fourth prize."

"Surely," said the trader, regretfully, "if we could take it."

The second said, hesitantly, "I have already recorded it."

"Eh? What is the use of that? We have nothing to give in exchange."

"But we have this. Give them anything."

The trader said, "What are you saying? They are too primitive to accept anything we could give them. It will surely be nearly a million years before they could possibly accept the suggestions of exogenous origin. —We will have to destroy the recording."

"But we know, Maestro."

"Then we must never talk about it. Our craft has its ethics and its traditions. You know that. Nothing for nothing!"

"Even this?"

"Even this."

The trader's sternly implacable set of expression was tinged with unbearable sorrow and despite his "Even this" he stood irresolute. The second sensed that. He said, "*Try* giving them something, Maestro."

"Of what use would that be?"

"Of what harm?"

The trader said, "I have prepared a presentation for the entire starship, but I must show it to you first, Explorer—with deep respect and with apologies for masked thoughts. You were right. There *was* something strange about this planet. Though the intelligences on the planet were barely first level and though their technology was primitive in the extreme, they had developed a concept we have never had and one that, to my knowledge, we have never encountered on any other world."

The captain said, uneasily, "I cannot imagine what it might be." He was quite aware that traders sometimes overpraised their purchases to magnify their own worth.

The explorer said nothing. He was the more uneasy of the two.

The trader said, "It is a form of visual art."

"Playing with color?" asked the captain.

"And shape—but to most startling effect." He had arranged the holographic projector. "Observe!"

In the viewing space before them, a herd of animals appeared; bulky, shaggy, two-horned, four-legged. They hesitated, then ran, dust spurting up beneath their hooves.

"Ugly objects," muttered the captain.

The holographic recording brought the herd to a halt, clamped it down to a still. It magnified, and a single beast filled the view, its bulky head lowered, its nostrils distended.

"Observe this animal," said the trader, "and now observe this artificial composition of a primitive concoction of oil and colored mineral, which we found smeared over the roof of a cave."

There it was again! Not quite the animal as holographed—flat, but vibrant.

"What a peculiar similarity," said the captain.

"Not peculiar," said the trader. "Deliberate! There were dozens of such figures in different poses—of different animals. The likenesses were too detailed to be fortuitous. Imagine the boldness of the conception—to place colors in pleasing shapes and combinations, and in such a way as to deceive the eye into thinking it is looking at a real object. These organisms have devised an art that represents reality. It is representational art, as I suppose we might call it.

"And that's not all. We found it done in three dimensions also." The trader produced an array of small figures in gray stone and in faintly yellow bone. "These are clearly intended to represent themselves."

The captain seemed stupefied. "Did you see these manufactured?"

"No, that I did not, Captain. One of my men saw a planetary being smearing color on one of the cave representations, but these we found already formed. Still, no other explanation is possible than that they were deliberately shaped. These objects could not have assumed these shapes by chance processes."

The captain said, "These are curious, but one doesn't follow the motive. Would not holographic techniques serve the purpose better —at such times as these are developed, of course?"

"These primitives have no conception that holography could someday be developed and could not wait the million years required. Then, too, maybe holography is *not* better. If you compare the representations with the originals you will notice that the representations are simplified and distorted in subtle ways designed to bring certain characteristics into focus. I believe this form of art *improves* on the original in some ways and certainly has something different to say."

The trader turned to the explorer. "I stand in awe at your abilities. Can you explain how you sensed the uniqueness of this intelligence?"

The explorer signed a negative. "I did not suspect this at all. It is interesting and I see its worth—although I wonder if we could ourselves properly control our colors and shapes in order to force them into such representational form. Yet this does match the unease within me. —What I wonder is how you came into possession of these? What did you give in exchange? It is *there* I see the strangeness lie."

"Well," said the trader, "in a way you're right. Quite strange. I did not think I could give anything since the organisms are so primitive, but this discovery seemed too important to sacrifice without some effort. I therefore chose from among the group of beings who formed these objects one whose mental field seemed somewhat more intense than that of the others and attempted to transfer to him a gift in exchange."

"And succeeded. Of course," said the explorer.

"Yes, I succeeded," said the trader, happily, failing to notice that the explorer had made a statement and had not asked a question. "The beings," the trader went on, "kill such animals as they repesent in color, by throwing long sticks tipped with sharpened stone. These penetrate the hide of the animals, wound and weaken them. They can then be killed by the beings who are individually smaller and weaker than the animal they hunt. I pointed out that a smaller, stone-tipped stick could be hurled forward with greater force and effect and with longer range if a cord under tension were used as the mechanism of propulsion."

The explorer said, "Such devices have been encountered among primitive intelligences which were, however, far advanced beyond these. Paleomentologists call it a bow and arrow."

The captain said, "How could the knowledge be absorbed? It couldn't be, at this level of development."

"But it *was*. Unmistakably. The response of the mental field was one of insight at almost unbearable intensity. —Surely you do not think I would have taken these art objects, were they twenty times as valuable, if I had not been convinced that I had made a return? Nothing for nothing, Captain."

The explorer said in a low, despondent voice, "There is the strangeness. To accept."

The captain said, "But surely, Trader, we cannot do this. They are not ready. We are harming them. They will use the bow and arrow to wound each other and not the beasts alone."

The trader said, "We do not harm them and we *did* not harm them. What *they* do to each other and where they end as a result, a million years from now, is not our concern."

The captain and the trader left to set up the demonstration for the starship's company, and the explorer said sadly in the direction in which they had gone. "But they accepted. And they flourish amid the ice. And in twenty thousand years, it will be *our* concern."

He knew they would not believe him, and he despaired.

Introduction to

ONE NIGHT OF SONG

For a couple of years now, I've been writing a monthly mystery story for *Gallery*, a "girlie" magazine (though I hasten to say that my mysteries are completely pure and undefiled). They're only a couple of thousand words apiece; they're supposed to be fair to the reader; and they're a lot of fun for me to do.

The only trouble is that I did "One Night of Song," and Eric Protter, who edits *Gallery*, regretfully rejected it (the only one he has ever rejected so far). The reason was a very good one. I had slipped up. Instead of doing a mystery, I had done a fantasy.

I asked Eric if I could submit the story elsewhere and he said, "Yes, provided you make just a few minor changes so that it is no longer part of the series—which I want to keep as an exclusive."

I made the changes, and then submitted the story to Ed Ferman. He took it and it appeared in the April 1982 *F & SF*. Frankly, I liked it better than any of the straight mysteries in the series, but Eric was absolutely right to reject it all the same. And as long as I can present it to you now, what difference does rejection make anyway?

17.

ONE NIGHT OF SONG

A s it happens, I have a friend who hints, sometimes, that he
can call up spirits from the vasty deep.

—Or at least one spirit; a tiny one, with strictly limited
powers. He talks about it sometimes but only after he has reached
his fourth Scotch and soda. It's a delicate point of equilibrium—
three and he knows nothing about spirits (the supernatural kind),
five and he falls asleep.

I thought he had reached the right level that evening, so I said,
"Do you remember that spirit of yours, George?"

"Eh?" said George, looking at his drink as though he wondered
why that should require remembering.

"Not your drink," I said. "The little spirit about two centimeters
high, whom you once told me you had managed to call up from
some other plane of existence. The one with the paranatural
powers."

"Ah," said George. "Azazel. Not his name, of course. Couldn't
pronounce his real name, I suppose, but that's what I call him. I
remember him."

"Do you use him much?"

"No. Dangerous. It's too dangerous. There's always the temptation to play with power. I'm careful myself; deuced careful. As you
know, I have a high standard of ethics. That's why I felt called
upon to help a friend once. The damage *that* did! Dreadful!
Doesn't bear thinking of."

"What happened?"

"I suppose I ought to get it off my chest," said George, thoughtfully. "It tends to fester—"

I was a good deal younger then [said George] and in those days women made up an important part of one's life. It seems silly now, looking back on it, but I distinctly remember thinking, back in those days, that it made much difference which.

Actually, you reach in the grab bag and whichever comes out, it's much the same, but in those days—

I had a friend, Mortenson—Andrew Mortenson. I don't think you know him. I haven't seen much of him myself in recent years.

The point is, he was soppy about a woman, a particular woman. She was an angel, he said. He couldn't live without her. She was the only one in the Universe and without her the world was crumbled bacon bits dipped in axle grease. You know the way lovers talk.

The trouble was she threw him over finally and apparently did so in a particularly cruel manner and without regard for his self-esteem. She had humiliated him thoroughly, taking up with another right in front of him, snapping her fingers under his nostrils and laughing heartlessly at his tears.

I don't mean that literally. I'm just trying to give the impression he gave me. He sat here drinking with me, here in this very room. My heart bled for him and I said, "I'm sorry, Mortenson, but you mustn't take on so. When you stop to think of it clearly, she's only a woman. If you look out in the street, there are lots of them passing by."

He said, bitterly, "I intend a womanless existence from now on, old man—except for my wife, of course, whom, every now and then, I can't avoid. It's just that I'd like to do something in return to this woman."

"To your wife?" I said.

"No, no, why should I like to do something to my wife? I'm talking about doing something for this woman who threw me over so heartlessly."

"Like what?"

"Damned if I know," said he.

"Maybe I can help," I said, for my heart was still bleeding for him. "I can make use of a spirit with quite extraordinary powers. A small spirit, of course"—I held my finger and thumb up less than an inch apart so that he was sure to get the idea—"who can only do so much."

I told him about Azazel and, of course, he believed me. I've often noticed that I carry conviction when I tell a tale. Now when *you* tell a story, old man, the air of disbelief that descends upon the room is thick enough to cut with a chain saw, but it's not that way with me. There's nothing like a reputation for probity and an air of honest directness.

His eyes glittered as I told him. He said could he arrange to give her something that I would ask for.

"If it's presentable, old man. I hope you have nothing in your mind like making her smell bad or having a toad drop out of her mouth when she talks."

"Of course not," he said, revolted. "What do you take me for? She gave me two happy years, on and off, and I want to make an adequate return. You say your spirit has only limited power?"

"He's a small thing," I said, holding up my thumb and forefinger again.

"Could he give her a perfect voice? For a time, anyway. At least for one performance."

"I'll ask him." Mortenson's suggestion sounded the gentlemanly thing to do. His ex-mistress sang cantatas at the local church, if that's the proper term. In those days I had quite an ear for music and would frequently go to these things (taking care to dodge the collection box, of course). I rather enjoyed hearing her sing and the audience seemed to absorb it politely enough. I thought at the time that her morals didn't quite suit the surroundings, but Mortenson said they made allowances for sopranos.

So I consulted Azazel. He was quite willing to help; none of this nonsense, you know, of demanding my soul in exchange. I remember I once asked Azazel if he wanted my soul and he didn't even know what it was. He asked me what I meant and it turned out I didn't know what it was, either. It's just that he's such a little fellow in his own Universe that it gives him a feeling of great success to be able to throw his weight around in our Universe. He *likes* to help out.

He said he could manage three hours and Mortenson said that would be perfect when I gave him the news. We picked a night when she was going to be singing Bach or Handel or one of those old piano-bangers, and was going to have a long and impressive solo.

Mortenson went to the church that night and, of course, I went too. I felt responsible for what was going to happen and I thought I had better oversee the situation.

Mortenson said, gloomily, "I attended the rehearsals. She was just singing the same way she always did; you know, as though she had a tail and someone was stepping on it."

That wasn't the way he used to describe her voice. The music of the spheres, he said on a number of occasions, and it was all uphill from there. Of course, though, he had been thrown over, which does warp a man's judgment.

I fixed him with a censorious eye. "That's no way to talk of a woman you're trying to bestow a great gift upon."

"That's just it. I want her voice to be perfect. Really *perfect*. And I now see—now that the mists of love have cleared from my eyes— that she has a long way to go. Do you think your spirit can handle it?"

"The change isn't timed to start till 8:15 P.M." A stab of suspicion went through me. "You hadn't been hoping to use up the perfection on the rehearsal and then disappoint the audience?"

"You have it all wrong," he said.

They got started a little early and when she got up in her white dress to sing it was 8:14 by my old pocket watch which is never off by more than two seconds. She wasn't one of your peewee sopranos; she was built on a generous scale, leaving lots of room for the kind of resonance you need when you reach for that high note and drown out the orchestra. Whenever she drew in a few gallons of breath with which to manipulate it all, I could see what Mortenson saw in her, allowing for several layers of textile material.

She started at her usual level and then at 8:15 precisely, it was as though another voice had been added. I saw her give a little jump as though she didn't believe what she heard, and one hand, which was held to her diaphragm, seemed to vibrate.

Her voice soared. It was as though she had become an organ in perfect pitch. Each note was perfect, a note invented freshly at that moment, besides which all other notes of the same pitch and quality were imperfect copies.

Each note hit squarely with just the proper vibrato, if that's the word, swelling or diminishing with enormous power and control.

And she got better with each note. The organist wasn't looking at the music, he was looking at her, and—I can't swear to it—but I think he stopped playing. If he were playing, I wouldn't have heard him anyway. There was no way in which you could hear *anything* while she was singing. Anything else but her.

The look of surprise had vanished from her face, and there was a look of exaltation there instead. She had put down the music she had been holding; she didn't need it. Her voice was singing by itself and she didn't need to control or direct it. The conductor was rigid and everyone else in the chorus seemed dumbfounded.

The solo ended at last and the chorus sounded in what was a whisper, as though they were all ashamed of their voices and distressed to turn them loose in the same church on the same night.

For the rest of the program it was all her. When she sang, it was all that was heard even if every other voice was sounding. When she didn't sing, it was as though we were sitting in the dark, and we couldn't bear the absence of light.

And when it was over—well, you don't applaud in church, but they did then. Everyone in that church stood up as though they had been yanked to their feet by a single marionette-string, and they applauded and applauded, and it was clear they would applaud all night unless she sang again.

She did sing again; her voice alone, with the organ whispering hesitantly in the background; with the spotlight on her; with no one else in the chorus visible.

Effortless. You have no idea how effortless it was. I wrenched my ears away from the sound to try to watch her breathing, to catch her taking in breath, to wonder how long a note could be held at full volume with only one pair of lungs to supply the air.

But it had to end and it was over. Even the applause was over. It was only then that I became aware that, next to me, Mortenson had been sitting with his eyes glittering, with his whole being absorbed in her singing. It was only then that I began to gather what had happened.

I am, after all, as straight as a Euclidean line and have no deviousness in me, so I couldn't be expected to see what he was after. You, on the other hand, who are so crooked you can run up a spiral staircase without making any turns, can see at a glance what he was after.

She had sung perfectly—but she would never sing perfectly again.

It was as though she were blind from birth, and for just three hours could see—see all there was to see, all the colors and shapes and wonders that surround us all and that we pay no attention to because we're so used to it. Suppose you could see it all in its full glory for just three hours—and then be blind again!

You could stand your blindness if you knew nothing else. But to know something else briefly and then return to blindness? No one could stand that.

That woman has never sung again, of course. But that's only part of it. The real tragedy was to us, to the members of the audience.

We had perfect music for three hours, *perfect* music. Do you think we could ever again bear to listen to anything less than that.

I've been as good as tone-deaf ever since. Recently, I went to one of those rock festivals that are so popular these days, just to test myself out. You won't believe me, but I couldn't make out one tune. It was all noise to me.

My only consolation is that Mortenson, who listened most eagerly and with the most concentration, is worse off than anyone in that audience. He wears earplugs at all times. He can't stand *any* sound above a whisper.

Serves him right!

Introduction to

THE SMILE THAT LOSES

The alphabet has seen to it that this story, which is related to "One Night of Song," comes immediately after it in the book. It's not a sequel, for it does not continue the plot line of the previous story, but it does make use of the tiny demon, which is the important point. It has appeared in the November 1982 issue of *F & SF*.

I intend to write a whole series of stories about the microdemon provided I can get editorial cooperation——or even if I can't. I am so fond of the situation and of the plot possibilities that I think I will write the stories even if I can't get them printed in the magazines. Then, when I have written about twenty of them, I'll see if I can't talk the soft-hearted Hugh O'Neill of Doubleday into doing the collection.

18.

THE SMILE THAT LOSES

I said to my friend George over a beer recently (*his* beer; I was having a ginger ale), "How's your implet these days?"

George claims he has a two-centimeter-tall demon at his beck and call. I can never get him to admit he's lying. Neither can anyone else.

He glared at me balefully, then said, "Oh, yes, you're the one who knows about it! I hope you haven't told anyone else!"

"Not a word," I said. "It's quite sufficient that I think you're crazy. I don't need anyone thinking the same of me." (Besides, he has told at least half a dozen people about the demon, to my personal knowledge, so there's no necessity of *my* being indiscreet.)

George said, "I wouldn't have your unlovely inability to believe anything you don't understand—and you don't understand so much —for the worth of a pound of plutonium. And what would be left of you, if my demon ever found out you called him an implet, wouldn't be worth an atom of plutonium."

"Have you figured out his real name?" I asked, unperturbed by this dire warning.

"Can't! It's unpronounceable by any earthly pair of lips. The translation is, I am given to understand, something like: 'I am the King of Kings; look upon my works, ye mighty, and despair.' —It's a lie, of course," said George, staring moodily at his beer. "He's small potatoes in his world. That's why he's so cooperative here. In *our* world, with our primitive technology, he can show off."

"Has he shown off lately?"

"Yes, as a matter of fact," said George, heaving an enormous sigh and raising his bleak blue eyes to mine. His ragged, white mustache settled down only slowly from the typhoon of that forced exhalation of breath.

It started with Rosie O'Donnell [said George], a friend of a niece of mine, and a fetching little thing altogether.

She had blue eyes, almost as brilliant as my own; russet hair, long and lustrous; a delightful little nose, powdered with freckles in the manner approved of by all who write romances; a graceful neck; a slender figure, that wasn't opulent in any disproportionate way, but was utterly delightful in its promise of ecstasy.

Of course, all of this was of purely intellectual interest to me, since I reached the age of discretion years ago, and now engage in the consequences of physical affection only when women insist upon it, which, thank the fates, is not oftener than an occasional weekend or so.

Besides which, Rosie had recently married—and, for some reason, adored in the most aggravating manner—a large Irishman who does not attempt to hide the fact that he is a very muscular, and, possibly, bad-tempered person. While I had no doubt that I would have been able to handle him in my younger days, the sad fact was that I was no longer in my younger days—by a short margin.

It was, therefore, with a certain reluctance that I accepted Rosie's tendency to mistake me for some close friend of her own sex and her own time of life, and to make me the object of her girlish confidences.

Not that I blame her, you understand. My natural dignity, and the fact that I inevitably remind people of one or more of the nobler of the Roman emperors in appearance, automatically attracts beautiful young women to me. Nevertheless, I never allowed it to go too far. I always made sure there was plenty of space between Rosie and myself, for I wanted no fables or distortions to reach the undoubtedly large, and possibly bad-tempered, Kevin O'Donnell.

"Oh, George," said Rosie one day, clapping her little hands with glee, "you have no idea what a *darling* my Kevin is, and how happy he makes me. Do you know what he does?"

"I'm not sure," I began, cautiously, naturally expecting indelicate disclosures, "that you ought to—"

She paid no attention. "He has a way of crinkling up his nose and making his eyes twinkle, and smiling brightly, till everything about him looks so happy. It's as though the whole world turns into golden sunshine. Oh, if I only had a photograph of him exactly like that. I've tried to take one, but I never catch him quite right."

I said, "Why not be satisfied with the real thing, my dear?"

"Oh, well!" She hesitated, then said, with the most charming blush, "he's not *always* like that, you know. He's got a *very* difficult job at the airport and sometimes he comes home just worn out and exhausted, and then he becomes just a little touchy, and scowls at me a bit. If I had a photograph of him, as he really is, it would be such a comfort to me. —*Such* a comfort." And her blue eyes misted over with unshed tears.

I must admit that I had the merest trifle of an impulse to tell her of Azazel (that's what I call him, because I'm not going to call him by what he tells me the translation of his real name is) and to explain what he might do for her.

However, I'm unutterably discreet—I haven't the faintest notion how *you* managed to find out about my demon.

Besides, it was easy for me to fight off the impulse for I am a hard-shelled, realistic human being, not given to silly sentiment. I admit I have a semisoft spot in my rugged heart for sweet young women of extraordinary beauty—in a dignified and avuncular manner—mostly. And it occurred to me that, after all, I could oblige her without actually telling her about Azazel. —Not that she would have disbelieved me, of course, for I am a man whose words carry conviction with all but those who, like you, are psychotic.

I referred the matter to Azazel, who was by no means pleased. He said, "You keep asking for abstractions."

I said, "Not at all. I ask for a simple photograph. All you have to do is materialize it."

"Oh, is that all I have to do? If it's that simple, *you* do it. I trust you understand the nature of mass-energy equivalence."

"Just *one* photograph."

"Yes, and with an expression of something you can't even define or describe."

"I've never seen him look at me the way he would look at his wife, naturally. But I have infinite faith in your ability."

I rather expected that a helping of sickening praise would fetch him round. He said, sulkily, "You'll have to take the photograph."

"I couldn't get the proper—"

"You don't have to. I'll take care of that, but it would be much easier if I had a material object on which to focus the abstraction. A photograph, in other words; one of the most inadequate kind, even; the sort I would expect of you. And only *one* copy, of course. I cannot manage more than that and I will not sprain my subjunctival muscle for you or for any other pinheaded being in your world."

Oh, well, he's frequently crotchety. I expect that's simply to establish the importance of his role and impress you with the fact that you must not take him for granted.

I met the O'Donnells the next Sunday, on their way back from Mass. (I lay in wait for them actually.) They were willing to let me snap a picture of them in their Sunday finery. She was delighted and he looked a bit grumpy about it. After that, just as unobtrusively as possible, I took a head shot of Kevin. There was no way I could get him to smile or dimple or crinkle or whatever it was that Rosie found so attractive, but I didn't feel that mattered. I wasn't even sure that the camera was focused correctly. After all, I'm not one of your great photographers.

I then visited a friend of mine who was a photography wiz. He developed both snaps and enlarged the head shot to an eight by eleven.

He did it rather grumpily, muttering something about how busy he was, though I paid no attention to that. After all, what possible value can his foolish activities have in comparison to the important matters that occupied me? I'm always surprised at the number of people who don't understand this.

When he completed the enlargement, however, he changed his attitude entirely. He stared at it and said, in what I can only describe as a completely offensive tone, "Don't tell me you managed to take a photo like this."

"Why not?" I said, and held out my hand for it, but he made no move to give it to me.

"You'll want more copies," he said.

"No, I won't," I said, looking over his shoulder. It was a remarkably clear photograph in brilliant color. Kevin O'Donnell was smiling, though I didn't remember such a smile at the time I snapped it. He seemed good-looking and cheerful, but I was rather indifferent to that. Perhaps a woman might observe more, or a man like my photographer friend—who, as it happened, did not have my firm grasp on masculinity—might do so.

He said, "Just one more—for me."

"No," I said firmly, and took the picture, grasping his wrist to make sure he would not withdraw it. "*And* the negative, please. You can keep the other one—the distance shot."

"I don't want *that*," he said, petulantly, and was looking quite woebegone as I left.

I framed the picture, put it on my mantelpiece, and stepped back to look at it. There was, indeed, a remarkable glow about it. Azazel had done a good job.

What would Rosie's reaction be, I wondered. I phoned her and asked if I could drop by. It turned out that she was going shopping but if I could be there within the hour—

I could, and I was. I had the photo gift-wrapped, and handed it to her without a word.

"My goodness!" she said, even as she cut the string and tore off the wrapping. "What is this? Is there some celebration, or—"

By then she had it out, and her voice died away. Her eyes widened and her breath became shorter and more rapid. Finally, she whispered, "Oh, my!"

She looked up at me. "Did you take this photograph last Sunday?"

I nodded.

"But you caught him exactly. He's a*dor*able. That's *just* the look. Oh, may I *please* keep it?"

"I brought it for you," I said, simply.

She threw her arms about me and kissed me hard on the lips. Unpleasant, of course, for a person like myself who detests sentiment, and I had to wipe my mustache afterward, but I could understand her inability to resist the gesture.

I didn't see Rosie for about a week afterward.

Then I met her outside the butcher shop one afternoon, and it would have been impolite not to offer to carry the shopping bag home for her. Naturally, I wondered whether that would mean another kiss and I decided it would be rude to refuse if the dear little thing insisted. She looked somewhat downcast, however.

"How's the photograph?" I asked, wondering whether, perhaps, it had not worn well.

She cheered up at once. "Perfect! I have it on my record player stand, at an angle such that I can see it when I'm at my chair at the dining room table. His eyes just look at me a little slantwise, so *roguishly* and his nose has *just* the right crinkle. Honestly, you'd swear he was alive. And some of my friends can't keep their eyes off it. I'm thinking I should hide it when they come, or they'll steal it."

"They might steal *him*," I said, jokingly.

The glumness returned. She shook her head and said, "I don't think so."

I tried another tack. "What does Kevin think of the photo?"

"He hasn't said a word. Not a word. He's not a visual person, you know. I wonder if he sees it at all."

"Why don't you point it out and ask him what he thinks?"

She was silent while I trudged along beside her for half a block, carrying that heavy shopping bag and wondering if she'd expect a kiss in addition.

"Actually," she said, suddenly, "he's having a lot of tension at work so it wouldn't be a good time to ask him. He gets home late and hardly talks to me. Well, you know how men are." She tried to put a tinkle in her laughter, but failed.

We had reached her apartment house and I turned the bag over to her. She said, wistfully, "But thank you once again, and over and over, for the photograph."

Off she went. She didn't ask for a kiss, and I was so lost in thought that I didn't notice that fact till I was halfway home and it seemed silly to return merely to keep her from being disappointed.

About ten more days passed, and then she called me one morning. Could I drop in and have lunch with her? I held back and pointed out that it would be indiscreet. What would the neighbors think?

"Oh, that's silly," she said. "You're so incredibly old— I mean, you're such an incredibly old friend, that they couldn't possibly— Besides, I want your advice." It seemed to me she was suppressing a sob as she said that.

Well, one must be a gentleman, so I was in her sunny little apartment at lunch time. She had prepared ham and cheese sandwiches and slivers of apple pie, and there was the photograph on the record player as she had said.

She shook hands with me and made no attempt to kiss me, which would have relieved me were it not for the fact that I was too disturbed at her appearance to feel any relief. She looked absolutely haggard. I ate half a sandwich waiting for her to speak and when she didn't, I was forced to ask outright for the reason, there was such a heavy atmosphere of gloom about her.

I said, "Is it Kevin?" I was sure it was.

She nodded and burst into tears. I patted her hand and wondered if that were enough. I stroked her shoulder abstractedly and she finally said, "I'm afraid he's going to lose his job."

"Surely not. Why?"

"Well, he's so *savage*; even at work, apparently. He hasn't smiled for ages. He hasn't kissed me, or said a kind word, since I don't remember when. He quarrels with *everyone*, and *all* the time. He won't tell me what's wrong, and he gets furious if I ask. A friend of ours, who works at the airport with Kevin, called up yesterday. He says that Kevin is acting so sullen and unhappy at the job that the higher-ups are noticing. I'm *sure* he'll lose his job, but what can I *do?*"

I had been expecting something like this ever since our last meeting, actually, and I knew I would simply have to tell her the truth —damn that Azazel. I cleared my throat. "Rosie—the photograph—"

"Yes, I know," she said, snatching it up and hugging it to her breasts. "It's what keeps me going. This is the *real* Kevin, and I'll always have him, *always*, no matter what happens." She began to sob.

I found it very hard to say what had to be said, but there was no way out. I said, "You don't understand, Rosie. It's the photograph that's the problem. I'm sure of it. All that charm and cheerfulness in the photograph had to come from somewhere. It had to be scraped off Kevin himself. Don't you understand?"

Rosie stopped sobbing. "What are you *talking* about? A photograph is just the light being focused, and film, and things like that."

"Ordinarily, yes, but *this* photograph—" I gave up. I knew Azazel's shortcomings. He couldn't create the magic of the photograph out of nothing, but I wasn't sure I could explain the science of it, the law of conservation of merriment, to Rosie.

"Let me put it this way," I said. "As long as that photograph sits there, Kevin will be unhappy, angry and bad-tempered."

"But it certainly *will* sit there," said Rosie, putting it firmly back in its place, "and I can't see why you're saying such crazy things about the one wonderful object— Here, I'll make some coffee." She flounced off to the kitchen and I could see she was in a most offended state of mind.

I did the only thing I could possibly do. After all, I had been the one who had snapped the photograph. I was responsible—through Azazel—for its arcane properties. I snatched up the frame quickly, carefully removed the backing, then the photo itself. I tore the photograph across into two pieces—four—eight—sixteen, and placed the final scraps of paper in my pocket.

The telephone rang just as I finished, and Rosie bustled into the living room to answer. I restored the backing and set the frame back in place. It sat there, blankly empty.

I heard Rosie's voice squealing with excitement and happiness. "Oh, Kevin," I heard her say, "how wonderful! Oh, I'm so glad! But why didn't you tell me? Don't you *ever* do that again!"

She came back, pretty face glowing. "Do you know what that terrible Kevin did? He's had a kidney stone for nearly three weeks now—seeing a doctor and all—and in terrible, nagging pain, and facing possible surgery—and he wouldn't tell me for fear it would cause me worry. The idiot! No wonder he was so miserable, and it never once occurred to him that his misery made me far more unhappy than knowing about it would have. Honestly! A man shouldn't be allowed out without a keeper."

"But why are you so happy now?"

"Because he passed the stone. He just passed it a little while ago and the first thing he did was to call me, which was very thoughtful of him—and about time. He sounded *so* happy and cheerful. It was just as though my old Kevin had come back to me. It was as though he had become exactly like the photograph that—"

Then, in half a shriek, *"Where's the photograph?"*

I was on my feet, preparing to leave. I was walking rather briskly toward the door, saying, "I destroyed it. That's why he passed the stone. Otherwise—"

"You *destroyed* it? You—"

I was outside the door. I didn't expect gratitude, of course, but what I *was* expecting was murder. I didn't wait for the elevator but hastened down the stairs as quickly as I reasonably could, the sound of her long wail penetrating the door and reaching my ears for a full two flights.

I burned the scraps of the photograph when I got home.

I have never seen her since. From what I have been told, Kevin has been a delightful and loving husband and they are most happy together, but the one letter I received from her—seven pages of small writing, and nearly incoherent—made it plain that she was of the opinion that the kidney stone was the full explanation of Kevin's ill humor, and that its arrival and departure in exact synchronization with the photograph was sheer coincidence.

She made some rather injudicious threats against my life and, quite anticlimactically, against certain portions of my body, making use of words and phrases I would have sworn she had never heard, much less employed.

And I suppose she will never kiss me again, something I find, for some odd reason, disappointing.

Introduction to

SURE THING

Here's another (the fourth and last) of the vignettes in this book. This one, actually, is my favorite among the four, and very nearly my favorite among all the short-shorts I have ever written.

If you don't sprain your diaphragm groaning, and snorting, and making unfavorable noises when you're finished, I shall be vastly disappointed.

19.

SURE THING

As is well known, in this thirtieth century of ours, space travel is fearfully dull and time-consuming. In search of diversion many crew members defy the quarantine restrictions and pick up pets from the various habitable worlds they explore.

Jim Sloane had a rockette, which he called Teddy. It just sat there looking like a rock but sometimes it lifted a lower edge and sucked in powdered sugar. That was all it ate. No one ever saw it move but every once in a while it wasn't quite where people thought it was. There was a theory it moved when no one was looking.

Bob Laverty had a heli-worm he called Dolly. It was green and carried on photosynthesis. Sometimes it moved to get into better light and when it did so it coiled its wormlike body and inched along very slowly like a turning helix.

One day, Jim Sloane challenged Bob Laverty to a race. "My Teddy," he said, "can beat your Dolly."

"Your Teddy," scoffed Laverty, "doesn't move."

"Bet!" said Sloane.

The whole crew got into the act. Even the captain risked half a credit. Everyone bet on Dolly. At least it moved.

Jim Sloane covered it all. He had been saving his salary through three trips and he put every millicredit of it on Teddy.

The race started at one end of the Grand Salon. At the other end, a heap of sugar had been placed for Teddy and a spotlight for

Dolly. Dolly formed a coil at once and began to spiral its way very slowly toward the light. The watching crew cheered it on.

Teddy just sat there without budging.

"Sugar, Teddy. Sugar," said Sloane, pointing. Teddy did not move. It looked more like a rock than ever, but Sloane did not seem concerned.

Finally, when Dolly had spiraled halfway across the salon, Jim Sloane said casually to the rockette, "If you don't get out there, Teddy, I'm going to get a hammer and chip you into pebbles."

That was when people first discovered that rockettes could read minds. That was also when people first discovered that rockettes could teleport.

Sloane had no sooner made his threat when Teddy simply disappeared from his place and reappeared on top of the sugar.

Sloane won, of course, and he counted his winnings slowly and luxuriously.

Laverty said, bitterly, "You *knew* the damn thing could teleport."

"No, I didn't," said Sloane, "but I knew he would win. It was a sure thing."

"How come?"

"It's an old saying everyone knows. Sloane's Teddy wins the race."

Introduction to

TO TELL AT A GLANCE

In February 1976, at the request of the magazine *Seventeen*, I agreed to write a science fiction mystery which would have a bicentennial angle. In response to that request, I wrote "To Tell at a Glance," making use of the same social background I had used in "Good Taste" (which appears in this collection) just a month earlier.

I thought the results were highly satisfactory but I, alas, am not the editor. I don't make the decisions in such cases. *Seventeen* was not satisfied and regretfully handed the story back to me.

I was left in a quandary. I had written what I imagined to be a story that would appeal to young women and I was reluctant to chance the standard science fiction magazines with it. Finally, I cut it in half and sent it to the *Saturday Evening Post*, which took it and ran it in their February 1977 issue.

The cutting, however, induced a deep melancholy in me, for despite *Seventeen*'s decision, I had a great fondness for the original story, and this is my opportunity to present it as it was to begin with.

20.

TO TELL AT A GLANCE

1

Elaine Metro waited with considerable composure. She had been a tourists' guide for two years now—almost—and having to handle men, women, and children from a dozen different worlds (to say nothing of Earth itself), keeping them happy and safe, answering their questions and meeting instant emergencies with instant action, gives one composure.

Either composure or breakdowns, that is, and Elaine had never broken down. She never expected to.

So she sat there and practiced, as she often did, being aware of her surroundings. The calendar gleamed the date at her—February 25, 2076—which meant that she was six days past her twenty-fourth birthday.

The mirror beside it reflected her face, or would if she just stretched a little to one side, and gave it a faint golden glow. That masked the natural paleness of her skin, and gave her blue eyes the illusion of light hazel, and her brown hair, the illusion of a touch of blonde. Rather flattering on the whole, she thought.

The news strip flashed on and off occasionally. There seemed nothing vital going on in the Orbit. A fourteenth colony was under construction, but that was nothing extraordinary.

There was a drought in Africa, back on Earth, but that was nothing extraordinary, either. Imagine a world that had no way of controlling its weather. Primitive!

But Earth was huge! —Like a million real worlds smashed together.

And yet it had so little room. Even Gamma, where Elaine had

been born and where she lived—even Gamma was a little too crowded. Fifteen thousand people and—

The door opened and Janos Tesslen came out. He was the Assembly Chairman and a good one, Elaine thought. At least, she had voted for him.

He said, "Hello, Elaine. Have I kept you waiting long?"

"According to the clock—fourteen minutes, sir."

Janos laughed briefly. He was a large man with eyes that smiled, sometimes, even when his lips didn't. His graying hair was crew cut, quite out of fashion, and it made him look older than the fifty he probably was.

"Come in, Elaine," he said. "Sit down."

She sat down, accepting the use of the first name quite naturally, even though she had never spoken to the chairman before. On a world like Gamma, where nearly everyone knows nearly everyone —why not?

Janos sat back on the swivel chair in his large room—larger than any private room Elaine had ever seen before—and said, "It's interesting that you should tell me you've been waiting fourteen minutes. Shouldn't you have simply said you waited only a little while?"

Elaine said, "I think precision in small things can be important."

"Very good. I'm glad you feel so for it is what I need of you. —Your grandparents came from the United States region of Earth, didn't they?"

"Yes, sir."

"And you've retained your American heritage, I suppose?"

"I've studied Earth history at college. American history was included—but I'm a Gammaperson."

"Yes, of course. So are we all. But you're a particularly special Gammaperson since you're going to save us all."

Elaine frowned slightly. "I beg your pardon—"

"Never mind that now. I've gotten ahead of myself. Since you are of American descent, I am sure you know that the United States was founded in 1776."

"Yes. This year is their Tricentennial."

"And that the United States was founded out of thirteen individual states. Also that there are now thirteen separate and functioning worlds in the Lunar Orbit; eight of them here in the L-5 position trailing the Moon, and five in the L-4 position preceding the Moon."

"Yes, sir. And a fourteenth is under construction in L-4."

"Never mind that. The Orbital World, Nu, was hastened, and the one now under construction, Xi, is being slowed, so that all through 2076 there will be thirteen Orbital Worlds, and not fourteen or twelve. Do you see why?"

Elaine said, dryly, "Superstition?"

Janos said, "Your sharpness cuts, young woman, but I do not bleed. The matter is *not* superstition. It's a matter of taking advantage of sentiment. The United States is the most important single region of the Earth Federation and if they are ready to vote for the establishment of an independent Federation of Orbital Worlds, this will be the year to do it. Combine the Tricentennial with the number thirteen and they couldn't resist, could they?"

"I can see there would be the impulse."

"And independence for us would be useful. The Earth Federation is a conservative force that limits our expansion. Once we are no longer tied to Earth, the Orbital Worlds could adjust to fit each other's economy more efficiently. We could outgrow these narrow limits in the Moon's orbit and head out for the asteroid belt where we would become a major force in human history. Do you agree?"

"Those who know seem to think so."

"Unfortunately there are strong forces on Earth against independence. Then, too, even though almost every Orbital Worlder is for independence, not all of them are for union. —What do you think of the Other Worlders, Elaine? You meet them constantly in your work."

Elaine said, "People are people, sir. But Other Worlders have different ways and I find them—unsympathetic at times."

"Exactly. And they find us—unsympathetic. And rather than have union, many of the people of the Worlds would refuse independence. Elaine, it's up to you to give us union."

Back to that, thought Elaine. She said, "What have I to do with it?"

"Listen," said Janos, gently, "and I'll explain. Those on Earth who are opposed to independence count on the hostility between the Orbital Worlds and do their best to increase it. What if some sabotage takes place here on Gamma, which is the strongest force for union in the Orbit? What if it is serious sabotage and it seems that some particular Other World is responsible. Anti-union sentiment would rise in Gamma and there would then be little likelihood of independence this year. Afterward, with the magic of '76 no longer pulling for us, it might not come for many years."

"We must guard against sabotage, then."

"Right! And so we do. That's where you come in. There are five people coming to Gamma. Ordinary tourists, apparently. There are many more than those five, of course, but it is those particular five, one from each of five different Orbital Worlds, who interest us. One of our agents on Earth—we have them, you know—"

"Everyone knows. Especially Earth, I think."

Janos put his head back as though to focus on her more efficiently. He said, "You have a way of saying these things that I like. —One of our agents got a message to us, badly garbled unfortunately. An Earthman is coming to Gamma, a skilled saboteur, and he's coming as an Orbital Worlder. The message should have told us the particular disguise he would be assuming, but that was the garbled part."

"I suppose you can't check with your agent because he is now dead."

"Unfortunately, he is. We did what we could to interpret the message and what we extracted could apply equally well to five people, at least four of whom are surely respectable Other Worlders and one of whom may be an Earthman in disguise."

"Refuse entry to all five, sir. Or let them in, arrest them all, and examine each thoroughly."

"But if we do that we offend the Other Worlds in question and run the risk of doing just what the sabotage would do."

"Once you locate the saboteur, your actions would have been satisfactorily explained."

"If they believe us. Then, too, the message was sufficiently unclear to leave it a distinct possibility that none of the five is a saboteur; that all are legitimate."

"Well, then, what is it you would have me do, Janos?"

Janos settled back in his chair and for a moment his shrewd eyes once again weighed her quality. He said, "You're a tourist guide and you're used to dealing with Other Worlders and with Earthpeople. What's more, your record shows you to be rather formidably intelligent. I'll see to it that those five are assigned to you for an official tour of Gamma; they can't refuse such a tour without being impolite; so impolite as to give us an excuse to hold them. You'll be with them for several hours, Elaine, and all you have to do is to tell us which one is the imposter—or perhaps that none of them is."

Elaine shook her head. "I don't see how that can be done. Whichever it is must have practiced for the task."

"Undoubtedly. I would suppose he had visited the Other World of which he is pretending to be a citizen; speaks, looks, and acts like one; has the proper papers and so on."

"Well, then?"

"But nothing can be done perfectly, Elaine. Find the imperfection. You have been on the various worlds in question. You know Other Worlders."

"I don't think I can—"

"If you fail," said Janos forcefully, "we may have to fall back on cruder methods and risk offending the Other Worlds. Or we may hang back, if you tell us there is no imposter, or take useless action if you spot the wrong one, and then who knows how much damage the sabotage may do to Gamma—quite apart from the failure of union. You must not fail."

Elaine's lips pressed tightly together. She said, "When does this start?"

"They're coming tomorrow. They'll be landing at Pier Two on the other side of the world." His thumb jerked upward in the almost inevitable gesture, and Elaine's eyes moved briefly upward in just as automatic a response.

It was natural enough. Gamma, like all the Orbital Worlds, was a doughnut-shaped structure, a torus. In Gamma's case, the hollow torus within which the population lived, was somewhat over two miles across. One could travel about three and a half miles along the hollow curve of the torus to reach the other side of the world, or cut upward through one of the three spokes that linked opposite sides of the torus.

Elaine remembered an Earthman laughing once at the Orbital habit of talking about the other side of the "world" in reference to the other half of the torus, but why not? Gamma was surrounded by space, just as Earth was.

Janos interrupted her train of thought. "You'll have to do it, Elaine."

She said, "I'll try to do it, sir."

"And you mustn't fail."

2

Elaine's two-room apartment was in Sector Three, and had the great advantage of being near the Center of Performing Arts. (She had had a youthful dream of being an actress but had lacked the voice for it—yet she still enjoyed being bathed in the atmosphere of the theater.)

At the moment, as she prepared for the rise to Pier Two, she wished earnestly that her voice had been better and her talents more marked—so that she would not now be a tourist's guide with an impossible task facing her.

She was dressed neatly. Her uniform fit snugly and she looked efficient—as she always did. She made an effort to look empty as well. It occurred to her that if she appeared to the five tourists to be too curious, too knowing, she would surely learn nothing. In fact, if she seemed too probing, she might also seem too dangerous to a desperate man. Someone prepared to sabotage a world would not hesitate to deal sternly with one young woman.

She looked up as she stepped outside. There was room within the torus to allow the raising of a forty-story building at the center, but twenty stories was the maximum allowed and ten stories was the average. The upper half of the torus was needed for the feeling of space and open air, to say nothing of allowing the entry of sunlight.

The louvers overhead were still opening at a rate appropriate to the early morning. The large mirror that floated in orbit with Gamma reflected sunlight inward and this bounced off smaller mirrors into the torus. The light bathed the structures on the ground side of the great doughnut and kept the temperatures within perfectly comfortable.

Elaine had never been on Earth, but she had read of it often enough and sometimes the even weather of Gamma made her long for just a little taste of Earth's disordered environment. Snow, especially. It was the one thing she couldn't properly imagine. Rain was something like a showerbath, fog something like steam, cold and hot like turning the proper taps in the steamrooms. —But what was snow like?

She wondered about that as she walked to elevator-bank Three and joined the line. There was not much of a wait since she had managed to avoid the rush hour of shift-change.

The elevator carried her up the spoke through a mile of slowly decreasing gravitation. It was the rapid rotation of the torus, one turn every two minutes, that produced that centrifugal effect that kept everyone and everything pressed against the outer side of the torus all around the doughnut with a force matching Earth-gravity. To everyone wherever he was on Gamma, the outer rim of the torus was "down" and the central hub was "up." And, of course, the other side of the World past the hub was also "up."

As Elaine went up the elevator, the speed with which it turned around the hub of the torus decreased, of course, and so did the centrifugal effect. She was down to less than half her normal weight by the time she passed the hospital area, where lowered gravity was useful in treating cardiac patients, respiratory cases, and so on.

Elaine enjoyed the sensation. She had once, during college, earned tuition money by serving as a nurse's aide and she knew the low-gravity sensation well.

Eventually, the elevator passed through the large spherical hub at the center of the torus, its movement carefully controlled by the central computer so that no elevator collided with any other as all converged at the hub in careful alternation. At the hub, the centrifugal effect was just about zero and, for the few minutes it took to pass through, she felt weightless. This was where Gamma's power station was located and (Elaine thought somberly) where the sabotage might take place.

The elevator passed through the hub and then moved along the spoke that connected with the other side of the world. The centrifugal effect was increasing again, and Elaine began to get the sensation of standing on her head. With the lack of effort born of long practice, she quietly inverted herself as, one by one, did the other passengers on the elevator. All were now standing on what had been the elevator ceiling some minutes before.

The sensation was that of moving down now, and of increasing gravitational pull. And then, when the pull had reached maximum and she was feeling (just a little regretfully) as heavy as she usually did, she was on the other side. The door opened and she stepped out. The other side of the world (she looked up briefly) was now the place where she lived.

3

Avoiding the rush hour, Elaine was late, which turned out to be troublesome. The other three guides, two men and a woman, were already there and clustered about the daily work sheet.

The woman, Mikki Burdot, saw her first and said, rather waspishly, "There she is."

Elaine's eyebrows lifted. "Naturally. I work here."

Mikki said, "It doesn't seem as though you do." She walked over on the cork-bottom shoes that added two inches to her diminutive height. She pushed her regulation cap off her forehead. That might be described as a nervous habit, but it did reveal her rich mahogany hair.

She went on. "You've got five people there. Exactly five. How's that for hard work."

Elaine reached for the work-sheet copies. "Five? That's all?"

"Five! I've got fourteen. Hannes has ten and Robaire has twelve. Fair division? I think not."

"It could be," said Elaine, "that they don't trust my work and are getting ready to relieve me of my duties."

"Phasing you out?" said Robaire. A dimple appeared on either cheek when he smiled, so he smiled often. "Exactly what I said. Then you'll be stony broke, with no chance of any other position, and you'll have to marry me. Right?"

Elaine said, "I've got you in mind, Robaire. Constantly! Just as soon as I'm stony broke. —Have you taken this up with Benjo Strammer? He's the one in charge of the work sheets."

"Yes, I did," said Mikki, "and he just said that's the way it was. Old—" The last word was lost in a mutter.

Elaine said, "All right. Look. Robaire, your twelve are mostly from Alpha, which means they'll be interested in our sports facilities, and that's your baby, right? Hannes has a lot from Mu, and they're all first generation and probably nervous about anything new, and we all know how fatherly he is."

"Paternal is my middle name," said Hannes, crossing his arms over his rather narrow chest.

"And Mikki, you've got them from Zeta, and most of the Zetans hate our guts, so they're going to need someone who looks little and helpless and very pretty. No one can hate you."

"The women can," said Mikki, softening.

"Yes, but the tourists you have are mostly men. Right? As for myself, I've got five, but they're from five different worlds. Each one is different. Each one will want to concentrate on something else, and I suspect each one is a VIP and will want special treatment and be impossible to please." She sat back and allowed a look of melancholy to pass over her face. "If anyone wants to change—"

"Not me," said Hannes. "My little Muans need me."

"And my Alphans," said Robaire, "must have someone who knows a football from a golf club."

Mikki said, "I never said I wanted to change. I just wish they could even it up more."

Elaine nodded and went to her own small office, no larger than sufficed to hold a small desk and, this time, Benjo Strammer. He was waiting for her. His hair was richly white and wavy, and he looked at her quizzically out of eyes nested in crow's-feet. He said, "You handled that very well, Elaine."

She said, "I take it you listened, Benjo."

"I had to. I was a little upset. That list came down to me that way. I didn't prepare it."

"Then we have to take it as given. Nothing else to do."

Benjo said, "But why, Elaine?"

"Why what?"

"Why did they make up the list for me?"

"Didn't they tell you, Benjo?"

Benjo shook his head and said, "No, they didn't."

"I guess they didn't want you to know, then."

"All right, but do *you* know?"

"If you're not supposed to know, you shouldn't even ask. Look, whatever it is, it's going to be touchy. Is the ship on time?"

"It's docking now."

"All right, then. Could you arrange to have my five tourists separated out as quietly as possible and brought in before the rest? I think I had better see them before we get started; try to get an estimate as to how I am supposed to handle this. You know, what I said to the others was probably right. I think they're VIPs and I don't want to goof it up."

Benjo looked sour. "I think it would be a lot better, Elaine, if they would cut me in on whatever's going on. If they keep me in the dark, then it's not my fault if I slip up."

"If it were up to me, Benjo, you could have it. Believe me when I tell you I don't want to touch this at all, whatever it is. Do you want it?"

"It came down for you specifically, didn't it? It's your thing. And if you want to see these people, you'd better use my office. This one isn't large enough. As for me, once they come in, I'll take a walk around the World."

A World walk was something he did every once in a while. It kept him in shape, he said. Elaine looked down briefly at her own flat abdomen and wondered if she could rely on that as a fact of nature for much longer.

4

Elaine sat on the corner of Benjo's desk, the corner nearest the door, with her arms crossed over her chest and one leg swinging. She had firmly refused to consider the problem the night before, feeling (quite rightly, she was sure) that if she did that she would spend most of the night wakeful and tense and be dim-witted today.

Now, however, there was no excuse to put it off further.

Problem: Five people, each from a different World. One of them might be (just *might* be) an Earthman pretending to be an Orbital Worlder. Assuming the Earthman knew his job, would there be any way he could give himself away? Was there something about the Orbital Worlds to which, even with practice, he could not adapt?

The trouble was, Elaine thought impatiently, that the Orbital Worlds had deliberately mimicked Earth conditions. Each revolved at such a speed as to produce Earth-normal gravities in the torus. Any Earthman would feel completely at home in this respect.

To be sure, gravity would drop off as one mounted the spokes, and an Earthman might not be able to avoid clumsiness there. The trouble was that not very many Orbital Worlders spent much time in the spokes, and most of them would be equally clumsy.

The typical Orbital-World atmosphere had the same pressure of oxygen that the Earth atmosphere had, but much less nitrogen so that the Other-World atmosphere was only half as dense as that of the Earth. That made little difference, though. Earthmen adapted to it almost at once. And why not? Earth had worse atmospheres than that—less pressure *and* less oxygen—on its mountains.

Orbital Worlds were much smaller than Earth, but what difference would that make? The vistas weren't as long in all directions as on Earth, and the horizon effect was quite different, but surely an Earthman could get used to that, too. The imposter, if there was one, would surely have lived on an Orbital World long enough to have become used to the effect.

To be sure, he might not know his way about Gamma, unless he had spent some time on Gamma. But then, people from the Other Worlds would not necessarily know *their* way about Gamma, either. Or, if the imposter *had* spent time on Gamma, might he know *too* much about it. No, there was nothing to say that any Other Worlder might not have read about Gamma before coming here for a visit. It might even be thought of as the natural thing to do.

Well, then, what about the Worlds they were supposed to come from? People from a particular Orbital World spoke in a particular way, had certain social and individual attitudes. Could the Earthman mimic these perfectly, or could he be expected to give himself away no matter how much he had practiced?

Elaine looked down at the desk and turned the work sheet so she could see the items.

Five Worlds. In order of age they were Delta, Epsilon, Theta, Iota, and Kappa. She had visited each one of them, and had read copiously about each one of them, in the line of duty. You can't understand tourists without understanding the societies that had molded them—and a guide had to understand tourists.

Delta was a rather dull World of work-bound people who spoke their language in a singsong way and did the same when they spoke the Gamman dialect. They tended to be large and fair in complexion, but that was only a tendency. There were tall people on each of the worlds, and short, and fair, and dark. You couldn't judge by physical appearance.

Epsilon was the most crowded of the Worlds, with a smaller-sized people, by and large, and a stronger infusion of descendants of Earth's East Asians than was true for most of the Worlds.

Theta had five of the six sections devoted to agriculture, instead of the usual three. It was the only one of the Orbital Worlds to go in heavily for cattle as opposed to smaller livestock. As it happened, of the five symphonies composed by Orbital-World musicians that were now part of the general repertoire of Earthly orchestras, three had been by Thetans.

Elaine stopped to think about that a moment. No, one couldn't make the easy generalization that Thetans were musical. Ninety-five of them could be musically illiterate and if the Thetan who was in the group should turn out to be so, that would prove nothing.

Iota was the great energy exporter of the Orbital Worlds. Each of the Worlds had solar energy as its prime source. Each had a large power station—considerably larger than the colony itself—absorbing sunlight and converting it to microwaves, some of which went to the World's own global hub, and some of which, if surplus there was, went to Earth. Iota's was the largest power station and it had the best facilities for beaming microwaves to Earth. It was quite understandable that Earth was presently more concerned with Iota than with any of the other twelve Orbital Worlds.

But that meant that Iota was the most pro-Earth of the Worlds, the least independence- and union-minded. Would an Iotan not be the most likely to cooperate with an Earth agent? On the other hand, might an Earth agent not be least likely to assume an Iotan disguise, since that would be most suspect?

How could she tell, she thought impatiently.

And what about Kappa, leisure-centered, culture-riddled? It was the most attractive of the Worlds she herself had visited. It meant she would have to keep her sharpest eye on the Kappan, since her own prejudices were involved there.

How could one tell a Kappan from a pseudo-Kappan? Or a Thetan from a pseudo-Thetan? Or any variety from a fake variety?

The trouble was that Earth was so various in its population types that any of the Orbital Worlders would be easily imitated by some particular Earthman or other.

But consider this— The agent, whoever he was, would have to be against independence, and against the union of the Orbital Worlds. Would he have to avoid showing this and be ostentatiously anti-Earth? Or would he realize that that sort of ostentation would in itself be suspicious. Or, considering that the agent did not know anyone was looking for him (or did he?), the question might not arise in either direction.

Would it be safer to try for something more subtle? If the independence and union forces were relying on the emotional values of the Tricentennial, could the conversation be maneuvered in that direction? Would the agent show impatience at the mention of 2076? Would he show anti-American sentiment?

But then might not some Orbital Worlders have such feelings of their own accord, without there being any need to have them Earthmen in disguise?

Elaine felt her mind moving into smaller and smaller circles, uselessly. What could she use as a criterion to tell the true from the false? Did any criteria exist?

Yet Janos had said: You mustn't fail.

She was about to surrender to the luxury of despair, when Benjo put his head inside the door and said, "Your tourists are here. Hope it goes well—and good-bye."

Elaine wondered if the good-bye might not turn out to have a particularly dreadful connotation. She composed her face as the tourists came to the door, and tried to compose her thoughts.

5

They were lined up before her, and Elaine spoke slowly and, she hoped, ingratiatingly.

"My name," she said, "is Elaine. If you would be more comfortable with my family name, it is Metro. No titles are in use on

Gamma, and the use of first names is common, but you may use any naming system you find convenient."

The Deltan seemed already disapproving. He was a tall man and broad-shouldered. He was made taller by a blockish hat he did not remove and by a long, slate-gray blouse that he wore down to mid-thigh. His heavy boots clumped when he walked and his bony, large-knuckled hands were lightly clenched.

He said, harshly, in a singsong tone, "How old are you?"

His name, Elaine knew from the chart, was Sando Sanssen, and from her knowledge of Deltan ways, she knew she would have to address him by his last name. "I am twenty-four years old, Mr. Sanssen."

"Do you know enough about this World, at your age, to be of use to us?"

His bluntness was Deltan—or was it overdone Deltan? Surely she had done nothing to warrant the bite.

She smiled and said brightly, "I hope I know enough. I am quite experienced at my work. In fact, my government is reposing considerable confidence in me, since they expect me to see to it that each of you sees all he can of whatever aspect of life on Gamma you wish to explore."

Ravon Jee Andor of Kappa caught her eye. He was of medium height, and his hair was very carefully shaped. It was blonder than it should have been by nature (Elaine was sure of this for it did not go with his dark eyes and complexion) and he was dressed with excessive ornamentation. He exuded a slightly pungent perfume that Elaine found attractive. (All that was Kappan, but was it too Kappan?)

He said with broad, somewhat sustained vowels, "If you generously wish to meet our desires, then you yourself, I think, would represent a Gamman life-aspect worthy of further study."

It was meant to be complimentary in the ornate Kappan fashion, Elaine was sure. She used his first two names as Kappan custom required and answered quite Kappan-fashion, "I am desolated, Ravon Jee, that this is, at the moment, impossible. Perhaps time will offer an opportunity."

"Get on with it, girl!" grunted Medjim Nabellan of Theta. Her richly black complexion (most Thetans, not all, were Blacks) was topped by crisp, gray curls, for the most part hidden under a broad-brimmed hat held to her chin by an elastic. Her clothes were gayly colored in broad stripes and she rolled her r's back in her throat. "Get on with it and don't waste your time humoring Kappan trash."

The Kappan bowed sardonically and did not lose his smile.

Elaine paused a moment. There was no reason the agent might not be a woman or a Black or both, and impatience at getting started might well be the primary and unconcealable emotion of anyone whose mission was to sabotage a world and who saw danger in any delay.

"I think it's silly to have a group with everyone from a different world," said Yve Abdaraman of Iota—the other woman of the group—in a drawl so pronounced as to make her sound sleepy. She was rather young, rather small, rather attractive in a light brown way (and she might have been well aware of this, for her costume was all in blending shades of brown). "If we're going to quarrel and snarl at each other, this is all going to be very unpleasant."

"I hope we *don't* quarrel and snarl, Yve," said Elaine (Iotans used first names as Gammans did), "and as soon as you each let me know what you particularly want to see—"

"Let's get started," said the fifth member, Wu Ky-shee of Epsilon, "and we can tell you on the way or we will waste time." He was plump and short, and his eyes had more than a little of the East Asian narrowing. He wore a skirtlike affair that reached nearly to the ground and he talked with the trace of a lisp.

—And he was another impatient one, Elaine thought.

Elaine said, "Since we are in one of the residential sections, then, we might as well walk through the streets to the university as a start. There we will find some interesting examples of Gamman architectural design—"

She herded them politely out ahead of her, circling them to take the lead, while her mind moved uselessly back and forth. Each one of them seemed worthy of suspicion, but not one of them seemed worthy enough.

If there were only something that held true for all the Orbital Worlds, and not for Earth—something so subtle and pervasive that an Earth-imposter could not guard against it and would give himself away— But what could such a thing be? Size? Something else?

She had to concentrate on her job. "This is the central building of Gamma University, built four years ago, with an illusion of curve just great enough to—" She talked on mechanically, but her mind, working in another direction, seized on the thought of the illusion of curve and went on from there—

6

They had walked leisurely past the pleasant homes of the section, each with their varying designs and their green lawns, all marked off ornamentally by light fencing material designed to produce differentiation rather than barrier. This section lacked the apartment house clusters that were to be found in the other two residential sections.

Elaine said, "We are coming to the airlock that separates this from the agricultural sector ahead."

"You keep the airlocks open, I see," said Sanssen. "Isn't that slipshod?" His pronunciation of the last word was so odd by Gamma standards, Elaine barely caught it. (Perfect Deltan, as nearly as she could tell.)

She said, "Not really. It is thoroughly automated. Any vibration associated with meteoric strike or internal explosion, any small loss in air pressure, will cause all airlocks to close, sealing off the six sectors, each from each. And, of course, they close during the night to keep the daylight of the agricultural sections from filtering into the residential areas."

"What happens," asked Ravon Jee, smiling, "if the meteor or whatever strikes the airlock machinery?"

"That is quite unlikely to happen. But if it does, it would not be fatal. All vital machinery exists in two complete sets widely separated, each one of which is capable of supplying the needs of the whole World."

She paused to make sure all her charges had managed the transition. It was just a matter of going up a flight of steps and down another; six up and six down, but the steps stretched the width of the torus and curved gently. Earthmen frequently found it amusing to walk the width of one step so they could find themselves slanting somewhat with respect to others in their party.

But though she watched the feet of all five, none seemed to hesitate or turn to one side in momentary curiosity.

Elaine sighed inaudibly. The Earthman, whichever he was, was well-schooled—or there was no Earthman.

7

Ravon Jee Andor had been at her elbow all through the agricultural sector, showing no interest in any of it. Now, as they entered the Cycling Center, he drew back, and looked unhappy.

"I don't have to get into *that*, do I? Animal wastes aren't my idea of delightful scenery."

Elaine kept the alertness out of her eyes as much as she could. She said, "You recycle wastes on Kappa, surely." (No Earthman was ever willing to visit the Center.)

"Not in my presence," said Ravon Jee. "Actually, I know nothing about all this engineering and statistics. —Come, dear girl, I'll wait out here. Let that Deltan go, he has the boots for it, and that farmwoman from Theta and the rest."

Elaine shook her head. "I appreciate your feelings but I can't leave you. I'm afraid my government would disapprove. Do come. I'll hold your hand, see?"

It was the kind of flirtatious gesture that no Kappan could refuse with honor. Ravon Jee, looking terribly unhappy, murmured, "In that case, lovely one, I would wade through muck, knee-high." (Elaine didn't think he would, though.)

She kept close to him as they passed through the antiseptic corridors. Most of the cycling process was hidden from view and was handled in completely automated fashion. Despite the manner in which Ravon Jee screwed up his face, there was only a faintly perceptible odor.

Sanssen looked at everything keenly, his large hands clasped behind his back. Wu Ky-shee, expressionless, took notes and Elaine managed to pass behind him and see what he was writing. It was in Epsilonian and even the script was unreadable to her.

Ravon Jee, still holding her hand, said, "I presume you will tell me that all this is essential."

"So it is," she said, "even, on a very large scale, on Earth."

He did not respond to the last comment. "A Kappan gentleman," he said, "remains unaware of such things."

She said, "What do you do on Kappa?"

"I'm a drama critic. I'm here to review the Gamman stage for my home paper."

"Oh, will you be visiting Earth for the dramatic festival in connection with the Tricentennial?" (She wondered if there were such a festival.)

"The what, my dear?" He looked blank.

"The American Tricentennial."

He said vaguely, "I don't know— Where is your theater district located?"

(Was his vagueness overdone? Did he really know nothing at all about the Tricentennial?)

She said, "It's on Section Four, the other side of the World." She started to make the inevitable gesture, but did not.

He looked up very briefly, as one always did, and said despondently, "Well, we'll get there eventually, I suppose."

Interesting, thought Elaine. Would that be the key?

                                    8

Medjim Nabellan said to her brusquely, "See here, guide, we are moving out of this farming district and I have seen no cattle."

"We have some, but not in this sector. We find cattle uneconomic. Chickens and rabbits can produce more protein more quickly."

"Bunk! You don't know how to do it properly. Your animal husbandry methods are well behind the times."

Elaine said, smoothly, "I'm sure our Bureau of Agriculture would be delighted to hear from you."

"I hope so. That's precisely why I am here and now that I have seen what you are doing here, any further touring is a waste of my time. I would like to go directly to the Bureau."

Elaine said, "I'm afraid I will be in trouble if you insist on leaving the party. My government will feel I have offended you."

"Nuts," said Nabellan grimly, her wide nose wrinkling. "Where can I find the Bureau?"

"On the other side of the world," said Elaine. This time she gestured firmly and Nabellan looked up. "If you leave now, the party may break up altogether. Please stay."

Medjim Nabellan said something under her breath but she made no further move to break away.

Elaine said in her pleasant guide's voice, "The agricultural sectors are bathed in sunlight at all times, but in the three residential sections, of course, it is sixteen hours light and eight hours darkness in alteration.

Wu Ky-shee said, "Do all Gammans sleep in unison?"

"No, of course not. They sleep when they please. In fact, some must work through the dark period."

"Why not allow each dwelling place to control its own sunlight, then? Useless conformity!" He made further notations in his book.

Yve Abdaraman said in her thin and very clear soprano voice, "Since Epsilon is the only World without standard day-night reflection, it must be you who are out of step. A night-interval reduces energy influx and keeps the temperature comfortable."

"Not at all," said Wu Ky-shee, raising his eyebrows. "If you imply Epsilon is hot, you are wrong. This day-night alteration is only a meaningless heritage from Earth."

Elaine tingled. A slur on Earth? She said, brightly, "I don't think we should ignore our Earthly heritage. The Tricentennial is here this year and a heritage of free—" She faded out, as neither reacted. Yve cast a look of impatience at her and then turned to the Epsilonian. "I have been on Epsilon," she said, "and found it hot."

"You may have found it too flexible and individual for your taste," returned Wu Ky-shee, stiffly.

Elaine said, "Please, won't you two follow me now? We have a long way to go to get to the other side of the World." She gestured, and automatically they responded. She went on, "We must catch up with the others."

Yve said, as all three hastened their steps, "The Cycling Center must have a computerized component. It would be a great help for me and my mission here if I could have access to that."

"I'm sure that can be arranged," said Elaine. "I believe our government is very open here."

(Her *mission*? Was that an incredible oversight? Or pure innocence? She was barely five feet tall—but would height prevent her from—)

Sando Sanssen was looking impatiently about. "You, Miss Metro, how much longer?"

"We'll be through soon, Mr. Sanssen. Is there anything you particularly want to see."

"The power station. I'm an electrical engineer, woman, and I am not interested in grainfields and fish pools."

"I'm not sure," said Elaine, soothingly, "if the hub is open to tourists—"

"I am not a tourist," said Sanssen, heavily. "I am an official of my government."

"Yes, of course. We are on our way up a spoke to visit a hospital area. Gamma is proud of its medical facilities and we would very much like for you to see it. While there, I will inquire for permission to enter the hub."

Sanssen nodded, but didn't look much mollified.

9

There was a hospital area in each spoke, six altogether. This one was higher up the spoke than the others since it dealt with low-gravity biological research.

All five of the tourists seemed at ease at low gravity, which was now little more than quarter-normal. Medjim Nabellan stumbled once but that seemed mere circumstance. Sanssen looked outraged at moving higher than he expected at one point, and came down with a clatter, but did not fall. But then, even Elaine sometimes forgot and took a giant step.

"I think you'll all be interested," she said, "in the low-gravity research we are doing here. That's one line of investigation that can't be carried on back on Earth at all, and while all the Orbital Worlds are active in this field, none has gone as far as Gamma. We are entering the laboratories now and there will be research assistants to describe the research and answer your questions. —Oh, Mr. Sanssen."

"Yes?"

"I just wanted to point out to you that we are only four hundred

meters from the hub. Now, I will try to get you an entry permit"—
they were alone now, the others having vanished into the hospital
area—"at Government Center, which is, of course, at the other side
of the World."

She gestured—and her heart beat high at his response. That *had*
to be it.

But there was no way in which she could keep her new knowledge from flooding her eyes and Sanssen saw it—and probably realized the mistake he had made. It was as if he suddenly dropped
his role.

"One moment, girl," he said, with no trace whatever of his Deltan accent. He moved toward her in a rush.

She evaded him like a matador side-slipping a bull with minimum motion. She couldn't, somehow, unblock her throat to call for
help. —Would he dare kill her? How would he explain her body?
Or must nothing stand in the way of his mission? Would he kill her
and then rush on to do what had to be done?

He turned and lunged, but his foot slipped on ground made far
more slippery than usual by low gravity. Elaine turned on tiptoe
and sidled past him in a low-gravity maneuver with which she was
well acquainted. He missed by a greater margin this time.

He stopped, turned, edged slowly between her and the door,
threw off his hat and, tearing open the static seam that held his
blouse together, threw that off, too. He was hard-muscled and
strong and his face was grim. He had a matter of minutes to get rid
of her before someone came, and he looked as though he were
ready.

She could call out now but, for the moment, she dared not waste
the breath for it. She kept her eyes on him as she swayed this way
and that, playing him carefully. He was being equally careful, no
longer disregarding the low gravity.

He moved forward in small steps, but she drifted away, watching, watching. She shifted direction and moved forward in a longer
glide, then whirled behind him and pushed. He flailed forward but
caught himself and was between her and the door again.

And then she tried to get to the door for one minute longer than
was safe, for his hand snaked out and seized her arm.

For a moment, they stood in tense stillness, and then his lips
stretched into a merciless smile and he drew her toward him. She

called out hoarsely and kicked at him, but he blocked that neatly with his hip. She wrenched desperately, but did not pull loose.

—And then a dark arm passed around the Earthman's throat, clamping down on his windpipe and yanking him erect. Elaine was loose.

"Thank you," she whispered.

Medjim Nabellan's expression was darker than her skin. "Has this Deltan animal been—"

"He's not a Deltan," said Elaine, gasping heavily now that it was over. She looked at the faces crowding around and said, "Please call the police, and please don't let go, Nabellan."

"No fear," said Nabellan, "unless someone wants to take over for a moment. Shall I break his neck for you?" She looked quite capable of it and the Earthman's eyes bulged out of his face.

"No, please," said Elaine. "I think he's needed alive."

10

She was back in Janos' office, two days after the earlier session with him.

He was utterly jovial now, as he said, "It couldn't have been better, Elaine. He was the man all right. Delta denies all knowledge of him, and whether that is true or not, they are forced to plump heavily for union now. We have played up Medjim Nabellan's part and Theta will strengthen its own pro-union stand. The Earth government is embarrassed and the American region's Tricentennial stand is now in an excellent position. While there are always unpredictables and unforeseens, I really think we will have independence and union before the magic year of 2076 is over. —But how did you do it, Elaine? How did he give himself away?"

Elaine said, "I had to think of something an Earthman would forget on an Orbital World even though the World was designed as like Earth as possible. At one point I began thinking of curves. Earth is a large World and its people live on an outside surface that curves down very gently. On the Orbital Worlds the people live on an *inside* surface that curves *upward*.

"On Earth, the 'other side of the World' is downward, far downward. In speaking of it, I imagine Earthmen point downward or make no gesture at all. They certainly don't point upward. On an Orbital World 'the other side of the World' is upward, and Other Worlders always point upward and look upward when they speak of it. You do, I do, we all do.

"So I tried it. I would mention the other side of the World to each one and point *downward* as I did so. It didn't matter that I did. Four of them looked upward anyway, quite automatically. It was just a brief glance in each case, but I could tell by that glance they were Orbital Worlders. When I tried it on Sanssen, his eyes followed my finger. He looked *down* and I knew he was an Earthman. He recovered at once but it was too late. I could tell at a glance, you see."

Janos nodded his head. "I would not have been that resourceful myself, Elaine. This will be worthwhile for you; you will be suitably rewarded."

Elaine said, "Thank you—but independence and union are the best rewards for all of us, aren't they?"

Introduction to

THE WINDS OF CHANGE

I have edited two anthologies along with Alice Laurance (a hard-working, intelligent, and good-looking woman, with whom it is a pleasure to work). The first was a mystery anthology, the second a science fiction anthology, and in both cases, the stories that were included were originals written for the volumes in question. What's more, in each case, the identity of the author was hidden and the reader was asked to guess that identity, if he cared to.

I wrote one of the stories in the science fiction anthology and that story was "The Winds of Change." I wonder, though, if I managed to hide my identity. A list of the contributors was placed at the beginning of the book, and I imagine anyone searching for an "Asimovian" story could scarcely fail to pick this one out of the lot.

But that doesn't matter. I honestly feel that in some ways this story (which the alphabet has fortunately brought to the very end of the story list) is the strongest in the book. That's why I'm using it for the title of the collection as a whole, aside from the fact I like the title. In fact, I consider the ending so strong that I'm going to forgo the "final word" I would ordinarily put in. I want no anticlimactic addition to the last page of this book as it now stands. (And don't look at it now! Read the story!)

21.

THE WINDS OF CHANGE

J onas Dinsmore walked into the President's Room of the Faculty Club in a manner completely characteristic of himself, as though conscious of being in a place in which he belonged but in which he was not accepted. The belonging showed in the sureness of his stride and the casual noise of his feet as he walked. The nonacceptance lay in his quick look from side to side as he entered, a quick summing-up of the enemies present.

He was an associate professor of physics and he was not liked.

There were two others in the room, and Dinsmore might well have considered them enemies without being thought paranoid for doing so.

One was Horatio Adams, the aging chairman of the department who, without ever having done any single thing that was remarkable, had yet accumulated a vast respect for the numerous unremarkable but perfectly correct things he had done. The other was Carl Muller, whose work on Grand Unified Field Theory had put him in line for the Nobel Prize (he thought probably) and the presidency of the university (he thought certainly).

It was hard to say which prospect Dinsmore found more distasteful. It was quite fair to say he detested Muller.

Dinsmore seated himself at one corner of the couch, which was old, slippery and chilly. The two comfortable armchairs were taken by the others. Dinsmore smiled.

He frequently smiled, though his face never seemed either friendly or pleased as a result. Though there was nothing in the smile that was not the normal drawing back of the corners of the mouth, it invariably had a chilling effect on those at whom he aimed the gesture. His round face, his sparse but carefully combed hair, his full lips would all have taken on joviality with such a smile, or should have—but didn't.

Adams stirred with what seemed to be a momentary spasm of irritation crossing his long, New Englandish face. Muller, his hair nearly black, and his eyes an incongruous blue, seemed impassive.

Dinsmore said, "I intrude, gentlemen, I know. Yet I have no choice. I have been asked by the Board of Trustees to be present. It may seem to you to be a cruel action, perhaps. I am sure you expect, Muller, that at any moment a communication will be received from the Trustees to the effect that you have been named for the presidency. It would seem proper that the renowned Professor Adams, your mentor and patron, should know of it. But why, Muller, should they reserve a similar privilege for me, your humble and ever failing rival?

"I suspect, in fact, that your first act as president, Muller, would be to inform me that it would be in all ways better if I would seek another position elsewhere since my appointment will not be renewed past this academic year. It might be convenient to have me on the spot in order that there be no delay. It would be unkind, but efficient.

"You look troubled, both of you. I may be unjust. My instant dismissal may not be in your mind; you may have been willing to wait till tomorrow. Can it be that it is the Trustees who would rather be quick and who would rather have me on the spot? It doesn't matter. Either way it would seem that you are in and I am out. And perhaps that seems just. The respected head of a great department approaching the evening of his career, with his brilliant protégé, whose grasp of concept and whose handling of mathematics is unparalleled, are ready for the laurels; while I, without respect or honor—

"Since this is so, it is kind of you to let me talk without interrupting. I have a feeling that the message we wait for may not arrive for some minutes, for an hour, perhaps. A presentiment. The Trustees themselves would not be averse to building suspense. This is their moment in the sun, their fleeting time of glory. And since the time must be passed, I am willing to speak.

"Some, before execution, are granted a last meal, some a last cigarette; I, a last few words. You needn't listen, I suppose, or even bother to look interested.

"—Thank you. The look of resignation, Professor Adams, I will accept as agreement. Professor Muller's slight smile, let us say of contempt, will also do.

"You will not blame me, I know, for wishing the situation were changed. In what way? A good question. I would not wish to change my character and personality. It may be unsatisfactory, but it is mine. Nor would I change the politic efficiency of Adams or the brilliance of Muller, for what would such a change do but make them no longer Adams and Muller? I would have them be they, and yet—have the results different. If one could go back in time, what small change then might produce a large and desirable change now?

"That's what's needed. Time-travel!

"Ah, *that* grinds a reaction out of you, Muller. That was the clear beginning of a snort. Time-travel! Ridiculous! Impossible!

"Not only impossible in the sense that the state of the art is inadequate for the purpose, but in the greater sense that it will be forever inadequate. Time-travel, in the sense of going backward to change reality, is not only technologically impossible now, but it is theoretically impossible altogether.

"Odd you should think so, Muller, because your theories, those very analyses which have brought the four forces, even gravitation, measurably close to inclusion under the umbrella of a single set of relationships, make time-travel no longer theoretically impossible.

"No, don't rise to protest. Keep your seat, Muller, and relax. For you it is impossible, I'm sure. For most people it would be. Perhaps for almost everyone. But there might be exceptions and it just might be that I'm one of them. Why myself? Who knows? I don't claim to be brighter than either of you, but what has that to do with it?

"Let us argue by analogy. Consider— Tens of thousands of years ago, human beings, little by little, either as a mass endeavor or through the agency of a few brilliant individuals, learned to communicate. Speech was invented and delicate modulations of sounds were invested with abstract meaning.

"For thousands of years, every normal human being has been able to communicate, but how many have been able to tell a story

superlatively well? Shakespeare, Tolstoy, Dickens, Hugo—a handful compared to all the human beings who have lived—can use
those modulated sounds to wrench at heartstrings and reach for
sublimity. Yet they use the same sounds that all of us use.

"I am prepared to admit that Muller's IQ, for instance, is higher
than that of Shakespeare or Tolstoy. Muller's knowledge of language must be as good as that of any writer alive; his understanding of meaning as great. Yet Muller could not put words together and achieve the effect that Shakespeare could. Muller
himself wouldn't deny it for a moment, I'm sure. What then is it,
that Shakespeare and Tolstoy can do that Muller or Adams or I
cannot; what wisdom do they have that we cannot penetrate? You
don't know and I don't know. What is worse, *they* didn't know.
Shakespeare could in no manner have instructed you—or anyone—
how to write as he did. He didn't know how—he merely could.

"Next consider the consciousness of time. As far as we can guess,
only human beings of all life forms can grasp the significance of
time. All other species live in the present only; might have vague
memories; might have dim and limited forethought—but surely
only human beings truly understand the past, present and future
and can speculate on its meaning and significance, can wonder
about the flow of time, of how it carries us along with it, and of
how that flow might be altered.

"When did this happen? How did it come about? Who was the
first human being, or hominid, that suddenly grasped the manner
in which the river of time carried him from the dim past into the
dim future, and wondered if it might be dammed or diverted?

"The flow is not invariant. Time races for us at times; hours van-
ish in what seem like minutes—and lag unconscionably at other
times. In dream states, in trances, in drug experiences, time alters
its properties.

"You seem about to comment, Adams. Don't bother. You are
going to say that those alterations are purely psychological. I know
it, but what else is there but the psychological?

"Is there *physical* time? If so, what *is* physical time? Surely, it is
whatever we choose to make it. *We* design the instruments. *We* interpret the measurements. *We* create the theories and then interpret those. And from absolute, we have changed time and made it

the creature of the speed of light and decided that simultaneity is indefinable.

"From your theory, Muller, we know that time is altogether subjective. In theory, someone understanding the nature of the flow of time can, given enough talent, move with or against the flow independently; or stand still in it. It is analogous to the manner in which, given the symbols of communication, someone, given enough talent, can write *King Lear*. Given enough talent.

"What if I had enough talent? What if I could be the Shakespeare of the time-flow? Come, let us amuse ourselves. At any moment, the message from the Board of Trustees will arrive and I will have to stop. Until it does, however, allow me to push along with my chatter. It serves its turn. Come, I doubt that you are aware that fifteen minutes has passed since I began talking.

"Think, then— If I could make use of Muller's theory and find within myself the odd ability to take advantage of it as Homer did of words, what would I do with my gift? I might wander back through time, perhaps, wraith-like, observing from without all the pattern of time and events, in order to reach in at one place or another and make a change.

"Oh, yes, I would be outside the time-stream as I travel. Your theory, Muller, properly interpreted, does not insist that, in moving backward in time, or forward, one must move through the thick of the flow, stumbling across events and knocking them down in passage. That would indeed be theoretically impossible. To remain *outside* is where the possibility comes in; and to slip in and out at will is where the talent comes in.

"Suppose, then, I did this; that I slipped in and made a change. That one change would breed another—which would breed another— Time would be set in a new path which would take on a life of its own, curving and foaming until, in a very little time—

"No, that is an inadequate expression. 'Time would, in a very little time—' It is as though we are imagining some abstract and absolute time-like reference against which our time may be measured; as though our own background of time were flowing against another, deeper background. I confess it's beyond me, but pretend you understand.

"Any change in the events of time would, after a—while—alter everything unrecognizably.

"But I wouldn't want *that*. I told you at the start, I do not wish to cease to be me. Even if in my place I would create someone who was more intelligent, more sensible, more successful, it would still not be *me*.

"Nor would I want to change you, Muller, or you, Adams. I've said that already, too. I would not want to triumph over a Muller who is less ingenious and spectacularly bright, or over an Adams who has been less politic and deft at putting together an imposing structure of respect. I would want to triumph over you as you are, and not over lesser beings.

"Well, yes, it is triumph I wish.

"—Oh, come. You stir as though I had said something unworthy. Is a sense of triumph so alien to you? Are you so dead to humanity that you seek no honor, no victory, no fame, no rewards? Am I to suppose that the respected Professor Adams does not wish to possess his long list of publications, his revered string of honorary degrees, his numerous medals and plaques, his post as head of one of the most prestige-filled departments of physics in the world?

"And would you be satisfied to have all that, Adams, if no one were to know of it; if its existence were to be wiped out of all records and histories; if it were to remain a secret between you and the Almighty? A silly question. I certainly won't demand an answer when we all know what it would be.

"And I needn't go through the same rigmarole of inquiry concerning Muller's potential Nobel Prize and what seems like a certain university presidency—and of this university, too.

"What is it you both want in all of this, considering that you want not only the things themselves but the public knowledge of your ownership of these things? Surely you want triumph! You want triumph over your competitors as an abstract class, triumph over your fellow human beings. You want to do something others cannot do and to have all those others know that you have done something they cannot do, so that they must then look up at you in helpless awareness of that knowledge and in envy and enforced admiration.

"Shall I be more noble than you? Why? Let me have the privilege of wanting what you want, of hungering for the triumph you have hungered for. Why should I not want the long respect, the great prize, the high position that waits on you two? And to do so in your place? To snatch it from you at the moment of its attainment? It is no more disgraceful for me to glory in such things than for you to do so.

"Ah, but you deserve it and I do not. There is precisely the point. What if I could so arrange the flow and content of time as to have me deserve it and you not?

"Imagine! I would still be I; the two of you, the two of you. You would be no less worthy and I no more worthy—that being the condition I have set myself, that none of us change—and yet I deserve and you do not. I want to beat you, in other words, as you are and not as inferior substitutes.

"In a way, that is a tribute to you, isn't it? I see from your expression you think it is. I imagine you both feel a kind of contemptuous pride. It is something after all to be the standard by which victory is measured. You enjoy earning the merits I lust for—especially if that lust must go unsatisfied.

"I don't blame you for feeling so. In your place, I would feel the same.

"But must the lust go unsatisfied? Think it out—

"Suppose I were to go back in time, say twenty-five years. A nice figure; an even quarter century. You, Adams, would be forty. You would have just arrived here, a full professor, from your stint at Case Institute. You would have done your work in diamagnetics, though your unreported effort to do something with bismuth hypochromite had been a rather laughable failure.

"Heavens, Adams, don't look so surprised. Do you think I don't know your professional life to the last detail—

"And as for you, Muller, you were twenty-six, and just in the process of turning out a doctor's thesis on general relativity, which was fascinating at the time but is much less satisfying in retrospect than it was at the time. Had it been correctly interpreted, it would have anticipated most of Hawking's later conclusions, as you now know. You did not correctly interpret it at the time and you have successfully managed to hide that fact.

"I'm afraid, Muller, you are not good at interpretation. You did not interpret your own doctor's thesis to its best advantage and you have not properly interpreted your great Field Theory. Perhaps, Muller, it isn't a disgrace, either. The lack of interpretation is a common event. We can't all have the interpretative knack, and the talent to shake loose consequences may not occur in the same mind that possesses the talent for brilliance of concept. I have the former without the latter so why should you not have the latter without the former?

"If you could only create your marvelous thoughts, Muller, and leave it to me to see the equally marvelous conclusions. What a team we would make, you and I, Muller—but you wouldn't have me. I don't complain about that, for I wouldn't have you.

"In any case, these are trifles. I could in no way damage you, Adams, with the pinprick of your silly handling of the bismuth salts. After all, you did, with some difficulty, catch your mistake before you embalmed it in the pages of a learned journal—if you could have gotten past the referees. And I could not cloud the sunshine that plays on you, Muller, by making a point of your failure to deduce what might be deduced from your concepts. It might even be looked upon as a measure of your brilliance; that so much crowded into your thoughts that even *you* were not bright enough to wring them dry of consequence.

"But if that would not do, what would? How could matters be changed properly? Fortunately, I could study the situation for a length of—something—that my consciousness would interpret as years, and yet there would be no physical time passage and therefore no aging. My thought processes would continue, but my physical metabolism would not.

"You smile again. No, I don't know how that could be. Surely, our thought processes are part of our metabolic changes. I can only suppose that outside the time-stream, thought processes are not thought processes in the physical sense, but are something else that is equivalent.

"And if I study a moment in time, and search for a change that will accomplish what I want it to accomplish, how could I do that? Could I make a change, move forward in time, study the consequences and, if I didn't like it, move back, unchange the change and try another? If I did it fifty times, a thousand times, could I ever find the right change? The number of changes, each with numberless consequences, each with further numberless consequences, is beyond computation or comprehension. How could I find the change I was seeking?

"Yet I could. I could learn how and I can't tell you how I learned or what I did after I learned. Would it be so difficult? Think of the things we *do* learn.

"We stand, we walk, we run, we hop—and we do it all even though we are tipped on end. We are in an utter state of instability. We remain standing only because the large muscles of our legs and torso are forever lightly contracting and pulling this way and that, like a circus performer balancing a stick on the end of his nose.

"Physically, it's hard. That is why standing still takes it out of us and makes us glad to sit down after a while. That is why standing at attention for an unfairly long period of time will lead to collapse. Yet, except when we take it to extremes, we do it so well, we're not even aware we do it. We can stand and walk and run and hop and start and stop all day long and never fall or even become seriously unsteady. Well, then, describe how you do it so that someone who has never tried can do it. You can't.

"Another example. We can talk. We can stretch and contract the muscles of our tongue and lips and cheeks and palate in a rapid and unrhythmic set of changes that produce just the modulation of sound that we want. It was hard enough to learn when we were infants, but once we learned, we could produce dozens of words a minute without any conscious effort. Well, how do we do it? What changes do we produce to say, 'How do we do it?' Describe those changes to someone who has never spoken, so that he can make that sound! It can't be done.

"But we can make the sound. And without effort, too.

"Given enough time—I don't even know how to describe the passage of what I mean. It was not time; call it 'duration.' Given enough duration *without* the passage of time, I learned how to adjust reality as desired. It was like a child babbling, but gradually learning to pick and choose among the babbles to construct words. I learned to choose.

"It was risky, of course. In the process of learning, I might have done something irreversible; or at least something which, for reversal, would have required subtle changes that were beyond me. I did not. Perhaps it was more good fortune than anything else.

"And I came to enjoy it. It was like the painting of a picture, the construction of a piece of sculpture. It was much more than that; it was the carving of a new reality. —A new reality unchanged from our own in key ways. I remained exactly what I am; Adams remained the eternal Adams; Muller, the quintessential Muller. The university remained the university; science, science.

"Well, then, did nothing change? —But I'm losing your attention. You no longer believe me and, if I am any judge, feel scornful with what I am saying. I seem to have slipped in my enthusiasm and I have begun acting as though time-travel were real and that I have really done what I would like to do. Forgive me. Consider it imagination—fantasy—I say what I *might* have done *if* time-travel were real and *if* I truly had the talent for it.

"In that case—in my imagination—did nothing change? There would have to be *some* change; one that would leave Adams exactly Adams and yet unfit to be head of the department; Muller to be precisely Muller and yet without any likelihood of becoming university president and without much chance of being voted the Nobel Prize.

"And I would have to be myself, unlovable and plodding, and unable to create—and yet possessing the qualities that would make *me* university president.

"It could be nothing scientific; it would have to be something outside science; something disgraceful and sordid that would disqualify you fine gentlemen—

"Come, now. I don't deserve those looks of mingled disdain and smug self-satisfaction. You are sure, I take it, that you can do nothing disgraceful and sordid? How can you be sure? There's not one of us who, if conditions were right, would not slip into—shall we call it sin? Who among us would be without sin, given the proper temptation? Who among us *is* without sin?

"Think, think— Are you sure your souls are pure? Have you done nothing wrong, ever? Have you never at least nearly fallen into the pit? And if you have, was it not a narrow escape, brought about more through some fortunate circumstance than inner virtue? And if someone had closely studied all your actions and noted the strokes of fortune that kept you safe and deflected just one of them, might you not then have done wrong?

"Of course, if you had lived openly foul and sordid lives so that people turned from you in disdain and disgust you would not have reached your present states of reverence. You would have fallen long since and I would not have to step over your disgraced bodies for you would not be here to serve me as stepping stones.

"You see how complex it all is?

"But then, it is all the more exciting, you see. If I were to go back in time and find that the solution was not complex, that in one stroke I could achieve my aim, I might manage to gain pleasure out of it but there would be a lack of intellectual excitement.

"If we were to play chess and I were to win by a fool's mate in three moves, it would be a victory that was worse than defeat. I would have played an unworthy opponent and I would be disgraced for having done so.

"No. The victory that is worthwhile is the one snatched slowly and with pain from the reluctant grip of the adversary; a victory that seems unattainable; a victory that is as wearying, as torturing, as hopelessly bone-breaking as the worst and most tedious defeat but that has, as its difference, the fact that, while you are panting and gasping in total exhaustion, it is the flag you hold in your hand, the trophy.

"The duration I spent playing with that most intractable of all materials, reality, was filled with the difficulty I had set myself. I insisted stubbornly not only on having my aim, but on my having that aim my way; on rejecting everything that was not *exactly* as I wanted it to be. A near miss I considered a miss; an almost hit I eliminated as not a hit. In my target, I had a bull's-eye and nothing else.

"And even after I won, it would have to be a victory so subtle that you would not know I had won until I had carefully explained it to you. To the final moment, you would not know your life had been turned wrong end up. That is what—

"But wait, I have left out something. I have been so caught up in the intensity of my intention of leaving us and the university and science all the same, that I have not explained that other things might indeed change. There would be bound to be changes in social, political and economic forces, and in international relationships. Who would care about such things after all? Certainly not we three.

"That is the marvel of science and the scientist, is it not? What is it to us whom we elect in our dear United States, or what votes

were taken in the United Nations, or whether the stock market
went up or down, or whether the unending pavane of the nations
followed this pattern or that? As long as science is there and the
laws of nature hold fast and the game we play continues, the background against which we play it is just a meaningless shifting of
light and shadow.

"Perhaps you don't feel this openly, Muller. I know well you
have, in your time, felt yourself part of society and have placed
yourself on record with views on this and that. To a lesser extent so
did you, Adams. Both of you have had exalted views concerning
humanity and the earth and various abstractions. How much of
that, however, was a matter of greasing your conscience because
inside—deep inside—you don't really care, as long as you can sit
brooding over your scientific thoughts.

"That's one big difference between us. I don't care what happens
to humanity as long as I am left to my physics. I am open about it;
everyone knows me as cynical and callous. You two *secretly* don't
care. To the cynicism and callousness that characterize me, you
add hypocrisy, which plasters over your sins to the unthinking, but
makes them worse when found out.

"Oh, don't shake your heads. In my searching out your lives I
discovered as much about you as you yourselves know; more, since
I see your peccadillos clearly, and you two hide them even from
yourselves. It is the most amusing thing about hypocrisy that once
it is adhered to sternly enough, it numbers the hypocrite himself
among its victims. He is his own chief victim, in fact, for it is quite
usual that when the hypocrite is exposed to all the world, he still
seems, quite honestly, a plaster saint to himself.

"But I tell you this not in order to vilify you. I tell it to you in
order to explain that if I found it necessary to change the world in
order to keep ourselves all the same, yet place me on top instead of
you, you wouldn't really mind. —Not about the world, that is.

"You wouldn't mind if the Republicans were up and the Demo-
crats were down, or vice versa; if feminism was in flower and professional sports were under a cloud; if this fashion or that in cloth-
ing, furniture, music or comedy was in or out. What would any of
that matter to you?

"Nothing.

"In fact, less than nothing, for if the world were changed, it would be a new reality; *the* reality as far as people in the world were concerned; the *only* reality, the reality of the history books, the reality that was *real* over the last twenty-five years.

"If you believed me, if you thought I were spinning more than a fantasy, you would still be helpless. Could you go to someone in authority and say: 'This is not the way things are supposed to be. It has been altered by a villain'? What would that prove but that you were insane? Who could believe that reality is not reality, when it is the fabric and tapestry that has been woven all these twenty-five years in incredibly intricate fashion, and when everyone remembers and lives it as woven?

"But you yourselves do *not* believe me. You dare not believe that I am not merely speculating about having gone back into the past, about having studied you both, about having labored to bring about a new reality in which we are unchanged but, alas, the world is changed. I have *done* it; I have done it *all*. And I alone remember both realities because I was outside time when the change was made, and *I* made it.

"And still you don't believe me. You dare not believe me, for you yourselves would feel you were insane if you did. Could I have altered this familiar world of 1982? Impossible.

"If I did, what could the world have been like before I tampered with it? I'll tell you— It was chaotic! It was full of license! People were laws to themselves! In a way I'm glad I changed it. Now we have a government and the land is governed. Our rulers have views and the views are enforced. Good!

"But, gentlemen, in that world that was, that old reality that no one can know or conceive, you two gentlemen were laws to yourselves and fought for license and anarchy. It was no crime in the old reality. It was admirable to many.

"In the new reality, I left you unchanged. You remained fighters for license and anarchy, and that *is* a crime in the present reality; the only reality you know. I made sure you could cover it up. No one knew about your crimes and you were able to rise to your present heights. But I knew where the evidence was and how it might be uncovered and, at the proper time—I uncovered it.

"Now I think that for the first time I catch expressions on your faces that don't ring the changes of weary tolerance, of contempt, of amusement, of annoyance. Do I catch a whiff of fear? Do you remember what I am talking about?

"Think! Think! Who were members of the League of Constitutional Freedoms? Who helped circulate the *Free Thought Manifesto?* It was very brave and honorable of you to do this, some people thought. You were much applauded by the underground. —Come, come, you know whom I mean by the underground. You're not active in it any longer. Your position is too exposed and you have too much to lose. You have position and power, and there is more on the way. Why risk it for something that people don't want?

"You wear your pendants, and you're numbered among the godly. But my pendant is larger and I am more godly, for I have not committed your crimes. What is more, gentlemen, I get the credit of having informed against you.

"A shameful act? A scandalous act? My informing? Not at all. I shall be rewarded. I have been horrified at the hypocrisy of my colleagues, disgusted and nauseated at their subversive past, concerned for what they might be plotting now against the best and noblest and most godly society ever established on Earth. As a result I brought all this to the attention of the decent men who help conduct the policies of that society in true sobriety of thought and humility of spirit.

"They will wrestle with your evils to save your souls and to make you true children of the Spirit. There will be some damage to your bodies in the process, I imagine, but what of that? It would be a trivial cost compared to the vast and eternal good they will bring you. And I shall be rewarded for making it all possible.

"I think you are really frightened now, gentlemen, for the message we have all been waiting for is now coming, and you see now why I have been asked to remain here with you. The presidency is mine and my interpretation of the Muller theory, combined with the disgrace of Muller, will make it the Dinsmore theory in the textbooks and may bring me the Nobel Prize. As for you—"

There was the sound of footsteps in cadence outside the door; a ringing cry of "Halt!"

The door was flung open. In stepped a man whose sober gray

garb, wide white collar, tall buckled hat and large bronze cross proclaimed him a captain in the dreaded Legion of Decency.

He said, nasally, "Horatio Adams, I arrest you in the name of God and the Congregation for the crime of devilry and witchcraft. Carl Muller, I arrest you in the name of God and the Congregation for the crime of devilry and witchcraft."

His hand beckoned briefly and quickly. Two legionnaires from the ranks came up to the two physicists who sat in stupefied horror in their chairs, yanked them to their feet, placed cuffs on their wrists, and, with an initial gesture of humility to the sacred symbol, tore the small crosses that were pendant from their lapels.

The captain turned to Dinsmore. "Yours in sanctity, sir. I have been asked to deliver this communication from the Board of Trustees."

"Yours in sanctity, Captain," said Dinsmore gravely, fingering his own pendant cross. "I rejoice to receive the words of those godly men."

He knew what the communication contained.

As the new president of the university, he might, if he chose, lighten the punishment of the two men. His triumph would be enough even so.

—But only if it were safe.

—And in the grip of the Moral Majority, he must remember, no one was ever *truly* safe.